Wrecked BY RUM

Bohemia Bartenders Mysteries
Book Two

LUCY LAKESTONE

Velvet Petal Press
Florida

About the Book

WHEN RUM COLLECTORS COLLIDE...

When mixologist Pepper Revelle joins the Bohemia Bartenders for what promises to be an entertaining, rum-soaked tiki convention in sultry South Florida, she expects divine ukuleles, sublime swizzles and a chance to know chief bartender Neil a little better. What she gets is chaos — the death of a high-profile rum collector, a cast of sneaky suspects and ten thousand limes to squeeze.

With one of their own under suspicion, Pepper and Neil set out to find the real killer. But behind the aloha shirts and cocktail parasols is a blender full of secrets. The centerpiece of the convention is a high-dollar tasting of rums that survived a shipwreck and other disasters, and when a precious bottle vanishes from the crime scene, everyone with a ticket is a suspect.

As Pepper tries to keep the insatiable crowd inebriated and her gregarious dog Astra sober, she finds peril under every palm tree. It seems like everybody's guilty of something. But who's guilty of murder? And can she and Neil find the culprit before they're smacked like the mint in a Mai Tai?

Wrecked by Rum is the second book in the Bohemia

Bartenders Mysteries, funny whodunits with a dash of romance set in a convivial collective of cocktail lovers, eccentrics and mixologists. These cozy culinary comedies contain a hint of heat, a splash of cursing and shots of laughter, served over hand-carved ice.

Chapter One

While I looked forward to making rum cocktails at an unpronounceable tiki convention in Fort Lauderdale, I wasn't fully prepared for a three-hour road trip with the man I couldn't get out of my head, his lovesick employee and a flatulent dog.

Neil, the leader of the Bohemia Bartenders, drove his roomy SUV through South Florida's bonkers traffic the way he did everything else, with cool, calm confidence. That cool was getting to me. On our recent adventure in New Orleans, we'd had a few moments of heat, but they'd all ended up being shaken and chilled over ice. Probably because they'd happened between moments of attempted murder and mayhem.

That was behind us now, though I still had the leather cord with the alligator tooth wrapped around my wrist, a good-luck token from a voodoo priestess that I hoped would get me through Hookahakaha with nothing more perilous than a hangover.

"Hey, Pepper. Tell me again why Melody is riding with Barclay?" Luke asked from the back seat, which he shared with my dog.

"She said she wanted to talk over rums with Barclay, plus she likes his car." Barclay drove a slick old BMW convertible and was a rum nut.

"I guess that's reasonable. He's a walking rum master class." Luke's glum tone belied his words. With his good looks, including shoulder-length, gold-streaked brown hair and tropical tattoos, he could have snagged just about any woman he wanted. Thing is, I was pretty sure he wanted Melody, a knockout blonde and one of my best friends.

Luke worked for Neil at The Junction Box, one of Bohemia's favorite craft cocktail bars. I was co-owner of Nola, a New Orleans-themed bar in our coastal Florida town. Barclay worked at a hipster bar in mainland Bohemia and Melody at a crappy hotel bar in Bohemia Beach, where she was the only one who knew what a muddler was.

Together, we were the Bohemia Bartenders, a group of elite (if I do say so myself) mixologists who went to events and made amazing drinks. As the newest member, I was just happy to be here, even if we did have a ton of work ahead of us at the tiki convention.

"And what the hell did you feed your dog this morning?" Luke added as Astra, an adorable caramel-and-white Cavapoo, grinned up at him with her tongue wagging and released another fart. It wafted throughout the car like an invisible dirigible, bounced about by the vents blasting AC in the eternal struggle against Florida's June heat.

"I fed her her normal gourmet dog food. My aunt wouldn't have it any other way." I neglected to mention that Astra had jumped up on my chair and snatched half of my eggs and bacon from the table when I was distracted by a phone call this morning. Her vapors were even more painful for me, given my nose had superpowers.

"What are you going to do with her while we're working?" Neil asked. Was he annoyed with me? I didn't find out till last night that my aunt was flying off to some natural healing conference in Arizona for the week and couldn't watch Astra. Or maybe I selectively forgot her telling me that. Aunt Celestine and I lived in adjoining halves of a duplex and shared custody of the dog, but I'd been hyper-focused on my business as Nola launched a new food menu.

"My partner at Nola said his younger sister would watch Astra while we're busy," I said. "She's a software genius in Miami with tons of vacation to burn, so it all worked out. I had to give up the tower room and book a double by the pool to accommodate both of us and the dog, but the hotel didn't mind. There's a waiting list for the tower rooms."

"Hmm," Neil said. "That's too bad. I have a tower room."

I looked at him sharply. Was he suggesting that it might be convenient for my room to be near his?

"They have great views from up there," he continued. "You can see the Intracoastal and the city from one side and the ocean from the other."

Ah. He was talking about views. Not us. Not that there *was* an us.

I had to remember that Neil had been preoccupied lately, too. His grandfather had been missing for a couple of months, and the family was in a holding pattern, waiting for news. Police had given up searching, even suggesting that his grandfather might have just gone on a trip, pointing out that there was no sign of foul play at his house. Its extensive collection of artifacts from his treasure-diving days was untouched, up to and including the ancient dildo collection. Not that I would go around touching ancient dildos voluntarily.

Neil seemed to take the situation in stride, but I knew he was worried. Whenever I asked him about it, he didn't say much. Not that he ever said much.

I really needed to stop chasing him. I'd had plenty of guys

before I met him, and there were plenty more out there. And this weekend, I needed to focus on the cocktails. I wanted to build my reputation. Neil already had an award-winning cocktail book. Nobody knew who I was.

"So, what's first on the agenda?" I asked.

"We drop our stuff at the hotel and then go right to Pau Hana for the opening presentation," Neil said. "We've got to whip up a welcome cocktail, and then we enjoy the program. But not you, Luke."

I glanced back at Luke, who was grinning. "Are you kidding? I can't wait to be Fizz Martin's personal errand boy."

Neil laughed. "If you're ever as famous as Fizz Martin, you can have an errand boy, too."

Fizz Martin was one of the best-known tiki bar impresarios in the country. A transplant from Australia, he'd started with a bar in San Diego during the early tiki revival and had expanded to locations in Chicago, Kansas City, Atlanta and New York, each venue unique and fantastic. He'd won all kinds of awards.

"He's been hinting on social media that he's about to sign up for a reality show," Luke said. "Maybe you should do something like that."

Neil made a noise that sounded like a dragon blowing its nose. "Never in a million years."

"Why not?" I asked.

He shot me a sidelong glance that was so full of irony, I winced. Right. Neil could do a seminar or present a cocktail with a great sense of theater, but he was an intensely private person. Maybe that's why I wanted to crack that coconut so badly. You know what they say about opposites.

I was much more of an extrovert than Neil was—just look at the differences in our clothes. Today I wore a colorful, low-cut dress that made no secret of my curves. It was patterned in parrots, tropical flowers and palm fronds that brought out my gray-green eyes, and I had a flamboyant floral adornment in my hair (complete with parrot), along with candy-red lipstick and my geeky cat's-eye glasses.

He was in khakis and a gray-blue guayabera shirt with a subtle pattern of tan palm fronds that ran down the front. His dark, red-flecked brown beard and mustache were trim— though at one time he'd had the bartender's handlebar 'stache, and people never stopped teasing him about it.

More to the point, he was a handsome nerd who loved making cocktails. And I couldn't get enough of him.

We were definitely opposite sides of a coin. But even though I was more of a mingler than he was, I had to admit I wouldn't want a camera crew following me around night and day either.

"Is that Barclay?" Luke asked. Amid the thickening traffic on I-95, we'd crept up on the little black convertible, whose cloth roof was wisely enclosed, given the June heat.

"They must've just stopped and gotten back on the highway, because Barclay drives a lot faster than you do," I said to Neil.

He gave me another look, this one seeming to ask, *And how do you know how fast Barclay drives?* Maybe because we'd taken a couple of field trips to Sanford to check out the drinks at Bitters & Brass and Suffering Bastard, but let Neil wonder.

Barclay had slowed down a bit more to let us pull up in the lane next to him. He was the kind of handsome magazines kill for, with short, wavy black hair, light-brown skin, amber-green eyes and a sly smile.

Melody gave us a thumbs-up from the passenger seat. Barclay waved and hit the accelerator, shooting away from Neil's SUV like a rocket leaving Cape Canaveral.

Astra barked.

"They look like they're having fun." Luke sighed.

"I just hope he doesn't get a ticket on the way down," Neil said.

I waved away the possibility. "We're past the biggest speed trap and officially in South Florida. He's not even driving fast enough to overtake your average Miami granny."

"Which means I'm not driving fast enough to pass a six-year-old on a skateboard," Neil said.

I chuckled. Astra barked again, and I let her clamber up to the front seat and get in my lap. Maybe she should've been secured in the back, but she was happy looking out the window as I ran my hands through her curly, silky fur. She made me happy, too.

About an hour later, we pulled up under the overhang at Wicker Wharf.

The hotel sat at one end of the causeway that led to the beach, across the Intracoastal Waterway from Fort Lauderdale. Long, two-story buildings wrapped around a landscape of pools and lush tropical greenery. On one side of this massive courtyard was the main building with the lobby, restaurants, meeting spaces and a retro tower that dominated the space. Room balconies poked out at angles all around the vaguely cylindrical tower, bringing to mind a giant game of Jenga. At the top, a spiky roof that resembled a UFO capped a round, glassed-in party space with a rotating floor. It used to be a restaurant, or so said the website that described all these amenities. I couldn't wait for our big event there tomorrow.

But for now, we had to check in and get our bartender butts over to Pau Hana.

"Fifteen minutes," Neil announced as we got out of the car.

My glasses immediately fogged up as the tropical heat smacked us in the face.

Neil and Luke started yanking suitcases out of the back while Astra dragged me over to a pygmy date palm and watered it thoroughly.

A moment later, Melody popped out of the lobby doors brandishing key cards. Her wiggle dress, blue splashed with red hibiscus flowers, flattered her annoyingly slender figure perfectly. Her blond hair was piled high and adorned with an arch of tropical flowers.

"Where's Barclay?" Luke asked.

"He went to park and load his stuff into y'all's room," Melody said, handing him and Neil their cards. "Can we all ride over together?"

"Sure!" Luke said, his mood brightening. Neil lifted an eyebrow at his enthusiasm, but the car was plenty big enough to take all of us.

I grabbed my key card from her. "Thanks. Has Gina checked in?"

"Yeah, she met me at the desk to give me your key. Ohhh, look at this sweet puppy," Melody cooed, bending over to scratch behind Astra's floppy ears. The Cavapoo panted happily. "Can I help you get her to the room?" Melody asked me.

"That would be awesome." I handed her Astra's leash. Then I slung my canvas messenger bag over my shoulder and grabbed the handle of my huge roller suitcase with one hand and the folded dog crate with the other before turning to Neil. "I've got to brief Gina on the doggy drill. I'll see you guys in a few."

"Fifteen minutes!" Neil said again.

I narrowed my eyes at him, and he laughed.

Chapter Two

"Still no joy in the pursuit of Mr. Rockaway?" Melody murmured after we left the guys and made our way through the vast lobby, whose wall of windows offered tantalizing glimpses of palms and pools.

"I've just about given up. He's pretty distracted, anyway."

"I know. I hope his grandfather turns up soon. But I still think he's interested. It's in the way he looks at you."

"Or laughs at me," I scoffed.

"He's laughing with you!" Melody grinned.

We passed through double doors that led to the corridor on the second floor of the first long hotel building. It wasn't so much a hallway as an outdoor walkway, open to the sky, and rooms flanked the endless passage. Occasional staircases led down to the first floor and the courtyard.

By the time we made a right turn for the next leg, I was out of breath.

"Here it is," Melody said halfway down the second eternal stretch of concrete.

"Thank Dionysus."

Astra barked as I dipped my card in the lock and pushed the door open.

"Hello?" I called. "Gina?"

"In here," came a soft voice.

I left my suitcase and the crate by the closet and headed down the narrow entryway, which opened up into a nice, big tiled room with two queen beds and the usual hotel furniture. Gina, whom I knew only from a phone call and my business partner Jorge's description, was sitting up against the pillows on one bed, legs outstretched, tapping away on a laptop computer. She looked up and smiled. She and her brother shared the same big, brown eyes that crinkled at the corners and the same long nose, but she was more slender. And younger, of course—the youngest of Jorge's four Listo siblings—early twenties, I guessed, so maybe four or five years younger than me.

I really needed to get Jorge to one of these cocktail events, but co-owning Nola was about as wild as he got. He was an engineer at the space center, and apparently his sister had the same techie tendencies.

"You're not supposed to be working. There are like three swimming pools out there." I returned Gina's smile and gestured to the sliding doors, where the inviting water sparkled under the palm trees. "I'm Pepper, by the way."

"Nice to meet you in person. I just wanted to get a few things done before you got here." She put the laptop aside and swung her legs over the side of the bed. She wore demure khaki shorts and a plain white T-shirt. "Is this Astra?"

"Sure is. She's such a sweetie," Melody said, popping off the dog's pink harness. Astra bounded over to Gina and stood on her hind legs, putting her paws on Gina's knees, demanding affection.

"Oh my goodness," Gina gushed. Her long, brown hair hung in her face as she bent over to pick up Astra, who proceeded to lick her nose. "Oh gosh." She held the dog away from her, just far enough that her tongue wouldn't reach. "She's so rumpled."

"It runs in the family." I unfolded the crate and snapped its walls into place. I pulled a blanket from the suitcase, fluffed it and stuck it inside the crate along with a couple of chew toys. I also extracted the dog food container and two bowls. "One of these is for water, one for food. She gets a scoop at breakfast and dinner. She will ask for more. Do not give her more. And don't give her alcohol no matter how much she asks for it."

Gina giggled. "She drinks?"

"She does *not* drink. At least not officially. I try to keep her away from my cocktails, but she sneaks a sip now and then. Mostly she enjoys chewing garnishes."

"Oh, I don't drink much anyway. We'll get along fine." Gina put Astra on the bed, and the dog leaned against her and gazed up at her with adoring eyes. "She's so cute!" Then Gina wrinkled her nose. After a second, it hit me too.

"I swear the gaseous emissions will stop soon. Just remember how cute she is."

Gina nodded and grinned, but she was waving away the fart cloud as she did it.

"She just peed," I continued, "so if you take her out every hour or so, she should be good. Poo bags are in that dispenser on the leash. If you want to leave, she'll be happy in the crate for a while. OK?"

"So you'll be back late, then?" Gina asked.

I nodded. "Probably. Enjoy yourself. I'll pick you up a wristband so you can sample all the pool party drinks starting tomorrow."

"They're going to be amazing," Melody said. "We're doing

an afternoon shift, and there are bars from all over the world doing pop-ups."

Gina looked kind of overwhelmed. "I'll probably just work. You all have fun."

"You sure you're OK?" At her nod, I ducked into the bathroom, emptied out and freshened up, then gave Astra a kiss on the head and headed back to the lobby with Melody.

"She's going to be in for a shock," Melody said.

"Gina? What do you mean?"

"You've never done Hookahakaha before, have you?"

"No. Is it wild?"

"Depends on who you meet." She wiggled her eyebrows at me, and I laughed. Melody always managed to meet someone fun. "It's a party scene for sure."

"Except we'll be working the whole time."

Melody wore a knowing look. "Oh, we'll have a little time for fun."

"This kind of work is totally fun for me anyway." Making cocktails was my passion. "There are the guys."

Barclay had joined Luke and Neil outside by the SUV. Barclay and Luke had changed into loud aloha shirts, and Neil had changed into a more modest one.

Like Luke, Barclay had tattoos—a dragon on one arm and what I'd learned were Korean characters on the other, reflecting a complex heritage he didn't talk about much. Music notes and flowers swirled up Melody's arms.

Neil had no visible ink, and I still didn't know if he was teasing when he'd hinted he had a tattoo. Mine was hidden, though he'd had a glimpse during a drunken moment. We hadn't talked about that much, either.

Regardless, the guys all looked deliciously tropical.

"Hey, Barclay." I smiled.

"Hey, dude," he said. It was so cute, him calling me *dude*. "Hey, Melody."

"Too bad we can't all fit in the Beamer," I said.

"I told you, it's a *Bimmer*," he teased.

Neil gave me the side-eye and beeped open the car doors. "Finally."

I leaned over and glanced at Barclay's vintage watch. "It's been *thirteen* minutes."

"Doesn't matter. We've got to go," Luke said. "Fizz Martin called."

"And?" I asked.

"He sounded a little drunk already." Neil opened his door. "He was yelling 'I have the nuclear football!' and said he needed us right away so he didn't have to guard it by himself."

"What the hell does that mean?" I clutched my bag and jumped into the co-pilot's seat again, leaving Melody to join the guys in the back rows.

"I'm not sure." Neil cranked up the SUV and pulled away from the curb, navigating the loop that would bring us back around to the road. "But we'd better go and find out."

Chapter Three

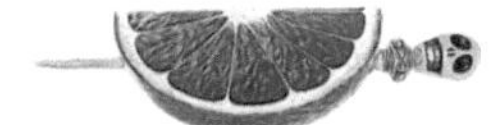

Pau Hana was one of the oldest tiki bars in America. It had been established during the first tiki craze in the 1950s, survived the ghastly era of fern bars and Long Island Iced Teas with its Mai Tais intact, and emerged on the other side with a new generation of fans.

The huge restaurant, with a dark bar that looked like the inside of a sailing ship and a lush garden in back, was a tropical island unto itself. Fort Lauderdale had grown up around it, but if you half-closed your eyes and ignored the looming furniture store next door and the surrounding traffic, you could imagine you were in a Polynesian paradise.

I'd been to Pau Hana once before. Aunt Celestine and I had stopped here during a road trip when I was a teenager. It was shortly after my parents sent me to live with her in Bohemia Beach, after Hurricane Katrina devastated our world in New Orleans.

Pau Hana was one of the reasons I fell in love with Florida. It had seemed so exotic at the time, yet somehow quintessentially Florida, especially among the palms and orchids in the garden. The dazzling floor show, with dancers representing islands and cultures of the Pacific, had completely captivated me. So did a sip of my aunt's Moonkist Coconut, served in a real coconut.

I'd heard a lot about Pau Hana's drink menu over the years, but I hadn't been fully initiated into the tiki cocktail revival until recently. I was excited to have this chance to come back as a mixologist and, let's face it, a demanding drinker.

"Happy hour is killer here," Barclay told us, nodding toward the bar off the lobby. He'd grown up in nearby Miami, and his parents lived here now, so he knew the place better than the rest of us.

I blinked, trying to get adjusted to the murky interior. It was always nighttime in Pau Hana.

"I doubt we'll have time for happy hour today," Neil said, adjusting the strap of the big bag of bar tools he carried on his shoulder. "I'll owe you all a drink if we can get through the next few hours. Fizz said he'd meet us in the kitchen."

A white-suited host greeted us and volunteered to lead us back. As we walked, I gawked at the layers of vintage South Pacific decor in the multiple dining areas that surrounded the stage. The prevailing theme was dark, carved wood, from the posts supporting the roof to the artifacts hanging from the walls.

Thatched overhangs made it seem as if huts were tucked under the high ceiling. Above, hanging lamps in a rainbow of muted colors and island styles added to the ambience. There was no audience yet, but a smattering of what I presumed were Hookahakaha volunteers and Pau Hana staff scrambled around, preparing for the event that would start later this afternoon.

As we pushed through the "in" door of the kitchen, the mysterious island lair was left behind in favor of a vast, brightly lit, colorless warren of prep and cooking areas. It was maybe 2 p.m., and the event was in two hours. Happy hour started at five. And already dozens of kitchen staffers were chopping and prepping huge bowls of food for the Asian-inflected Pau Hana menu.

The host led us through a maze, eventually pointing us around a corner to a smaller prep area next to one of the biggest ice makers I'd ever seen. The niche was stuffed with several prep tables, sinks, a door labeled "STOREROOM," refrigerators and boxes of produce.

There we found Fizz Martin clutching a small, rough wooden box branded with an old-looking logo of a ship and a faint "JAMAICA." He was animatedly talking to a cluster of about ten tiki types. No mistaking the clothes of the tiki 'ohana. It was like a radioactive flower garden had blossomed in the gray backstage of Pau Hana. Plus they had badges around their necks that indicated they were all convention staff or VIPs.

Fizz looked slightly older than his publicity photos, close to forty, I guessed—dimpled and boyishly good-looking, but with a little gray in his wavy, longish, light brown hair and goatee. A pinkness of cheek suggested he'd imbibed early and often.

"Almost four hundred men came out to fight the fire," Fizz was telling the group in his charming Australian accent. His voice crescendoed with his unfolding tale. "They fought the fire with pumps and with boats. Rivers of flaming rum poured out of the warehouse, still on fire, sizzling into the waterways that would take the burning liquor to the Thames and oblivion. There was *blue fire* on the river. The firemen got drunk from the fumes!" There were exclamations among his rapt audience, and Fizz's gray eyes shone with excitement.

"The entire city of London glowed to the light of rum fire that night. Some firefighters were set afire themselves when flaming rum sprayed out at them, and they had to be doused with chemical extinguishers. They battled the blaze to exhaustion but in vain. The fire burned for almost three days, fueled by some four million pounds' worth of rum, the equivalent of more than 375 million dollars today. But it was truly priceless, a huge stock of spirits from the Caribbean. Some sixty-five hundred casks went up in flames, the jewels of the West Indian rum trade."

Now the crowd moaned in mourning, Barclay among them. He must have seen how confused I was, because he leaned over and whispered in my ear. "He's talking about the London docks fire in 1933."

"Oh, right." I pretended to understand as Fizz continued.

Neil, on my other side, harrumphed and put down his tool bag, either unimpressed or already well-acquainted with the facts.

"To this day," Fizz said, "we don't know the true extent of what was lost. Many of the records were destroyed in the Blitz during World War II. The assumption is that all of that rum from the famous Rum Quay is lost to time."

As more among the audience murmured for the elixirs they would never taste, Fizz's voice dropped to a whisper. "But I know a secret, and I'm going to share it with you." The tikiphiles were immediately silenced by his theatrical urgency and leaned forward so they wouldn't miss his revelation. I found myself doing the same thing, caught up in the drama.

"The historians' assumptions are wrong," Fizz said so softly, he was almost drowned out by the drone of the air-conditioning. "Because right here in my hands is the last known bottle of London dock rum to survive the fire in 1933."

"Holy hell," Neil breathed as the rest of the crowd gasped, shouted and applauded.

"Oh, Fizz!" one slim woman with shortish, white-blond

hair said from the heart of the crowd. In her thirties, she wore all black and had an aging punk rocker vibe, and her eyes shone with emotion. She also looked vaguely familiar. Had I seen her at Cocktailia in New Orleans?

"That's wild," Barclay said under his breath.

"Why isn't your head exploding?" I asked him as the tiki folks shouted questions at Fizz. "Isn't that like the holy grail of rum collectors?"

"One, my head *is* exploding, and yeah, it would've been the holy grail, but no one thought it truly existed till now. I mean, I heard stories when I visited London last summer, but I didn't know what to believe. This is amazing."

"And my bartenders are here! Neil!" Fizz called out.

Of course Neil knew Fizz. Neil knew everybody.

"Nice to see you again," Neil said with a smile, reaching out to shake Fizz's hand. At least, the hand that didn't have an iron grip on the wooden box.

Neil introduced us all. Fizz ignored Barclay's enthusiasm, kissed Melody's hand with a little too much effusion, eyeballed my cleavage, and perused Luke with amusement as Neil said, "And here's Luke Wisnia, your dogsbody for the day."

"Ha, *Twilight,*" Fizz said with a grin.

"What?" Luke looked confused.

"You look like one of those teenage vampires. I'm calling you Twilight. OK, Twilight. You stick with me like glue. And if I don't have this box in my hands, then you have the box. Someone must be with the box at all times."

"Um, I'm not a security guard," Luke said as Barclay and Melody snickered.

"Don't worry, man," Fizz said. "We're surrounded by people, including your team. And hardly anyone knows what's in this box. And none of you are going to tell, right?" Fizz called out to the rest of the tikiphiles, who were starting to break up to attend to whatever tasks awaited them before Fizz's opening program.

A chorus of assent seemed to calm Luke a bit.

"I have some questions about that rum," Barclay said as our team gathered around Fizz.

"Later, my friend. You guys have a drink to make for me, right?"

"For you and a hundred and fifty other people," Neil said. "It's from your book. The Molokai Mermaid."

"Oh, that's a tasty one," said the blond woman I'd overheard earlier, her wide, light brown eyes alight with enthusiasm.

Fizz reached out and wrapped an arm around her, pulling her close. "You know my wife, Kim, right?"

Neil shook her hand, and we all said hi. "You were at the awards at Cocktailia, weren't you?" I asked.

"Good memory," said Kim, smoothing Fizz's rumpled hair. "We won best American cocktail bar that night for our New York place."

"One of my proudest moments. So were you surprised, honey?" Fizz asked Kim.

"I'll say! Just when I think you can't surprise me any more, you actually track down a bottle of London dock rum!" He grinned and pulled her in for a quick kiss. "You'll have to have a special case built for it," she added.

"Well, I have an even bigger surprise. I'm going to let people taste it."

Her eyes widened. "You what?"

"You'll see." He laughed.

What did Fizz have planned? Kim seemed about as clued

in as I was. I guess that's what you get if you marry the equivalent of a circus ringmaster.

"Get to work, you guys," Fizz said. "I want to go over my presentation one more time. Twilight, you're with me. Kim, can you supervise these fine mixologists?"

"Sure," she said as a less than happy Luke followed Fizz. "But I think Val will be more help."

A woman who'd been hovering on the edge of our group moved closer. "I was just waiting until Mr. Martin finished entertaining us." Her dry tone matched her expression. I guessed she was about thirty and almost as tall as Barclay, our tallest member. (I was the shortest.) She had bright pink hair cut short with bangs that fell into her pale face and heavy eye makeup.

"Great to see you, Val," said Neil. My radar activated at his warm tone. How did he know *her?* "What have you been up to?"

"Consulting, these days. And supervising the cocktails for Hookahakaha."

"Miss your bar?"

"Sometimes. But this kind of work gets me out of New York regularly, which isn't a bad thing."

She introduced herself to the rest of us, and I learned her name was Val Helena. I knew that name. She'd owned a fabulous craft cocktail bar in New York, got written up in all the magazines, but it went under a few years ago.

"I've got stacks of limes and oranges awaiting your ministrations," she said. "You ready?"

Now that the small crowd had cleared, I could see the boxes of fruit looming like the tower at our hotel. Holy crap.

Neil elbowed me. "Ready?"

I turned to him. "I think so?"

Val laughed. "This is nothing. I've ordered ten thousand limes for the weekend."

I tried to contain the launch of my eyebrows. "Great."

"Why don't you start squeezing the citrus? Keep count," Neil said to me. "I'll get you final numbers in a sec."

Barclay and Melody got to work making the garnishes from orange slices, cherries and mermaid-tail picks. With Kim looking over his shoulder, Neil spent a few minutes double-checking his calculations for the batched drink, given we had to fill a hundred and fifty cups ("totally biodegradable," Val told us). Kim went off to check the projector setup, and Val helped with the garnishes.

I spotted a coat rack with a couple of clean white aprons on it and grabbed one. Wearing that and thin vinyl gloves extracted from a box on the counter, I started slicing and squeezing. With one of Pau Hana's electric juicers, of course. It wasn't like I was behind my bar in Bohemia on a slow night, where I'd lovingly squeeze each lime fresh as I crafted a cocktail.

Neil oversaw the mixing of the light and dark rums, the juices and the allspice dram in a big, clear bucket as we lined up the cups. Then he got out his Lewis bag, filled it with ice cubes and started pounding it with a mallet. It was a noisy, violent way to make crushed ice, but it was also snobbishly vintage, so it was perfect for Neil.

I couldn't help sneaking glances as he slammed the hammer over and over into the canvas, shattering the ice inside. There was wiry muscle built into his trim frame, and I'd had only teasing glimpses of that body so far. And his nerdy focus was incredibly sexy. So sue me for looking.

By the time I was done producing a couple of gallons each of lime and orange juice, you could've licked my glasses and gotten your daily dose of vitamin C. Beyond the noise of the kitchen, I could hear the rumble from the restaurant—the guests were arriving.

Fizz appeared with Luke in tow. Luke clutched the wooden box with the London dock rum and also had a big bag that looked like a padded cooler slung over his shoulder. He seemed disgruntled and nervous.

"You ready?" Fizz asked us, peering into the clear, square buckets. He looked up at Melody and winked. "Dip me up one of those, sweetheart."

Barclay rolled his eyes. Luke's face went sour. Neil, still flushed from beating the hell out of the cubes, showed no reaction as he scooped crushed ice into a cup and handed it to Melody.

As Fizz hovered, she ladled in the drink and garnished it, then handed it over. Fizz put his hand over hers as he eased the cup out of her grasp, bathing her in his glowing gaze. Melody just quirked her mouth into a half smile and raised an eyebrow.

Fizz took the cup, regarding it with pursed lips. "These are better in a tiki mug, but whatcha gonna do?" He tipped up the drink, drained it in one go, smacked his lips and let out a satisfied sigh. "Thank you, darlin'," he told Melody. "If I do say so myself, I make a damn good drink. OK, Twilight. I want you in the wings with that thing. Everyone's in place. Time to serve!"

"Hang on a minute," Val said.

Fizz looked her in the eye, meeting her glint of hostility with one of his own. "You have a problem?"

The lean, tall cocktail manager crossed her arms. "No, but I don't want to start serving until after you've started. It's dark enough in there. I don't need our people tripping over everyone still milling around."

"Not a problem, because I'm starting right now. So serve."

I didn't like the way he said *serve*.

Val didn't say anything at all, just stared him down till he spun on his heel and headed around the corner and out of sight, trailed by Luke.

I could've sworn I heard Val say "dick" under her breath.

Chapter Four

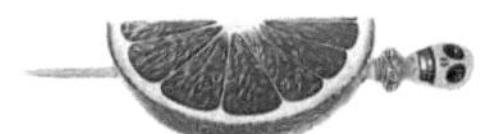

Crushed ice. Cocktail. Garnish. Scoop, pour, decorate, over and over and over. We made up the drinks, and then the cups went onto the big, circular trays. The trays had to be carried into the dining area of Pau Hana, and since there were only a few volunteers helping us, I got to join the tray carriers while my colleagues prepped and loaded more drinks.

Balance had never been my strong suit, but I wore flats with my flashy tropical dress because I knew I'd be on my feet all day. Those shoes saved me, because it was as dark as a bat's butthole when I handed my apron to a volunteer, grabbed a tray and eased out of the bright kitchen into the gloom of the South Seas hideaway. I moved slowly, balancing the edge of the huge, heavy platter of drinks on my shoulder.

The only real light came from the dimmed lanterns and Fizz Martin's slide show, currently paused on a photo of him. In spite of what he'd said, Fizz hadn't taken the stage yet, but a film crew had set up in the aisle between the lower dining area and the elevated one in the back, ready for the star. Looked like the same documentarians I'd seen at Cocktailia.

A guy in a grass skirt and aloha shirt was up there playing ukulele, finishing a Hawaiian tune I didn't recognize. He sang the last few words, strummed his final cord and leaned into the microphone.

"Everybody ready for some Hookahakaha?" he shouted.

"Yeah!" responded the crowd, a colorful sea of floral prints in the dimness.

"Everybody ready for some *cocktails?*"

"YEAH!" they shouted back.

"Well, here they come! So please keep your seats and put your hands together for the Man with the Muddler, the Titan of the Tiki Bar, Mr. *Fizz Martin!*"

The "yeahs" exploded into hoots and hollers and shouts of "Fizz! Fizz! Fizz!" as many in the crowd leapt to their feet. I hovered in an aisle with the tray, not wanting to compete with the commotion.

Fizz strolled onto the stage from the back stairs, his hands in the air, accepting his acclaim. In one hand, he carried a huge stick. No, not a stick. Since Fizz was the Man with the Muddler, I realized that's what he carried, though a muddler that size would only fit into a glass the size of a garbage can. The dark wooden club looked more like something Fred Flintstone might carry around, but it was elegantly carved with tiki-style faces.

The crowd settled, and I started moving. I held the tray steady as another volunteer took cups off it and distributed them down the long, crowded tables at the front of the room.

For the next ten minutes or so, I only had glimpses of Fizz's presentation as I moved back and forth to the kitchen with the other team of volunteer servers, bringing out loaded trays and distributing the cocktails around the dining area. But I got the idea. He was talking about the history of tiki, the great founders of the fanciful watering holes that served Caribbean-influenced drinks in Polynesian-pop settings. With nods to Don the Beachcomber and Trader Vic, Fizz claimed the glory for much of the tiki revival, even though brilliant bar folk from all over the country, from New Orleans to San Francisco to New York, paved the way for him. It was all I could do not to roll my eyes.

At last, we finished delivering the drinks. Melody personally presented a fully garnished cocktail in a tiki mug to Fizz himself, to audience applause and his broad wink. Then Neil, Barclay, Melody and I stood in a dark corner of the dining room next to the elevated back seating area, close to the kitchen, where we had a great view of the stage.

We also had a great view of Luke. He was in the dark hallway next to and slightly behind the stage where performers could enter and exit. He still held the wooden rum box and the big bag Fizz had given him.

Even from here, I could tell from Luke's body language that he was anxious. I couldn't say I blamed him. He held many thousands of dollars' worth of rum in his hands, and what the heck was in the bag? Personally, I'd want to be armored in bubble wrap.

"Now, I know we have some of the most discriminating rum connoisseurs in the world in this audience," Fizz was saying against a backdrop of an image of the Molokai Mermaid cocktail from his book, "because where would tiki be without rum?" He held up his cocktail and took a sip through the straw. "Do you like my drink?"

There were cheers from the audience, and many folks raised their cups. At least they liked the cocktail, even if Fizz didn't bother to mention the Bohemia Bartenders.

"I have something very special to show all of you. As you saw on the Hookahakaha schedule, we have a Gold Tooth Rum Tasting scheduled for Sunday. And the price was a little steep, right?" His slide show shifted to an image of a happy guy with multiple gold teeth, and Fizz pointed at him with his muddler. "Like this Tongan fellow, our guests might have to give up their gold teeth to pay for it."

There were laughs from the audience.

"A thousand bucks to taste rum, you ask? Why would anyone spend that? Well, first of all, half the proceeds go to a charity that gives culinary scholarships. So these folks are generous. But I daresay the real reason these nine people signed up was because I promised them that the tasting would be absolutely spectacular. And I'm a man of my word.

"Not only that, I like to play fair. It shouldn't only be the richest of our 'ohana who get to try what I have in store. Come here, Twilight!" He gestured for Luke to come up on the stage, and Barclay and Melody snickered again. I only smiled. Neil was impassive. He probably didn't like his employee being humiliated, and I liked him for that.

"So what I'm saying," Fizz continued, "is that we sold chances on the tenth ticket for just twenty-five dollars, also to promote the charity, and we're going to draw that name now."

The buzz among the audience rose as Fizz set the muddler and his mug on the stage and dug around in the big bag Luke held. The slide show shifted to an image of Wonka's Golden Ticket. I've always loved that movie. The old one, anyway.

Fizz pulled a tiki mug out of the bag Luke was holding, a mug I recognized as coming from his San Diego bar. I'd just started a small collection of mugs myself, and I knew this one was a popular item. He shook it, indicating something was in it, then reached in and pulled out a tiny, folded piece of paper. With one hand, he flicked it open. "And the winner is ... Conan Cray!"

There was a collective sigh and a smattering of applause

from the audience. Most of them knew who Conan Cray was. He was famous in the tiki community. I'd met the wizened rum collector and mixologist in New Orleans. There was very little he didn't know about rum. Or chemistry, for that matter.

Cray rose from his seat and ambled toward the stage. He wore a white linen suit and a white straw hat with an elaborate tropical headband, not to mention a huge grin. Fizz leaned down and handed him the tiki mug. Then they shook hands.

"Can't wait to see what you have for us," said Cray. Fizz just winked as everyone applauded.

"Lucky bastard," Barclay muttered.

"Did you buy a chance?" I whispered.

"Two," he said. "All I could afford."

"And now," Fizz said, "I'm going to tell you a little story about what our Gold Tooth tasters are going to enjoy."

As the slides changed on the screen behind him, Fizz talked about not the London dock rum, as I expected, but a legendary bottle of Wray & Nephew 17-Year-Old that he pulled from Luke's bag. It rested in an open-face wooden box. Crowd noise built as Fizz explained that this wasn't literally a seventeen-year-old rum—it was, in fact, bottled in the 1940s and contained rums that went back to 1915. It was also ridiculously rare, and the bottle was worth more than fifty thousand dollars.

"But that's not all. Here, Twilight." Now Luke, who'd faded to the back of the stage, looked really grumpy as he stepped forward again, and some in the audience laughed. Fizz reached into the bag and pulled out another bottle wrapped in burlap. He unrolled the rough fabric slowly, maximizing the drama, as the image behind him changed to that of a classic sailing ship.

This squat bottle looked ancient, weathered, almost

pearlescent, with wax dripped over the top. "How many of you have heard of the *Lord Archibald?*"

Only a few responded, but there were also a few gasps. Once again, I had no idea.

"It was a British ship tasked with pursuing pirates in the Caribbean, but its captain wasn't so good at his job. So he chose piracy instead. He acquired all manner of treasures, it's said—emeralds, gold, silk, opium ... and rum."

Fizz paused for dramatic effect. "The ship went down in the Caribbean in 1746, lost in a hurricane. Some hundred and twenty souls were lost at sea, as was the rum. At least until the ship was recovered about ten years ago. The exact contents of the treasure have been closely guarded, but I have managed to obtain one of the few intact bottles of rum that were still on board. And this is it."

Now the crowd was really excited. Even Barclay and Melody applauded, but when I looked at Neil, he had a glazed look in his eyes. OK. That was weird.

Fizz rewrapped the bottle and handed it back to Luke, who stowed it in the bag with the Wray & Nephew.

"But that's not all!" Fizz shouted. His voice boomed through the darkness, around the big central room, the satellite dining rooms, the upper eating area behind us, cutting through the noise. The crowd immediately settled.

And then, as the slide changed to a dingy black and white photo of ships and docks, he went into his dramatic story of London's West India Docks fire, adding even more detail ("As nearby spice warehouses burned, peppercorns exploded, hitting firefighters like BBs!"). As Fizz finished—"and I alone have the last surviving bottle of rum from the fire!"—he opened the wooden box. Gingerly, he extracted an aged, dark bottle with a ragged label and held it high above his head.

He got a standing ovation. And if a human being could glow, that's what Fizz Martin was doing right now.

Like any good performer, he didn't let the crowd's enthusiasm wane. He quickly boxed the London rum and handed it back to Luke, who stepped off the stage and into the shadows. Only this time, Luke came over to us.

"I don't want to be alone with these goddamn bottles," he whispered as Fizz settled the crowd.

"We'll protect you," Barclay teased, but all of us tightened up around Luke as curious gazes followed the keeper of the bottles before Fizz spoke again.

"Now I'd like you all to take a look at this little movie my staff has put together about our next bar project. I'm excited to announce we are bringing the Fizz Martin brand to Miami!" There was more thunderous applause. "I'll be right back!"

As the movie cranked up, with Fizz on-screen talking about his history, his other bars, his legend, his *blah blah blah,* all to beautiful images of his bars, the man gathered his props and strode up to us. And he looked right at Melody. "You got any more of my Molokai Mermaid back there? I need to wet my whistle before I go back on stage."

Melody, whom I'd never seen fazed by a guy, looked momentarily taken aback. She glanced at Neil, who gave her a look as if to say, *Whatever you wanna do.*

She shrugged. "We have a little left over. I can dish you up a drink."

"I love a woman who can dish me up a drink." Fizz grinned. Luke moved to follow them. "Hang on, Twilight. You've been kinda fidgety. Why don't you head to the loo and meet me back out here in"—he looked at his smart watch—"ten minutes? The video will be done by then. I'll take this."

Smooth as honey syrup, Fizz handed Melody the giant

muddler and his tiki mug and slid the box with the London dock rum away from Luke. Fizz put an arm around Melody's shoulders and steered her back to the kitchen. To her credit, I saw her inching away from him as they walked.

"I don't like him," Luke murmured, articulating my own thoughts.

"We don't have to deal with him after today," Neil said, keeping his voice down as the movie played on and the crowd laughed at the funny bits.

"And Melody can handle herself," I added.

Luke nodded, resigned. "I guess I might as well go pee then. Will you hold onto this?" He held out the bag. Barclay took it with reverence, and Luke headed off in the other direction.

"Fizz is a piece of work," Barclay whispered. "But I'd still like to try his rum."

"You and everybody here," I answered.

The movie droned on for several more minutes, then a new slide popped up showing Fizz's flagship bar in San Diego.

But there was no Fizz. Melody hadn't come back, and Luke, designated errand boy, hadn't either. Kim stood up behind the projector, her head swiveling, looking around for her husband. The documentary crew used the break to fiddle with cameras and switch out memory cards. The crowd started to whisper.

"Pepper, check the kitchen. Barclay, check the bathroom and see if Luke fell in," Neil said. "I'll take the bag." He put the rum bag on the floor next to his bag of bar tools.

Barclay smirked and headed back toward the lobby and the restrooms. I gave Neil a sidelong glance but headed for the kitchen. There was no reason Neil couldn't go check. But maybe since I was friends with Melody, he thought it might be better if I was the one to—what? Discover her *in flagrante delicto?* That wasn't Melody's style at all. She loved men, but she'd never put up with any kind of serious advances from someone like Fizz Martin.

I pushed through the swinging door, blinked a few times to get used to the bright light, then made my way through the maze and around the corner to the obscure nook where we'd prepared the Molokai Mermaid.

And screamed.

Chapter Five

By the time I realized I'd stopped screaming, I began to notice other people around me gasping and shouting.

"Stand back!" I said instinctively. I'd seen enough *Law & Order* to know they shouldn't be standing so close. They might track through the blood.

Because there was a lot of blood. And Fizz Martin was lying on the cold, gray tile—

Did I mention there was a lot of blood?

And it was chaos. There was stuff everywhere, not just blood. Orange slices. Cherries. What looked like pieces of dishware or something. People were shouting, calling 9-1-1 ... I could dimly hear them asking for police and an ambulance and telling them to come back to the kitchen.

And ... *oh my God.*

Someone stood up slowly from where they'd been crouched behind a metal prep table. I hadn't seen him at first.

Luke.

His hands covered in blood.

At least he's alive, was the first thing I thought. And the second thing was: *Why is he holding the muddler?*

He dropped it to the floor with a clatter.

With a sick feeling, I realized the carved wooden club also was covered in blood.

This did not look good.

THE NEXT HALF hour was a whirlwind. I remembered a few things: The manager checking Fizz's pulse and telling everyone to get back but telling Luke and me specifically not to go far. The first wave of police arriving and pulling Luke aside. Neil showing up and wrapping an arm around me.

That's when I became aware that I was trembling. Trembling and cold. Neil's calm presence helped, and slowly, that red haze that had filled my vision faded, at least if I didn't look back toward the corner.

"They just told everyone in the other room that Fizz had to leave suddenly, so everyone headed into the bar," Neil said. "They're shutting down the dining room."

"I hope they don't have to shut down the whole restaurant," said the manager, a handsome, tan guy with a name tag that said "Pip" whose grim face didn't match his happy Hawaiian shirt.

Priorities. Gotta love 'em. You've got a dead guy in your kitchen, and you're worried about the crab rangoons.

Barclay and Neil flanked me, and I wondered where Melody was. Luke was across the space, being watched carefully by one of the first cops who'd arrived at the scene. I snuck a glance at the carnage. The body still lay there.

"Why don't they cover him up?" I whispered to no one in particular.

"They don't want to destroy any evidence," Barclay said.

Oh, right. I should know that from *Law & Order*.

The detectives arrived after the EMTs and the first cops, along with more cops who started putting up yellow tape and securing the scene. Crime-scene techs arrived about the same time and began their painstaking work.

There were two detectives. I could tell from the badges and civilian clothes. The woman, petite and tan with black curly hair, in no-nonsense dress pants and blouse, went to work parsing who was who. She said a few words to the cop watching Luke, who nodded and looked attentive and glared at Luke while the woman began to scan the scene. Luke's head was down and his eyes were closed. Maybe he was trying to shut the scene out of his head. I wish I could.

The male detective came our way first.

"Hi, Dad," Barclay said.

My mouth dropped open. "He's—you—"

"Detective Flores," he introduced himself with an almost-smile. The detective, wearing a charcoal sport jacket, was tall and handsome, his skin a shade darker than Barclay's topaz. He had even greener eyes.

He turned to his son. "I can't say I'm happy to find you here, but I'm glad you're OK. When I heard there was a death at Pau Hana, I worried."

"I'm OK." Barclay looked a little flustered, a rarity for him. "This is Neil, who runs the Bartenders. And this is Pepper. She found the—the body."

It sounded so stark. I mean, I knew Fizz Martin was dead ... but *Fizz Martin was dead.* How someone so much larger than life could be robbed of it so quickly and completely was beyond my immediate comprehension. I was still in shock, I guessed. I could've used a Jet Pilot about now. I would never drink a Molokai Mermaid again.

"Pepper. Last name?" Detective Flores pulled a notebook out of his jacket pocket.

"Revelle." I spelled it for him and gave him the contact info he asked for.

"Can we talk for a minute?"

"Uh, sure." I looked at the others and followed the detective around the corner and through the main kitchen to a quiet back hallway. I had an immediate sense of relief to be away from the carnage, even if I was about to be questioned by Barclay's dad. "So you're a Fort Lauderdale detective?"

"I've been here for about five years. Before that, Miami." He leaned a shoulder against the wall next to me and crossed one leg over the other, pen at the ready. The movement revealed the gun at his hip, under his jacket.

"Don't you have to, uh, recuse yourself because of Barclay?"

"Why? Did he kill the victim?" The tone was casual, but there was an edge. Maybe worry?

"No. Absolutely not. Barclay was in the dining room with us when Fizz went back to the kitchen. Barclay went to fetch Luke from the bathroom at the same time I walked into the kitchen and found Fizz. There's no way, I don't think. Unless he has some kind of speedy superpower I don't know about."

"He was good at track, but no." Detective Flores looked amused. And maybe relieved. "I think we're OK, then. You'd better start from the beginning."

So I told him about Fizz and his rare bottles of rum. How he talked about the London dock rum, then introduced all the bottles on stage, with Luke carrying them around until Fizz took the London dock rum box. How Fizz talked Melody into pouring him a drink and how she went into the kitchen with him.

"Melody? You work with her, right? I believe Barclay's mentioned her."

"Yeah, she's one of the Bohemia Bartenders. Melody Curtain." *Oh, shit.* Was I incriminating Melody?

"And what was her relationship with Mr. Martin?"

"What? She had no relationship. He just asked for a drink."

"Are you sure about that?"

"I hate to speak ill of the dead, but Fizz was a lech, OK? And Melody and I are good friends. She would've told me something like that. She probably felt like she couldn't say no to pouring him one of our cocktails. He's the big celebrity, and our team was here to support him today."

"Was Melody in the kitchen?"

"I assume she poured him his drink. But she wasn't there when I went back there."

"What about since then?"

I shook my head regretfully. "I haven't seen her since she went to the kitchen with Fizz." A dark thought occurred to me. "Do you think she's OK?"

"I expect so," said the seemingly unflappable Detective Flores. "Detective Cruz and I will want to speak with her. We'll take a look around, but if she's not here, make sure you get her in touch with us when you see her."

Great. Now I had a double worry. Luke was in trouble, and Melody was missing. Or a suspect. Or both.

"So, tell me about Luke."

"Luke is a good guy. Luke Wisnia." I spelled it for him. "He works for Neil Rockaway, who owns a bar in Bohemia, where we're all from."

He nodded. Of course he knew that. His son was one of us.

"Did Luke have any issues with Fizz Martin?"

"Not really. I mean, no."

"Not really?"

I swallowed. "Luke was a big fan. He was assigned to be Fizz's assistant today. Fizz gave him a nickname, and he didn't like it much, but Luke's kind of a, well, he's a nice guy." Luke was a wimp. But in a cute way. "Not the kind of guy who would kill somebody."

"Mm-hmm," the detective said, taking more notes. "Tell me about what you saw when you came into the back kitchen."

I nodded and took a deep breath. "Fizz was lying there. There was a lot of blood. And then Luke stood up. He was in the back corner. He was holding the muddler."

"That baseball bat thing?"

"Yes. It was a prop Fizz used for his presentations. It's supposed to look like a cocktail muddler."

"Big cocktail."

"I could use one about now."

He snorted. "Let's walk back. Did Luke say anything to you?"

"No," I said as we started walking. "I mean, I didn't give him much of a chance. I screamed my head off. He dropped the muddler. Luke kind of held his arms around himself like he was cold. He was shaking his head. He looked scared, to be honest. And then people started arriving, and the first officer on the scene pulled him over to the corner and made him wait there."

Detective Flores sighed. I had a feeling it didn't look good to him either.

"Oh my God," I exclaimed just as we rounded the corner and walked past a cop who was talking to Pip the manager and keeping everyone else away.

"What?"

"His wife. Fizz's wife. Someone needs to tell her. She was

running the projector for the show, Fizz's presentation. She was in the dining room. Her name is Kim."

"She hasn't been in the kitchen?"

"Not since earlier when we were all prepping drinks."

Neil was suddenly at my side. He was good at that. "Everything OK?"

"Do you know Kim Martin?" Detective Flores asked him.

"Yes."

"You haven't seen her since we left the room?"

"No," Neil said, stroking his trim beard. It was the closest thing to a nervous tic he had.

"Then she might not know what happened. Do you think you can see if you can find her?"

Neil's jaw set in a firm line. What a rough thing to ask him to do. But it was probably better than having the cops pushing through the crowd in the bar, looking for a woman they didn't know.

"I'll see what I can do," Neil said. He handed me the bag with the precious rums and his bar bag, then headed past Pip and the cop on the perimeter and out of the kitchen.

"Please wait a moment," the detective said to me, and walked toward Detective Cruz. They exchanged a few words, then really started scanning the mess on the floor. I couldn't help but follow their search. What were they looking for?

Barclay had been hovering at the edge of the mess. His eyes shifted to mine, then back to the scene. It was like he was drinking it all in. Good, because I didn't want to.

I went to him. "What did I miss?"

"They took a lot of pictures."

"What do you think they're looking for?"

He looked at me. "You really don't know?"

"Why would I know?"

"You gave them the whole story, right? What is the one thing Fizz wouldn't let out of his sight?"

I reluctantly scanned the scene again. The bits of what I thought was a plate I now recognized as pieces of the green ceramic tiki mug Fizz had been carrying. The muddler was still lying on the tile, a bloody mess and a good guess as the murder weapon. And before he gave it to me just now, Neil had ended up with the bag of bottles.

But not the box. Not the nuclear football.

The London dock rum was gone.

Chapter Six

"Maybe you should be a suspect," I teased Barclay.

"Who? Me? I have no interest in owning his dock rum. I'd have loved to taste it, sure, but owning something like that is a huge responsibility. It's like owning the *Mona Lisa*. You have to protect it. Respect it. I have enough to worry about."

"Whereas Fizz treated it like a carnival attraction."

"Maybe." Barclay shrugged. "I think somebody really wanted it. And that's what my dad is looking for. But he's not going to find it here. It's long gone."

Indeed, the detectives were opening the stainless-steel cabinets in this part of the kitchen and not turning up much except bowls and cooking pans.

Who wanted the rum badly enough to kill Fizz Martin for it?

I turned to Barclay. I'd had enough of the crime scene. And he was much nicer to look at anyway. But when he was looking over my shoulder, his eyes widened, and I turned to follow his gaze.

Neil was on the other side of the perimeter cop, just beyond the wide-open doorway that would lead visitors right into the shocking view of the crime scene. He waved and pointed, and I got it immediately. Next to him was Kim

Martin, who looked increasingly worried as she took in the cop and the noise from the scene that she couldn't yet see.

Neil was trying to protect her from seeing the crime scene. He was such a good guy. No wonder I had the hots for him.

I nodded, stepped forward and waved for Detective Flores's attention. He saw me and moved toward us, and I pointed toward Neil. The wall still blocked Kim's view. Detective Flores stepped out and around the perimeter cop and led Neil and Kim out of sight. And then I heard a terrible cry of anguish.

Just when this day couldn't get any worse.

Kim rushed around the corner and saw the whole horrible scene, the bewildered detective and Neil right behind her. Then she cried out again, turned and crashed right into Neil. He gingerly patted her back and whispered comforting words until she quieted a bit, then the detective again led her to the doorway.

Barclay elbowed me, and I looked up. "If you're going to watch," he said quietly, "we might as well hear them, too."

He was so bad. And so right. We edged over toward Neil, who was still close to the doorway, looking grim. I reached out and squeezed his shoulder. He nodded. And I listened.

Kim was teary as she described operating the projector during the show. "I had no idea he even bought that rum until this morning," she told the detective. "Fizz was always collecting something. He loved having the rarest rums. It wasn't my thing. I mean, I help create the menus, manage the business, but I left all that to him. It was just part of his persona, you know? And he loved it."

"Did anyone try to buy the rum from him?"

"I told you, I didn't know anything about it, so I have no idea. He didn't share his deals with me."

"Why? Were they illegal?"

"Would he announce to a room of a hundred or so people something he got illegally? Don't be ridiculous." She pushed her white-blond hair back and sniffed. "Everybody loved him. I don't see how this could've happened. You think a thief did it?"

"Could be. Do you know Melody Curtain?"

"No." Her eyes narrowed. "Melody—there was a Melody with the Bohemia Bartenders. What does she have to do with it? Did she kill Fizz?"

"We'd just like to ask her some questions."

"That's not good," Barclay whispered.

"Melody was in the bar," Neil whispered back.

"What?" I breathed. "Does she know what's going on?"

"I don't think so," Neil answered, "but we'd better hook her up with the detectives to clear up any misunderstanding."

I bit my lip. I had a bad feeling Melody being a suspect was my fault. But I had to tell Barclay's dad about Melody going back to the kitchen with Fizz, didn't I? And I knew she was innocent. Unless—unless Fizz tried something he shouldn't have. As much as she loved to flirt, Melody wouldn't put up with much crap from any guy.

Detective Flores was writing down Kim's contact information. "Where were you just now?" he asked her.

"The bar. There was an announcement that Fizz left the building. I figured he was on one of his quests, so I shut down the projector and went to the bar with everyone else."

"Quests?"

"Rum. Or whatever. The presentation was almost over anyway. And if he had a lead on a rare bottle of anything, he wouldn't hesitate to go after it."

"He wouldn't have texted you or anything?"

Kim gave him a funny look. "Fizz doesn't text."

Detective Flores raised one eyebrow. "OK. Thank you. I'm sorry for your loss. We might want to talk to you again, all right? Do you need anything?"

"No, thank you," she croaked. "I just want to go back to the hotel."

"We can give you a ride."

"No. That's nice of you, but I'd rather be alone. And I have a van here. For all of our convention stuff." A sob escaped her, and she wandered off, her hand on her head.

"Should I go with her?" I whispered to Neil.

Neil shook his head. "She wants to be alone. I get that."

Pip the manager pulled Detective Flores aside and had some heated words with him. Dinner would be off tonight while investigators double-checked the dining room for anything unusual, but the detective told Pip they'd do their best to finish processing the scene by the next day's dinner service.

"But we need to prep hours in advance!"

"As long as your people don't come in here, that's fine," the detective told him. "The M.E. isn't even here yet. A scene like this might take us fifteen, twenty hours to process. You're lucky the bar is operating. We could've shut down the whole restaurant."

Pip's shoulders slumped, and he headed off as the detectives put their heads together again. Now they approached Luke. Cruz and the cop that had been guarding our friend grabbed Luke by the arms, tugging him out of the room.

"Wait! I didn't do anything!" he cried out.

"We just need to ask you some questions, and it will be better to do that down at the station," Detective Flores said as he watched them leave the room. He shot a remorseful glance at us. At least he had the decency to look sorry about it.

I'd found Luke with a bloody club in his hands. I'd want to question him, too. But I knew in my heart he didn't do it.

"I need to get him a lawyer. Now," Neil said. "Pepper, get Melody. Make sure Detective Flores talks to her before he throws them both in jail, OK?"

"Right. OK."

Neil headed out, taking his bar bag but leaving the rare rums with me. I handed the bag to Barclay. "Please tell your dad to wait a minute. Tell him I can get Melody for him."

"No problem. Pepper?"

"Yeah?"

"Breathe, dude."

I blinked. Then I breathed. "OK. I'll be right back."

I WENT out the kitchen door that led me into the dining room. With dinner service canceled, there were just a few of the wait staff cleaning up the last of the cups and glasses, tiki mugs and appetizer plates people had used during the seminar.

A few of the tiki people were walking through, on their way out to the garden, I supposed. And there were several in the lobby and gift shop area chatting and laughing, spilling out from the crowded bar.

Inside the bar, colorfully dressed tiki folk shouted at each other over the surf band, elbow-to-elbow as they enjoyed fancy drinks and the bar's below-decks atmosphere. It was like being in the belly of a ship, with wood and ropes and nautical accoutrements, along with slanted windows that always had fake rain falling against them to increase the sense of cozy warmth inside.

It was more than cozy warmth, though. It was June, the air-conditioning was struggling, and the air steamed like a tropical jungle. The only people dressed appropriately were the barmaids, who had barely-there wraps around their wee butts and tiny bikinis around their luscious boobage. I mean, I had luscious boobage, but I didn't have the tiny figures these ladies did. I was sure they earned every penny they got in tips, not just because they looked great but because they were dealing with a sweaty mass of demanding, drunken revelers.

Even in my tropical dress, I felt like an outsider. Maybe because I had just found a body in the cold, gray kitchen.

I shook myself, breathed again and began the hunt for Melody. I had to push between packed tables on my left, the bar on my right and throngs of people standing in the middle. I slipped past the band on the far end and took a right to scope the rest of the L-shaped bar. And there I saw Melody, squeezed into a crammed alcove in the back, sitting on the lap of some guy dressed in a white sailor suit, hat and all. She was drinking something tall and frosty.

"Pepper!" she shouted when she saw me. "You have a lot of catching up to do!"

I tried to smile, but it just didn't happen. "What are you drinking?"

"Cobra's Fang. *Ssssss.*" Melody made a snake noise and curled two fingers into a fang shape and clawed them into my arm. "You need one of these."

There was never a statement more true, but there was no time. "Can I talk to you for a minute?"

"You'd better talk loud!"

"Outside? Please?"

She pouted.

"I'll take care of it," Sailor Boy said with a grin, tapping the bill on the table. "Go ahead. Come back soon."

"Thanks for the seat. I'll see you later." Melody kissed his cheek, leaving a bright red lip stamp, then got up and followed me out. "This better be good, Pepper," she shouted in my ear as I cleared a path and we spilled out into the lobby.

"It's not. It's bad," I said, leading the way toward the kitchen.

"What do you mean? Is everybody OK?" She halted in the middle of the nearly empty dining room.

I lowered my voice. "Our people are OK. For now. Listen, did you hear what happened to Fizz?"

Her eyes grew wide. "Oh, shit. Is he pissed at me?"

Good. She didn't kill him. I knew that in my heart, but hearing her assuming he was still alive took a weight off my mind. "He's not pissed at anyone. He's dead."

Melody took a staggering step backward. Her drink sloshed in the tall glass. Then she slurped the entire thing down with her straw and set the glass on a nearby table.

She took a heaving breath. "What happened?"

"He was murdered in the kitchen. The cops want to talk to you. And I should tell you, by cops, I mean Barclay's dad. He's a Fort Lauderdale police detective."

She just stood there blinking for a minute. "Is this a joke?"

"Would I joke about this? No. And think before you talk, OK? You might've been the last person to see him alive. Other than the person who killed him, that is. And there's something else you should know."

"What?"

"They've taken Luke in for questioning. I found him with the body, holding the bloody muddler."

"Fuuuuuu—"

"Melody Curtain?" The deep voice boomed out of the

dimness. It was Detective Flores, trailed by Barclay, coming from the direction of the kitchen.

Melody stood straighter. "Yes? You must be Barclay's father. It's so nice to meet you. I've heard a lot about you."

She had? That's right. She and Barclay just spent three hours in the car together. Plus they'd been friends awhile, too. And I had to hand it to her. Melody knew how to pull herself together in a hurry.

"Detective Flores," he said with a half smile. He gestured to a table. "Can we talk?"

Chapter Seven

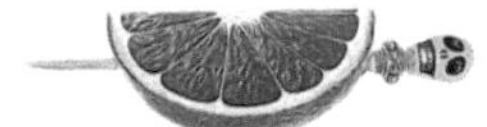

Melody snuck a glance at me, then sat at the table with Detective Flores. The party girl was now sober and serious. Well, except for the nutty floral tiara she was wearing.

At the detective's significant look, Barclay and I retreated to a short hallway off the lobby that led to the gift shop. Barclay still carried the bag with the remaining rare rums. We stood next to a display case set into the bamboo-lined wall that showed tropical shirts, leis, island instruments, jewelry, purses and tiki mugs.

"She didn't do it," I told him.

"Of course she didn't. She would never do something like that unless it was self-defense." Barclay raised an eyebrow. "It wasn't self-defense, was it?"

"I don't think so. She was shocked to hear Fizz was dead. But she also asked if he was pissed at her, so I wonder what happened."

"If my dad was pissed at her?"

"No, silly. Fizz. He must have done something, or she did something, or—frankly, my head hurts."

"We could get a drink."

"Always a good idea, but I want to wait and see how Melody does."

He nodded, and we looked at the display case to pass the time.

"I have a thought," I said.

"You always have many thoughts."

"But most of them are dirty."

He laughed.

"See that big bag?" I pointed to the largest bag in the display case. It featured a cartoony, toothy hula girl with a fringe (actual fringe) skirt, flowers and parrots. "I think we need that."

"Not my style," he joked.

"We need it for the rums! If someone is after rare rums, they might want these bottles, too." I gestured to the bag he carried. "Everybody saw Fizz's bag on stage. It's like carrying around a target."

"Right. And the best disguise at Hookahakaha is the loudest bag we can find. I like the way you think."

A few minutes later, we'd bought the hula-girl bag and stuffed Fizz's original bag into it. Then we drifted back out to the lobby, where we could look into the dining room and see the interview in progress. Detective Flores was taking more notes. We could only see Melody's back.

"That's some crown she's wearing on her head," Barclay said after a few minutes.

"I have one that's even more outrageous. I made it myself."

"More outrageous than that?" He grinned, and those amber-green eyes twinkled. It was nice to see someone smiling again.

"Totally. You'll see. Assuming we get to the point where we get to have fun again."

"The show must go on," he said. "Look. I think they're done."

The detective and Melody now stood, and we took that as our cue to wander over.

"Stay out of trouble," Detective Flores told Barclay.

"And take it easy on Luke," his son replied. "He didn't do it. He's a good guy."

"Good guys sometimes do bad things. But I'll keep it in mind." Detective Flores smiled for real this time, and his whole face got in on the action, echoing Barclay's. *Damn.* God save me from good-looking men. He handed Melody and I business cards. "Pepper, I'll let you know if I need anything else. Keep your eyes open and call me if you remember anything. All of you, be careful. If Luke isn't our man, then there's still a killer out there."

And then he was gone, heading back to the kitchen and the crime scene.

Melody huffed. "I need a goddamn drink."

WE HAD A FEW MINUTES' wait in the crowded bar, where we pretended nothing was wrong. We said hello to Dick and Dale, a couple of handsome guys we knew from Cocoa Beach who were trailed by a posse of ridiculously good-looking guys in matching aloha shirts.

"Bachelor party," Dick said with a grin. He was the thin, muscular one.

Dale looked more like a husky, hunky bodyguard. "Ours," he added. "We're getting married here on Sunday."

"That'll be gorgeous!" Melody said. But like all the women staring after the group with longing eyes, I'm sure she was thinking, *They are ALL gorgeous, and are any of them interested in girls?*

I also ducked behind a pole when Mr. Mixy squeezed by with his entourage. He used to be a barback in Bohemia and, unfortunately for me, a temporary-insanity boyfriend. He'd since become a famous mixologist in L.A. with a big, dark beard that resembled a fluffy Muppet and a pretentious series of popular online videos, making me further regret my past life choices. Not that I broke up with him—oh, no, that's the one good choice I *did* make. I regretted being involved with him at all and having to avoid him at conventions. I was better at recognizing narcissists now. At least I tried to learn from my mistakes.

Finally, we got our potions of choice and walked through the dining room to the back part of the building. There were smaller dining rooms there, along with the big Chinese ovens and the double doors that led to our destination: the garden.

The early evening sunlight was a little startling, given we'd been in the dark recesses of Pau Hana for hours. But the faux waterfall in its weirdly green pool was soothing and cooling, and the breeze rustling in the thick palms that crowded around the path eased the pain of the summer heat. Gentle Polynesian music and recorded bird sounds added to the tropical atmosphere.

We found a little path that headed into the middle of the thicket, which was dotted with South Seas tikis, and sat at a tiny metal table amid the rocks and greenery.

"Where's Neil?" Melody asked.

"He went to get Luke a lawyer." I took a long draw of my rum-heavy Jet Pilot, with its hint of tart lime, the sweet spice of falernum and a whisper of absinthe, and some of my tension melted away. This was the kind of drink that smacked you in the ass and kissed you silly at the same time. Not that I'd kiss and tell.

"So what did you tell my dad?" Barclay asked, savoring his Mai Tai.

"The truth." Melody slurped her fresh Cobra's Fang.

"Yeah, but what's the truth? What happened when you took Fizz back to the kitchen?" I asked.

"You mean, when *he* took *me* back to the kitchen. What a jerk. Sorry. It sucks that he died, but ..."

"What happened?" Barclay pushed.

Melody raised her eyebrows, took another sip, then set her drink down. "We went to the back corner, where there was still a little of the cocktail left in one of the buckets. He set down that stupid rum box ..."

"You mean stupid expensive," Barclay said, and I snorted.

"Yeah, whatever." Melody rolled her eyes. "I think he wanted his hands free. And just to be clear, I set down that overgrown muddler so I could pour him his drink. Not that he couldn't do it himself. I garnished his mug properly, because that's what we do. And I handed it to him."

"And?" I asked. I had a feeling she enjoyed drawing this out.

"He took a sip and said, 'This is delicious, but I bet it's not as delicious as you are.'"

"Oh, please," Barclay said.

"I've heard worse lines," I said. "But not from a married putz." The dappled sunlight fell across Melody's pretty face, sexy dress and blond up-do. No doubt Fizz took one look at her, licked his lips and decided she would be his conquest du jour. "What did you say?"

"I said, 'I'm scrumptious, but you'll never find out just how much.' I went to leave, and he grabbed my arm and yanked me in and laid a big kiss on me."

Barclay grimaced.

"So," I asked, "does that mean your lipstick will still be on him? And your DNA?"

"Gross. Will you stop with the crime scene forensics already? I told the detective what happened, including that my prints were on the muddler and the mug, since he made me carry them," Melody said. "The point is, I pulled away and smacked him and got the hell out of there."

"Ooo, smacked him. So old-school," Barclay said.

"It felt good," she admitted.

"So is that when the tiki mug got broken?" I asked.

Melody shook her head. "The good detective asked me that too, and no, I don't think so. I didn't see him drop it or hear anything shatter. Plus, Fizz's phone started ringing as I went around the corner, and I heard him answer it. So Detective Flores said they would look at his phone records and figure out who called him. As I left, I even heard him say something like, *Hola,* Kokomo! I'm drinking a cocktail I invented, living my best life and looking for my next wahine,' so if the caller can verify that, they'll at least know he was still sipping when I left. I was back there three minutes, tops."

"And then where did you go?" I asked.

"Well, Sergeant Pepper," she teased, "I went out the back hallway that leads to the lobby."

"There's a back exit?" I asked. Multiple exits meant multiple entries. Multiple ways to access the crime scene.

"I believe there are multiple exits from the kitchen to other parts of the restaurant and the outside. I went past the back bar and got out to the lobby. Then I went to the bathroom, and then I figured I might as well check out the gift shop, because they have some adorable dresses, and the last thing I wanted to do was hear more of Fizz's foolishness. And then everyone was headed to the bar, so that's where I went."

"Can someone confirm where you were?" Barclay asked.

"Besides the sailor," I added.

She quirked her mouth. "The attendant was in the bathroom and took my dollar for the towel, and we had a nice chat about the carvings in there. And the gift shop is holding my purchase for me, so yes on both counts, just like I told your dad. Who said he might have to question me again, by the way, but I don't think he thinks I did it."

I breathed out a big sigh. "That's good. That just leaves us to worry about Luke."

And whether he killed Fizz Martin.

Chapter Eight

Barclay used an app to summon a ride for our trip back to the hotel, since Neil had taken the car and we hadn't heard anything from him. I'd texted him twice to no avail.

I had visions of Luke being fingerprinted and led off to jail. Putting Luke in jail would be like throwing a steak into the lion enclosure at the zoo. But I figured Barclay's dad was a fair guy, even if he wasn't the only one who would determine Luke's fate.

The truth was, it was hard to imagine just how Luke got in that position in the Pau Hana kitchen, with a bloody murder weapon in his hand, if he *hadn't* killed Fizz.

I tried to put all of that out of my mind as we pulled up at Wicker Wharf. The sun was low in the sky, and the light was golden. It should've been a relaxing tropical evening. But the big lobby's electronic chill music did anything but chill me out with its relentlessly annoying high-hat beat.

I tried to shake off the day as we headed toward registration. In the secondary lobby near the vendor hall, which hadn't opened yet, the mood lifted. Big tikis dominated the space. A ukulele trio of guys in Hawaiian shirts, straw hats and fluffy leis were jamming and singing silly songs, and one of the visiting bar teams gave out cocktails from a tiki-hut bar. Folks stood around chatting in their bright retro clothes. This was a happy place, especially because news of Fizz's demise apparently hadn't arrived here yet.

We picked up the team's swag bags, wristbands and badges, and I bought an extra drink wristband for Gina so she and Astra could enjoy the pool parties while I was working. As Barclay said, the show must go on.

We also picked up cocktails from the tiki bar, which came in orange Hookahakaha cups.

Melody took a sip as the lime-wheel and parasol garnish poked her in the nose. "Mmm, I love a good Jungle Bird."

The rum drink was especially delicious because this one was made with fresh pineapple juice, not that nasty canned stuff. "But it makes me think of Luke," I said.

"Explain," Barclay said after sipping his. "Ahhhh."

"Because he has parrots and monkeys tattooed all over his arms?" Melody guessed.

"Jungle birds. Exactly." I quaffed half the drink as we moved back to the big lobby—and, to my great relief, saw Neil and Luke coming in through the main doors.

"Luke!" Melody cried out. Hmm. Maybe Melody was more invested in Luke than she was letting on?

She was the first to hug him, and we all followed. I hugged Neil, too, who just looked embarrassed.

"Stay here. I'll get you guys a drink," Melody said, and Barclay, Neil, Luke and I sat in a cluster of cushy chairs in the orbit of the vast, open-air lobby bar.

"Are you OK?" I asked Luke.

He nodded but didn't say anything. He was pale, and his normally perfect shoulder-length hair was frizzy and askew. He looked like he'd just survived the Hindenburg disaster.

"I called a friend of my father's who does criminal law," Neil said. "He came to the station right away."

"So they didn't charge you with anything?" Barclay asked Luke.

Neil answered again. "No. Wait a sec. Melody should hear this, too."

The suspense was killing me.

OK, maybe that wasn't the best phrase to use right now.

After an awkward couple of minutes, Melody came back with a fresh round of Jungle Birds for all of us. Don't ask how she balanced five cups in her arms. She's a professional.

Luke took his drink, looked at Melody with gratitude and took a deep sip. Then he let out a tremendous sigh and leaned back. His eyes got kind of shiny. "This was the worst day ever."

"I'm sorry, man," Barclay said, "but it could've been worse. You could still be there."

"That's true," Luke said.

"The question is, why aren't you? What happened?" I shook my head. "I'm so sorry, Luke. I didn't mean to scream like that when I saw you, but—"

"It's OK, Pepper. I should've screamed when I saw him, too." Luke took another sip. Color started to return to his face. "When I got back there—saw everything—I just shut down. And then ... I was worried. I didn't know what to think. Melody had been the last person to see him, and she had the muddler."

"But I left him there, totally alive and well in all his asshole glory," Melody exclaimed, then lowered her voice. "Sorry. I know. He's gone."

"Don't be sorry. We know what he was." Barclay turned back to Luke. "But what happened, man?"

"I guess I should've gone straight to the dining room from

the bathroom, but I peeked in and didn't see Fizz with you guys, so I thought it might be better to head back to the kitchen to see what he was up to and make sure he got back on time. I didn't want to walk in front of the whole audience in the dining room, so I went through one of the back hallways. I can't even tell you which one, now. It's a maze back there."

Pau Hana was huge. It was easy to see how he could've gotten lost. I leaned closer, keeping my voice low so no one could overhear. "So you went back to the kitchen, and what did you see?"

"What you saw. Fizz lying on the floor. The mess. The blood. The muddler—it was lying on him, right on top of his neck, so I picked it up so I could feel his pulse. It's what they always do in the movies. I don't even know if I was doing it right." Luke put down his empty cup on a side table. Neil, who hadn't touched his drink, handed his cup to Luke, who took another deep sip. "Anyway, I didn't feel anything except numb, and then a bunch of thoughts were screaming through my head." He lifted his eyes to Melody's. "I thought about you."

"About me?" she said.

"You went back there with him. I thought maybe—maybe you killed him. And I didn't want anybody to know. I mean, I'm sure you had a good reason if you did. And I felt sick to my stomach. I huddled there behind the prep table to try to get my thoughts together. I still had the muddler in my hand, I guess. I don't even remember. That's when you came in, Pepper."

"And what did the cops think of all this?" I asked.

"Well, thanks to Neil, I talked to the lawyer right away, and I told him I didn't want to tell them anything if it meant incriminating Melody."

"Silly boy," Melody said. "I wouldn't kill that blowhard. I smacked him, though."

Luke erupted in a laugh. "Oh my God." He covered his mouth for a moment, his eyes wide, surprised at his own reaction. "Well, I didn't say much during the first part of the interview, and they were getting really frustrated with me and told me I was going to be charged with murder. And then they started asking me about Melody, and I figured out that they didn't think you were a suspect. So I told them about you going back there with him and that it was several minutes before I went to check on him and found him like that."

"I think it helped that Luke hadn't fled the scene," Neil said. "Plus, his clothes."

"What about his clothes?" I asked.

"There was no blood spatter on them," Neil answered. "His hands were bloody from the muddler, but if he'd bashed Fizz's face in, there would've been blood all over his clothes."

Melody made a funny noise. When I looked over at her, she was as white as a bourbon milk punch. She took a big gulp of her drink and sat back in the chair and closed her eyes.

"You're not going to faint on me, are you?" I asked.

"No," she squeaked. "Carry on."

"Sorry," Neil said. "But that's how the lawyer laid it out for me later, after they released Luke. I don't think they've ruled him out entirely, but they know the facts don't add up. He's still a person of interest."

"And the London dock rum is missing," I said. "If Luke was going to kill Fizz for the rum ..."

"Barclay might've." Luke wore a little smile. I was relieved to see it.

Barclay chuckled. "Never." Though he clutched the hula girl bag with the other rums a little more tightly.

I gave Barclay the side-eye. "I was ready to turn in Barclay, too, but let's not give his dad a heart attack. Anyway, the rum is missing. It makes sense that the killer was the thief who stole the rum."

"It won't be easy to narrow down who that might be. Everybody knew about that rum," Neil said. "Fizz started with the story in the kitchen earlier today, and then he told the entire audience about it. They all saw the box, too."

"Yeah, but is it going to be some rando klepto from the Hookahakaha crowd?" I asked.

Neil shot me a droll smile. "Rando klepto? It could've been. It's not like this was a thoughtfully planned heist. It was a crime of opportunity. It could've been anybody."

"But more likely," Barclay said, "it was someone serious about rum or someone who knew how to sell the bottle to someone serious about rum."

"So we should start with the rum collectors," I said. "Talk to everybody with a ticket to the Gold Tooth Rum Tasting. Even if they're not in the market for stolen rum, they might know who is."

"Whoa," Neil said. "We have a lot to do here. We've got to serve drinks for a couple of hours poolside tomorrow, plus we're prepping most of the day for the Tiki Skyliner party in the tower tomorrow night. And we have a packed agenda for most of the weekend. We don't have time to play Nancy Drew."

"You say 'Nancy Drew' like it's a bad thing." I glowered at him. "Nancy Drew rocks. And we have to find the real thief."

"Why?" Neil asked.

"Because of Luke," Melody said.

"Yeah, Luke," said Barclay. "I've heard enough of my dad's work stories to know that if they can't find a perfect suspect, they might go back to the second-best. And a jury is going to love a guy with bloody hands holding the murder weapon who hated to be called 'Twilight.' Right, Twilight?" he said to Luke.

A slow, reluctant smile took over Luke's face. "Right. And I appreciate it, guys. But I don't want anybody getting killed. I'll be fine."

Neil sat up in his chair, and we all leaned in to hear him. "Pepper, I get your point. And Luke, you know I'm on your side. But we have to be careful." He eyed each of us in turn, then settled back on me. *"Careful,* Pepper. Remember New Orleans?"

"So you're not going to fire me if I sniff around a little?" I don't know why I was so excited.

"I won't fire you," he said, his gray eyes intense. "As you once pointed out, we're all partners. Sniff around a little. But be careful, OK? And I want to be along for the ride whenever possible."

I raised an eyebrow and pursed my lips at him. *Oh, Neil.* If he only knew how I loved his inadvertent double entendres.

And I couldn't wait to start sniffing.

Chapter Nine

When you're sweating at 7 a.m., you know you're in South Florida.

The air-conditioning in the hotel room wasn't too bad, but it struggled with the June heat, and I ran a little hot anyway. Especially with a snoring, warm little bundle of fur curled up in the crook of my arm.

We'd stayed in the hotel bar last night for another couple of hours, talking things out, eating expensive hamburgers and, of course, drinking. The bar drinks were substandard, so Neil had run up to his room and quietly brought back a pitcher full of Rum Barrels that we shared until we all pleaded exhaustion and turned in. I'd tried luring Gina out to the lobby by text, but she said she was enjoying a movie on TV. At least I was confident Astra was happy.

The dog wasn't happy now, though, as the sky brightened outside. She'd climbed onto my chest, squishing my boobs and filling my face with fish breath. She kneaded my skin, making me yelp—it was time to get her daggers trimmed. Still half asleep, I tried petting her with my eyes closed and settling her down, but she wouldn't have it. She kept creeping up my chest until her face was right against mine.

"OK, beast," I groaned. I glanced over at Gina. She was still asleep. That Rum Barrel I'd brought her before bedtime must've knocked her out cold, but she sure seemed to like it, telling me she'd never had a drink that good before.

That's because she never had a Bohemia Bartenders drink before. I loved introducing naive drinkers to the good stuff.

I shuffled Astra off me, went to the bathroom and pulled on light blue-and-white-striped lounge pants and a white tank top with a built-in bra. I added my dark sunglasses and leather sandals, tied up my caramel-brown hair in a ponytail and leashed up the pup in her little pink harness to take her on her morning constitutional.

We slipped out the door, then went down the corridor to the next available staircase to the ground floor. That led us right out to the lush, green lawn, which was dotted with beautiful old palm trees, mostly coconut palms and royals. I spotted an iguana climbing slowly up the trunk of one of them, giving me the stink eye when I moved closer to check him out. So we wandered toward the sprawling pools, with their geometric arches that doubled as waterfalls, and meandered around the edge.

Convention volunteers were setting up the last of the cabana bars. Later, they'd be staffed by some of the coolest tiki bartenders from around the world.

Astra tugged me along, watering bushes as we went, and I followed, looking around idly. This was not an early crowd, and only a few people were poolside. One was a stocky guy with round, pink cheeks and a red mustache and beard, wearing a white sea captain's hat with his aloha shirt, white shorts and sandals. He lounged in a long chair and sipped from a travel coffee mug that said *World's Best Drunk*. He was reading the sports section of the local newspaper. My eye was drawn to a headline on the news section lying by his feet.

I gasped, and the guy looked up.

"Good morning," he said, looking a bit puzzled. "What a cute dog. Does she normally eat doughnuts?"

"What? Oh, shit!" I yanked Astra away from the man's plate. I hadn't seen it sitting under his lounge chair. "Damn it. I'm so sorry." My continuing campaign to stop cursing seemed to be headed in the opposite direction. I unsuccessfully tried to pull the last of the doughnut out of Astra's mouth. She gulped and grinned, her mouth covered in pink icing and sprinkles. "She prefers bagels with cream cheese, actually."

He laughed. "No problem. She did me a favor. I've already had two. What's her name?"

"Astra. And I'm Pepper. Can I buy you another doughnut? Or another coffee?"

"Oh, this isn't coffee." He winked. "Here, have a seat." He smiled and gestured to the lounger next to his. I sat sideways on it and kept an eye on Astra, who was sniffing around for crumbs. "I'm Cap Calder," he said, touching the bill of his hat. "But some folks just call me Captain."

"I can't imagine why," I said, and he laughed. "Do you have a boat?"

"I have a car that looks like a boat. I'm sure you'll see it later," he said to my puzzled expression. "Truth is, I hate boats."

"Oh, gosh, me too. I mean, I don't mind a canoe or a kayak, but if I ride on any other kind of other small boat, I turn completely green."

"I'm OK on boats," he said, "but I just think there are more efficient and pleasant ways to get inebriated. When it gets hot, I prefer to sit over there"—he gestured to a corner of the courtyard—"on my patio in the shade and watch the pool and sip my very good rum."

I could respect that. "Well, it's nice to meet you. I didn't mean to interrupt you, only do you mind if I look at your paper for a minute?" I gestured toward the news section lying at the end of his lounge chair.

"Knock yourself out. I always go for the sports first anyway."

"Thanks." I picked it up and looked more closely. The headline was at the bottom of the front page: *Bar impresario dies at tiki restaurant.* The story went on to say Fizz Martin had died at Pau Hana and the death was suspicious. Police said they had "several leads," but the story was low on details. Maybe the cops were withholding them to see what they could shake loose. The missing rum wasn't mentioned. But there was a short bio of Fizz enumerating his various accomplishments, nothing that couldn't be had from a Wikipedia entry. Maybe he'd get a better obituary later. The guy had proven himself kind of a jerk, but he'd also had a huge impact on the bar and tiki community, and his death was going to cause shock waves.

"What are you reading there?" Cap asked.

There was no point in trying to hide it. I handed over the section. "Some bad news for Hookahakaha."

Cap took the paper, scanned it and stopped at the story. His mouth opened slowly and his eyes widened as he scanned it. "Well, shit."

"Yeah. I know."

"I was at the seminar yesterday. I just thought he left the building. That's what they said."

"I guess his soul left the building but not the rest of him."

Cap looked at me closely. "You know something about it?"

"I know it was suspicious, like the paper said." I wasn't going into the gruesome details with someone I'd just met. "Did you notice anything strange about yesterday?"

"The only thing I noticed is when my drinks started to get

low. Then I ordered more. The Molokai Mermaid was fantastic, but I ordered a few of Pau Hana's drinks to tide me over until happy hour."

A few? Those drinks would knock anybody on their ass. Anybody except Cap, I guessed.

"I sure wish I could've gone to that Gold Tooth Tasting," he said wistfully. "Some really fine rums he had. You don't think they'll still have it, will they? I didn't get a ticket, but a lot of people paid a lot of money for that."

"That's an excellent question." What would the organizers do? Neil had taken the hula-girl bag with the other two bottles from Barclay and was planning to ask the organizers and Kim Martin what to do with them. Maybe that show would go on, too.

I realized Astra had found the sports section and was chewing her way through the baseball news.

"No, girl!" I yanked the paper out of her mouth and left it on my chair. "I'd better get her going. She's not empty yet."

"Understood," he said. "Nice to meet you. See you later?"

"I'm one of the bartenders, so no doubt you will. I'll be out by the pool with something tasty later today."

"I'll be there!" Cap said. "See you later!"

After Astra left a deposit in the Bank of Poo, which I withdrew with a plastic bag and tossed in an appropriate receptacle, I headed back to the room, thinking. If the newspaper had the story, everybody would know about Fizz.

Gina was in the shower when I got back to the room, so I fed Astra her *real* food and settled on the bed to check my phone. Sure enough, on the Hookahakaha app's announcements page, there was a somber message saying that Fizz had passed on and a tribute was in the works. It had even fewer details than the newspaper story, but that was just as well. It also said the Gold Tooth Rum Tasting would go on as scheduled, run by Conan Cray, our friend and rum expert, and ... Neil! Regrettably, the London dock rum was no longer on the agenda, the notice said without revealing why.

I texted Neil. "What, you didn't have enough to do already?"

"You saw the announcement, I take it," he wrote back. "You busy? I could use some help in the kitchen."

Astra barked and ran over to Gina, who was emerging from the bathroom, to demand her morning petting. Gina was already dressed in a cute sundress. It even had a tropical pattern. She'd fit right in.

"How are you this morning?" I asked as she petted the dog.

"I feel good. I sure slept hard. I'd like to try another drink or two today, if that's OK. That punch was really good, and I'm thinking maybe I can learn something about cocktails. I was googling this morning while you were out and realized it's kind of a gap in my education."

"You should absolutely try some drinks today. Starting at noon, there will be bars rotating in and out of the cabanas around the pool, and they all have fantastic mixologists. That's what the wristband is for."

"Oh, yeah. The wristband." She found hers on the end table and slipped it on. "Thanks. You have to work?"

"Yeah, after a quick shower. Astra already ate and did her business."

Astra looked at me and barked.

"But she can have a treat or two. Later. She also had a doughnut."

Gina looked horrified. "You feed her doughnuts?"

"Astra fed herself a doughnut." I went over, picked up the

dog and gave her some love. "Astra feeds herself all manner of things. Just don't let her start drinking."

I put her on the bed and turned back to my phone and Neil's text. "Give me a few minutes and I'll meet you in the kitchen," I typed.

"Good," he replied. "I have a couple thousand limes and some ideas on where you can start sniffing."

Chapter Ten

The hotel kitchen wasn't quite as big as Pau Hana's, but it was still a bit of a maze, with access to the restaurant, back elevators, a service hallway and the ballroom, where the vendors were finishing setup. I knew all of this because I got thoroughly lost on my way there.

I found the Hookahakaha crew in a prep area off the main kitchen. There were a few cheesy party-store tiki decorations up—leis, lanterns, green plastic fringe. A bulletin board was covered with schedule information. There were maybe a half dozen people already working at big stainless-steel tables, and more trickled in behind me.

Val was one of them, her pink hair still wet. She wore a T-shirt that said "Drinks Well With Others," black cropped cargo pants and combat boots.

"If I get some Earl Grey in the next five minutes, I might not kill someone," she said at a significant volume as she set down a rough-looking canvas bar bag. It was almost as beat-up as my fat messenger bag, which held a few basic bar tools and a bunch of other stuff besides. I idly fingered the small hole in the side, a souvenir of New Orleans. I'd have to get a cool patch or pin to plug that up.

Val laid out tools at her station, which was marked off with yellow masking tape on the metal table and labeled in black marker. Some smart-ass had written on the tape: *Abandon hope, all ye who enter here,* along with arrows and *VAL-halla!* Similar tape was on the walk-in cooler, labeled *Hookahakaha bars only—THIS MEANS YOU!*

One of the guys gave Val a wave and disappeared, coming back a few minutes later with a steaming mug, its teabag tag fluttering. He set it on the table in front of her.

"What's the status?" she asked him. I took a closer look at his badge. It said "Cocktail Coordinator," so he was one of her hired helpers. Val's badge said "Cocktail Queen."

They looked over a sheaf of papers and started writing a long list on a white board while I found Neil. He was at his own prep table with an industrial squeezer and boxes and boxes of limes. Blue tape marked "Bohemia Bartenders" outlined his work station. I realized other tables had similar zones. These people were serious about their territory.

"How long have you been here?" I asked him. I swear, the man didn't sleep.

"A couple of hours. You look nice."

I got all tingly inside. "Just my work clothes," I said. Though the loose army-green crop pants, scoop-neck white T-shirt and black vest were all designed to enhance my finer points. My chunky black sneakers were cute and great for standing. And my hot-nerd retro glasses kept juice out of my eyes, even if they weren't actually designed to help my vision. My hair was tied up with a tropical-patterned scarf, Rosie-the-Riveter-style. "You look nice, too."

He wore long khaki shorts and a nice Junction Box black T-shirt and cap, advertising his home bar. Truth is, I would've thought he looked nice in anything.

"Do you want to squeeze, or do you want to slice?" he asked.

"What are you sick of doing?"

"I could use a break from the squeezer. But beware. It's the squeezer of death."

"Fine by me. I'm not afraid."

"You will be," he said in a Yoda voice, and I cracked up. "Let me demonstrate."

The Yoda voice was appropriate, because the squeezer looked like a miniature R2D2, without all the buttons. It had a chrome base and a white top with a hood that looked kind of like an astronaut's helmet, only imagine a helmet with no face guard. Just a hole where you sacrificed your hand to the squeezer gods.

Neil cranked it up. He reached in through the hole in the helmet with one of the lime halves he'd cut and pressed it down against the screaming-fast reamer spinning in the middle. Juice dribbled out the spout below into a square container. The juicer had all the finesse and volume of a jet engine and none of the safety features.

"Mother of God," I said.

"I know. You sure you're up for this?"

I tried to look brave. "How bad can it be?"

"Well ..." Neil nodded toward the white board, which now was covered with lists of ingredients and numbers.

I looked more closely. "Does that say *eight hundred ounces* of lime juice?"

"Yeah. And we're saving all the shells for garnishes. But I've halved a ton of limes already."

"Of course you have."

He laughed. "I'll work on the lime wheels."

"Yeah, that should be easy. Only nine hundred of those." The other numbers were mind-boggling too, from five hundred pineapple slices to four thousand mint sprigs. I guess

I shouldn't have been surprised. We had to supply not only a dozen bars doing stints in staggered shifts at the pools this afternoon, but the Tiki Skyliner party tonight.

"Hey, do you have enough swizzles for this afternoon and tonight?" I asked. We were among the featured bartenders at the party, and Neil was so excited about it, he'd ordered custom Bohemia Bartenders swizzle sticks—sky blue with a happy skull, plumeria flowers and a heart molded into the plastic, and our name on the shaft. I'd already stolen a few of them for my collection.

"I have the swizzles. And the two hundred pineapple shells on that prep list are for us, too. Barclay and Luke will be coring the pineapples a little later. Melody's supposed to decorate our station in the tower this morning. And before you get started," he said, lowering his voice, "Cray is getting us a list of ticket-holders for the Gold Tooth Tasting."

"Ooo, suspects!"

"Don't jump to conclusions. But if they are suspects, I don't want you talking to them alone. I'm going with you."

Oh, goody! "You don't have to," I said, trying to play it cool.

"Yes, I do. I think we can catch some people this afternoon before our stint at the pool party."

"Sounds like a plan."

Cray had won the tenth ticket to the tasting. I wondered who the other nine lucky bastards were. I'd met Cray in New Orleans, and while he was an obsessive collector, I couldn't see him doing something as dreadful as killing Fizz Martin. Though if a bottle of London dock rum came to him through the grapevine? The temptation to own that unique piece of history might be too great to resist.

Making craft cocktails seems pretty glamorous in videos like Mr. Mixy's, with nice, clean hipster clothes, sexy lighting and all the messy parts edited out. But the truth is, it's damned hard work. As I tried to avoid losing a finger in the squeezer of death, some twenty other bartenders and volunteers were now working in the kitchen to fulfill the demands of Val's master list, making guava honey syrup, snipping mint, stripping basil leaves, cutting oranges, chunking watermelon, slicing their way through stacks and stacks of boxes of produce ... it was crazy impressive. Each had a work area designated by blue masking tape—not yellow, like the queen's—and Val was quick to scold anyone who strayed out of their spot or screwed around with tools or ingredients or was distracted by gossip—because the name "Fizz" leapt several times out of the chatter as the bartenders tried to suss out what happened at Pau Hana.

Despite her grumpiness, or because of it, Val had earned her crown. Her knife work was dazzling, and she ran the whole operation like a general on D-Day. In fact, her glower every time I tried to chat with Neil had me working twice as fast. Maybe I didn't really need all ten fingers?

By the time we'd finished beating the limes into submission, I smelled like a juice factory and my squeezer hand was painfully cramped from repetitive motion and constant terror. Neil doffed his hat, leaving it at his station, and stretched. We gave a nod to Barclay and Luke, who were busy coring pineapples, and headed out into the sunlight.

It was just after noon, and the poolside bars were cranking up. The adjoining pools, sparkling blue in the sunshine, were crowded now, with lots of retro bathing suits and straw hats in evidence and plenty of people in the water. Under the swaying palms, a DJ played exotica and surf music.

"Wanna get a drink?" I was already sweating in the tropical heat. Puffy clouds were building in the pale blue sky and moving inland, promising storms later.

"Lunch first, I think. Unless you want to see me drunk."

"Oh, Neil, I so want to see you drunk."

"But then you'll just take advantage of me," he quipped.

I laughed. Because I'd certainly consider it. And I was relieved to know that he was still interested in flirting with me.

We took the few steps up to the poolside cafe and sat across from each other at a table under an umbrella. We pulled out the menus that were propped up between the napkin box and condiment carrier, and in a couple of minutes, a server took our order. Neil got a mahi sandwich. I got quesadillas. They were the cheapest thing on the menu, and they weren't cheap. We also got plain old water and gulped it like it was going out of style, still hydrating after all our work in the kitchen.

I was just checking the schedule on my convention app as we waited for our food when I felt a presence in front of me and looked up. It was an elegantly wrinkled man in a white suit with a broad white hat, and he was grinning.

"Mr. Cray!" I said.

"Hello, darlings. It's Kayanne, isn't it?"

"They still call me Pepper," I said, smiling because he remembered my real name.

"And they still call me Cray."

"Would you like to join us?"

"Indeed I would. I was invited."

"Thanks for coming, Cray," Neil said, standing and pulling out a chair for the older gentleman, so he was at a right angle to both of us. "I'm buying."

"Excellent. How are the cocktails here?"

"Frankly, we didn't want to take the chance, not with all the bar pop-ups waiting for us," Neil replied.

"I expect that's wise." Cray sat and hung his hat on the

back of the chair. "I'll order some lemonade." He waved at our server and put in an order for lemonade and oysters Rockefeller.

Conan Cray seemed like the kind of man who would take his lemonade on the veranda. Though he had a Southern accent, he wasn't native to New Orleans, where I'd met him. Native New Orleans folks, me among them, didn't really have a classic Southern accent. But Cray did have a gothic old multi-story house in New Orleans where he kept his extensive rum collection and a modern mixology/chemistry lab that came in handy during our last visit.

"Where are you from, Mr. Cray?" I asked him. "I mean, obviously you live in New Orleans, but I'm curious about your accent."

"Savannah, my dear. Born and bred. And maybe dead, someday. They have such nice cemeteries in Savannah."

"So does New Orleans," I said.

"Yes, but I don't like the idea of being buried in a crypt. I'll feel safer in the cool, dark ground."

OK, that was creepy. But he said it with a smile.

"Do you have the list?" Neil asked.

"I do indeed." Cray pulled a piece of paper from inside of his jacket. "They were kind enough to print this for me in the business center. I'm not much for reading off these little screens." He patted the chest pocket of his jacket, where I could see the outline of a phone. "This is why I don't belong to the online rum group where all the cool kids like to chat."

He pulled a pair of half-frame eyeglasses from the same pocket and perched them on his nose as he unfolded the paper. I couldn't quite see what was on it, though I sure tried.

"What can you tell us about the Gold Tooth tasters?" Neil asked.

"Well, there's obviously one extremely well-connected collector on this list, but I think we can rule him out." Cray looked up and raised a mischievous eyebrow at us. Neil chuckled and I smiled.

"Don't keep us in suspense," I said. "Who looks like they'd really, really want some London dock rum?"

"Well, the real question is, who wouldn't?" Cray said. "Of all the names of people I know on this list, every single one of them would be delighted to get their hands on that bottle. But perhaps that is not the question."

"What do you mean?" Neil asked.

"I like to ask, 'What doesn't belong here?' Or to be more specific to the situation, who doesn't belong? And there's a name here I've never seen associated with rum collecting. Someone who doesn't love rum coming to a tasting like this? They have to have an ulterior motive."

Chapter Eleven

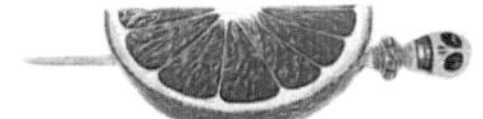

n ulterior motive? Why would anyone with a ticket to the tasting have an ulterior motive?" I asked Cray.

"A gut feeling," Cray said. "Take a look."

Neil snatched the list from Cray's outstretched hand before I could, shooting me a *Ha!* sort of look that made me want to smack him and kiss him at the same time.

He scanned the list. "Are you talking about Number Eight plus one? That name looks really familiar to me."

"Well, perhaps she is a rum collector, then," Cray said.

"Who is it?" My patience had run out.

"Greer Allighant," Neil said. Then his head snapped up. "Greer Allighant! I do know her! And no, she's not a rum collector that I know of. More of an art collector, or at least she used to be. I thought she was living on cruise ships. Ez, whose band plays a lot at my bar, told me all the details. Greer used to live in Bohemia Beach and came into my bar once or twice."

"Is she the sort who would murder for a treasure?" Cray asked casually.

Neil shook his head. "Not from what I hear. A really cool older lady."

"And what is older, exactly?" Cray teased.

Neil smiled. "Just an expression. But we'll talk to her. I'm more interested in some of the other names on this list."

"Give me that!" I exclaimed, reaching over and yanking the paper from his hands.

"Easy," Neil said. "I can't afford a paper cut. The lime juice will be hell."

Cray chuckled, and the waiter came with our pricey hotel food. It looked pretty good. But I only took a second to take a bite of quesadilla before looking closely at the list.

I couldn't help a little gasp, and then I looked up guiltily.

Neil had caught me, of course. "What?"

"Nothing. Nobody." I took another bite of quesadilla so I didn't have to talk.

His eyes narrowed. "Pepper?"

Then Cray stared at me, too, until I finished chewing, which was really awkward.

"OK. Fine. I just happened to notice Mark Fairman on the list."

"Do you think he might be a suspect?" Cray said.

"I don't know."

Neil assumed a wry expression. "But Fairman did take quite an interest in Pepper in New Orleans."

"We barely spoke!" I said. But he was right. I'd only run into Mark a couple of times, but the English owner of Fairyland Distillery was sex on a swizzle stick, redheaded and muscular and, oh, that accent in that deep, husky voice ... and he sniffed around me like I was a glass of his very fine gin. I took a long drink of water and tried to get myself under control. "Anyway, he's rich, isn't he? So he might be in the market for a bottle like this. Or he could've hired someone. He's also strong. He could've, you know, killed somebody."

"Strong, huh?" Neil said. Now he didn't seem so wry. More like annoyed.

"Oh, hell, I don't know." I turned back to the list, ignoring Cray's knowing smile. "Hey, Dick and Dale are on this list."

"Guess they couldn't bring the whole bachelor party," Neil said. "We'll see what they know, ask them to let us know if they hear anything. I know them and feel OK about looping them in. They're good guys. I don't think they'd do anything to Fizz, and I really don't think they'd have the money to buy that bottle, either."

"But if they don't have the money," Cray noted, "stealing it would be the obvious option."

"Oh, crap." There was one person on this list I'd prefer to avoid.

"Now what?" Neil asked. Maybe he hadn't recognized my stupid ex-boyfriend's real name.

"Mr. Mixy. Or as he's known to the DMV, Stephan Sully. I do *not* want to talk to him."

"That's OK," he said. "I can do it."

"But I want to interview everyone!" Ugh. I didn't want to be left out, but Mr. Mixy?

"Your call, Sergeant Pepper." Now Neil had the spark of triumph in his eyes. "Think he could've killed Fizz?"

"Honestly, I think he's capable of anything that would bring him notoriety. But he wouldn't like maintaining that beard in jail."

Cray chuckled again. "I still think this Greer person is worth talking to. And I think you should talk to Nigel and Lottie. They know everyone."

"They don't know me." I looked at their names on the list. "Nigel and Lottie Dashwood. Who are they?"

"Professional bon vivants from London," Neil said. "They

travel the world to cocktail events and distilleries. They were at Cocktailia."

"I must've missed them."

"They blog about everything and have sponsors," Neil continued. "So they really do know everyone. It might behoove you to get to know them if you want to meet more people and get known yourself."

"Huh." I wasn't really into schmoozing just to further my career, but they sounded interesting. I looked back at the list. "That leaves one more name. Arnold Preiss. That's—no. That's not the tech guy, is it?"

"Indeed it is. The ErthOrbyt CEO. Where they get those dreadfully spelled names, I'll never know." Cray dabbed at his mouth with the cloth napkin. "He's gone hard into collecting in the past couple of years. I guess he got tired of climbing mountains and wanted to do something with his millions."

"Billions," Neil corrected. "He's gone hard into tiki, too. He has a home in West Palm, and he's always posting pictures of his tiki bar. It's next-level."

"He's got a decent palate," Cray said. "He took me out to a very generous dinner in New Orleans one night and picked my brain. He's legit in spite of his money."

Cray was one to talk. You didn't get a house like his or a collection like his without spending some scratch.

"And what about you, Mr. Cray?" I couldn't help asking. "Would you be in the market for a bottle of London dock rum?"

He finished one of his oysters and looked at me with a twinkle. "Now, that's a very interesting question. I have certain bottles in my collection that I have just because I enjoy owning them. I never plan to taste them. I know myself too well, and if I took a sip, I would eventually drink the whole thing, and then I wouldn't have it anymore. So I preserve a few very special bottles because the pleasure of knowing I have them is greater than the pleasure of tasting them.

"That said, I don't think I could get ahold of a bottle of rum that survived the West India Docks fire and not have a taste of it. I'm terribly curious about it, and that's why I was so delighted to win a golden ticket to the tasting. Did the fire or smoke affect the rum in any way before it was bottled? And does the taste reflect where it's been all these years? And where *has* it been all these years? That's something I dearly wanted to find out from Fizz at the tasting. And now I'll never have the chance to ask him or to taste it.

"So would I jump at the chance to get a bottle of London dock rum?" he mused. "Theoretically, if it wasn't attached to murder? Oh, yes, Kayanne Pepper. Like any true collector, I believe I would."

Cray's admission, or idle musing, depending on one's point of view, gave me something to think about as Neil settled the bill and we said farewell to the genteel old collector. How many collectors were like him? And how far did their obsessions stretch? Collecting was, by definition, obsessive. It was about having All The Things. Would they pay someone to obtain such a bottle or jump at the chance to get one, no matter how it came into their hands? Would a normally nonviolent person who had to have the rarest bottle of rum in the world step over the line and kill for it?

Chapter Twelve

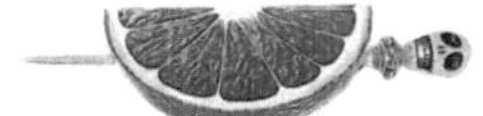

Cray donned his hat and headed for his room to get out of the heat, while Neil and I judged we had just enough time to hit the pool cabana bars and button-hole any Gold Tooth tasters we met.

A few of the international bars were doing the early shift at the pool party. We stopped first at the Italians' booth, picked up cocktails and ran into Dick and Dale right way. They were dressed in matching aloha shirts, different ones from the day before. I took a sly look around. Yeah, there was the rest of the ridiculously handsome bachelor party, lounging by the pool in their swimwear.

I popped my eyes back in their sockets and turned to Dick and Dale. Neil was asking them about their plans for the Gold Tooth Tasting.

"We thought it would be a nice wedding present for both of us," said Dick. He took a sip of the Italian bar's Bitter Mai Tai, which was dosed with Campari and garnished with mint, a cherry and a lime shell. I had a feeling I'd touched that lime shell at some point this morning.

"Yeah, but I'm bummed we won't get to try the London dock rum," Dale added. Beefier and broader of shoulder than Dick, he also seemed to be sweating more. The Florida heat took no prisoners.

"Is that why you bought tickets? Did you know Fizz would have the London rum?" I asked.

"It was a total shock to us," Dick said. "We only heard about it at Pau Hana yesterday. I got the impression it was a surprise when Fizz announced it. Wasn't it?"

"I thought so too," I admitted. "Though he told a few of the volunteers about it before his presentation."

"Terrible thing that happened to him," Dale said. "Did you guys hear any of the details?"

"We don't know much more than what was in the news," Neil said diplomatically.

The problem with our plan to ask everybody about the rum was that every time Fizz's name was mentioned, an image of him lying on the floor came back to me. I sipped a little more of the drink and tried to focus on what Neil was saying.

"I'm working with Cray to make sure the tasting will still be outstanding, so I hope you'll get your money's worth. And Kim Martin has generously allowed us to include the shipwrecked rum and the Wray & Nephew 17 on the menu."

"Fantastic," Dick said.

I glanced at Neil, and he nodded.

"Hey," I asked the guys, "can we let you in on a little secret?"

"I'd be upset with you if you didn't," Dick said with a lilt, and Dale laughed.

I leaned in, and they did the same. "The London dock rum was stolen."

Dick and Dale exchanged a look. "So it's true," Dale said.

I almost dropped my cup. "What?"

"There's a rumor going around that the rum was stolen when Fizz—well, when it happened," Dick said. "We heard it this morning over breakfast."

Damn. So much for gauging surprised or not-so-surprised reactions to the news that the rum was missing.

"Well, if you guys hear anything, see anything, can you let us know?" I asked. "One of our people is kind of mixed up in this, and it would be a load off our minds if we could figure out what really happened."

That was vague enough to protect Luke, I hoped, although if the rum rumor was rampant, there might be even more colorful gossip going around about our fellow Bohemia Bartender.

The guys assured us they'd keep their ears open, and we moved on to the next cabana, where we tried a delicious banana-themed drink from a French bar. Then we stood next to the pool, sipping and looking for victims. I mean, suspects.

"Ah, there they are," Neil said.

I followed his gaze to the other side of the pool, where a handful of people were clustered around a couple who were talking, smiling and waving their hands around. They looked to be in their early thirties. She was slender and dark-skinned, with a great smile, gorgeous big curly hair, warm brown eyes and animated eyebrows. He was a bit thicker, pale, with a thin brown beard and mustache, a jolly demeanor and a retro hat.

"The bloggers?" I asked.

"Nigel and Lottie. Let's go say hi."

Lottie was mid-story, delivered in a lovely, crisp English accent. "Well, that's when the driver threw his cigarette at Nigel, and because Nigel had spilled the 151 all over his trousers, they caught fire! I've never seen a man move so fast."

"I left them burning in a little pile outside the entrance of the Savoy and walked to Charing Cross in my knickers," Nigel said in an amusingly languid voice to the group's laughter. "Lottie pretended not to know me."

"Well, you were the one who'd insisted on that dreadful hired car, you smelt of burnt rum, and you were *completely* trolleyed. But at least everyone let us alone on the tube." She kissed his cheek to the merriment of the crowd.

"Neil!" Nigel said when he noticed us listening. "I swear, I barely recognize you without the twirlable mustache. Everyone, this is Neil Rockaway of the Bohemia Bartenders. We should chat. I'm overdue for a write-up of your cocktail book."

"That's kind of you," Neil said in his typical self-effacing fashion.

The hangers-on drifted off as Neil and I sat next to the couple. "This is Pepper Revelle," Neil said. "She owns an excellent New Orleans-themed cocktail bar in Bohemia."

His compliment warmed me. Actually, I probably couldn't be any warmer, but I was pleased just the same.

"I'm Lottie, and this is Nigel," said the female half of this dynamic duo.

"Great to meet you." I didn't want to confess I hadn't read their blog yet. I got the feeling I should have.

"You know, we're overdue for a trip around Florida," Nigel said. "New bars in Orlando and thereabouts we have to investigate. We'll have to make a stop in Bohemia."

"But we are going there next month," Lottie said to him. "The Bohemia Beach Film Festival, remember? It has a cocktail theme this year."

"Oh, that's right," Nigel replied, though his expression suggested he was still a bit fuzzy.

"Excellent," Neil said. "We're making drinks for that."

"Perfect time to visit my bar," I added. "Sazeracs on the house anytime you want to drop by."

"You're on," Lottie said. "Are you having a good time? I

mean, other than what happened last night. Poor Fizz. What a tragedy."

"And the rum gone, too. A nearly equal tragedy," her husband said.

Apparently everyone at Hookahakaha really did know about the missing rum.

Lottie elbowed him. "Now, now."

"I was looking forward to it, anyway," Nigel said, looking sheepish.

"You have tickets to the Gold Tooth Tasting?" I asked.

"Indeed we do," Lottie said. "I was relieved to see that Neil and Cray will be taking care of us."

"We'll do our best to make it memorable, though we can never fill Fizz's shoes," Neil said.

The quirk of Lottie's mouth was telling.

"I think it's safe to say we're all right with it." Nigel lowered his voice. "Not to speak ill of the dead, but I didn't think much of Mr. Martin."

"Why not?" I asked.

"He was a handsy bastard," Lottie said with an ironic smile.

"Oh, no, not you too," I said, then covered my mouth.

"Did he approach you, Pepper?" Lottie asked with interest. I had to remember these two were writers. Bloggers. Maybe they didn't get personal in their posts, but I didn't want to give them any ammo until I'd checked out their stuff.

"Not me, no. I heard a story from a friend. Really," I said to her skeptical look.

"I'm sorry to hear that. I fended him off. No harm done," she said. "But Nigel has refused to go into any of his bars since."

"I don't mind going now," Nigel said, sipping on his drink. "Seems like the least we can do to support Kim."

I cocked my head. "Does she need the support?"

"Well ..." Nigel hesitated.

Lottie looked at him, then at us. "We've heard Fizz was stretched pretty thin, but obviously he was doing well enough if he was planning to open a new bar in Miami. She'll be all right."

"You haven't heard any rumors about where that London dock rum might've ended up, have you?" Neil asked.

"Sure haven't, but I'd kill for a sip." Nigel blanched, a layer of pale on pale, when he realized what he'd said. "Bloody hell, that came out wrong."

Lottie squeezed his shoulder. "It's all right, darling. We know what you meant." She turned to us. "One of your fellows was at the scene, I hear?"

Whoa no. She knew about Luke. "We just want to make sure that if there's any information that can keep the cops on the right track, we pass it on," I said. "So if you hear anything ...?"

She nodded. "Understood. We'll let you know."

"What are you drinking there? Looks nice," Neil said of their matching cocktails, which were garnished with orange peels and a fancy swizzle stick.

"It's a quite tasty Saturn," Nigel said. "Old Alastair's done nicely with this one. Of course, it helps that it has Fairyland's Frilly Fairy Gin in it."

I turned to Neil, my mouth only slightly agape. "Alastair?"

Nigel smiled. "Alastair Markham. You know him? He's representing The Dandy Tipple, his London place. Have you been?"

"Not yet," Neil said, not mentioning his history with Alastair. Neil had attended Oxford at the same time as Alastair for a short while and left when he discovered his future was destined for mixology instead of astronomy. And Alastair had a demented fixation on what he perceived as an ongoing rivalry between them.

Funny Alastair hadn't shown up for cocktail prep this morning. Of course, he probably took joy in making his underlings do the hard work.

"Maybe we should give that Saturn a try," Neil said. "We'll see you around?"

There were friendly goodbyes as Nigel shook Neil's hand and Lottie gave me a surprising little hug. I liked her. I liked both of them. I didn't want to think they could be killers, but there seemed to be no love lost between them and Fizz Martin.

Neil and I walked away and disposed of our empty cups in a waste can that smelled strongly of rum. Thank Dionysus the drinks were small. I had a little buzz going, and I had to keep it together for not only our pool shift later but the big tower party tonight.

A loud peal of laughter drew my attention, and I looked several lounges away to see a pretty woman being fawned over by not one but three happy guys.

Wait.

"Is that Gina?"

"Who's Gina?" Neil asked.

"My roommate on this trip. Jorge's sister. Astra's dog-sitter."

Sure enough, Astra was sitting at Gina's feet with a bowl of water at her side, gnawing on somebody's flip-flop. The dog must've sensed me, because she looked up and saw me, then stood and started barking.

"Oh, my sweet little baby. I'd better go say hi before the hotel bans her for being too loud."

Gina looked up at the racket, smiled and waved as we strolled over. She had a nice one-piece bathing suit on under a gauzy white cover-up and was sipping a cocktail, no laptop in sight. One of the guys asked her if they could get her another drink.

"Oh, I'm not sure. I've already had two," she told him.

"You haven't had this one. I promise, you'll love it," he said, and he was gone.

"Neil, this is Gina."

"Nice to meet you." He shook Gina's hand as I leaned down to pet Astra, who panted happily.

"You doing OK?" I asked Gina.

"I'm great! This is really nice," she said, looking around at the party scene. "I've never been to anything like this before."

I leaned in so her fan club, who were at the moment arguing over which demerara rum they liked best, didn't hear me. "Just watch these drinks. They're pretty strong."

"Oh, I'm totally in control," she whispered back. "Don't worry. Astra and I are just fine."

I nodded. She seemed OK. A little looser than yesterday, but maybe that was a good thing. "Whose flip-flop?" I asked at normal volume.

"Larry's. That guy who just left to get me a drink? It's his. He says he was planning to buy new ones anyway."

Yikes. I hoped Astra didn't chew anything more expensive than a flip-flop. I gave the dog one more ruffle, and she smiled at me. *Aw.* She was such a good dog—mostly—and I felt a little guilty for not spending more time with her. But she seemed to be having fun.

"See you later," I said to both of them, then headed back toward the cabana bars with Neil. "Are you sure you want to talk to Alastair?" I asked him.

He raised an eyebrow. "I think it's a good idea to remind Alastair that I will always be a pain in his ass."

I laughed out loud. Neil had a little ornery streak that was doubly amusing when he revealed it because he was civil to a fault most of the time.

We strolled toward the booth featuring The Dandy Tipple, Alastair's bar. They had a cool art deco font in the signage and pretty cocktails lined up. There was quite a crowd in front of it, so much so that we couldn't see if Alastair was in there. But as we walked up, the crowd seemed to part, revealing not Alastair but a vision in a white suit right out of *Miami Vice*, with sexy scruff and dark red hair, turning toward us with a Saturn in his hand.

A wicked grin took over his face. "Hot Pepper!"

I resisted the urge to fan myself. At that moment, he had no idea *how* hot.

Chapter Thirteen

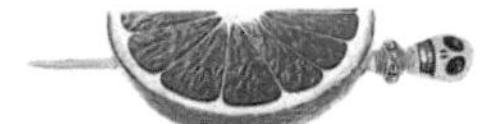

"**P**epper! What a treat. And Neil, my friend," Mark Fairman said, approaching us with drink in hand. That slightly gruff, deep voice with the yummy English accent reminded me all over again how attractive the broad-shouldered redhead was and how I absolutely did not need this kind of distraction right now.

Over Mark's shoulder, I caught a glimpse of another familiar face—Alastair Markham, staring out from behind his bar with a look of surprise and annoyance, the mighty swoop of his fair boy-band hair wilting in the heat. Neil would be pleased that he'd gotten under Alastair's skin without having to say a single word to him.

"You'll be mixing it up at the party tonight, won't you?" Mark asked Neil.

"Indeed we will. You're sponsoring The Dandy Tipple?"

"A bit of cross-branding. Alastair's bar is doing quite well in London. So this is good for both him and Fairyland Distillery. We have a rum now, did you know?"

"A spiced rum, isn't it?" Neil asked.

"Spot on. We take the young rum from Jamaica and age it in oak with cinnamon and ginger and a few *secret spices*." Mark leaned over me when he stage-whispered *secret spices*. His warm breath appeared to be seasoned with rum and secret spices, too. I didn't mind. Though his face was a little pink.

"You should wear a hat," I said. "Don't underestimate the Florida sun. You'll go home looking like a pomegranate."

He lowered his voice. "I could use some help with sunscreen later." Oh, no. Points off his hotness for a seriously bad line.

"You have a ticket to the Gold Tooth Tasting, don't you?" The grain of irritation in Neil's voice made me smile.

Mark took a big sip of his drink before answering. "I do indeed. Bloody awful what happened to Fizz. And I feel a bit like I've been teased with that promise of the London dock rum, only to hear we won't get to taste it. Do you think you might get Kim to change her mind?"

Ah. Mark seemed clueless, a point in his favor. "I guess you haven't heard? The rum was missing from the scene," I told him.

"Stolen, then? Well, good luck to whoever snatched it." His tone was sarcastic. "They certainly won't be able to enjoy it properly."

"Why not?" Neil asked.

"You're obviously not a collector. Sure, you see the nefarious stolen-art collector in films sitting down in his secret room with a brandy and his Van Gogh"—he pronounced it like "van cough"—"but I believe collectors of rare bottles want everyone to know what they have and then to brag about the experience of having it. Or tasting it."

"Which they can't do unless they want to be accused of murder," I said.

"Or accessory to murder," Neil added. "What a mess."

"A most unfortunate mess," Mark said.

Unfortunate. A very British way to describe a murder.

"If you hear anything about the London dock rum, would you let us know?" I asked. "We have a friend who made an *unfortunate* appearance at the crime scene, and we'd like to make sure justice is done."

"'Justice is done.' Sounds so Old West," Mark said. "You ever dress up as a cowgirl, Hot Pepper?"

So Mark was a little weirder than I thought. Still cute, though. And I was OK with a certain amount of weird.

"Can't say I have. A saloon girl, once, for one of those vintage photos when I was on vacation." It sounded sexier than it was. The feather boa made me sneeze.

"A saloon girl?" His amber eyes seemed to glow. "Thank you. Now I have an image I shall carry with me all day."

Oh, lord.

"Speaking of all day, we have to get going," Neil interrupted. "Lots on the agenda."

"Right. Carry on. I'll see *you* later." Mark grinned at me, then spun and headed to the next cabana bar.

"That was—interesting," I said at the same time Neil said "awkward."

I smiled puckishly at him. "Speaking of awkward, shall we get a drink from Alastair?"

"Hrrrmmph."

"Just this one, and then, I promise, I'll go get ready for our pool shift."

Alastair and a couple of lovely women who were helping him had several drinks lined up on the bar already, so we grabbed a couple right away. I wasn't sure what nefarious ingredients Alastair would put in a drink he was preparing expressly for Neil, so taking a pre-made cocktail seemed like the safest route.

"How's it going, Alastair?" Neil asked politely, though there was the faintest hint of humor under his even tone.

Alastair pushed his drooping bangs back and bared his teeth in an approximation of a smile. "Absolutely fantastic. Our Saturns are the hit of the party."

I took a sip. "Very nice." It was. But hit of the party? He was trying too hard.

Alastair's brow furrowed. "What are you doing here?"

"All the things you're doing," Neil said. "Only we're helping prep in the kitchen, too."

Alastair's mouth opened, then closed. There was no doubt he knew exactly what we were doing here if he'd seen any of the program. And Neil's little zing had caught him off guard.

"Someday you'll graduate from barback. Or maybe you won't. Since you didn't graduate from *Oxford.*" Alastair cackled. I rolled my eyes. Neil just made a little bow, and we turned away, catching a glimpse of Alastair's frustration at our refusal to bite at his insults.

"What is his problem?" I asked when we were out of earshot.

"You'd think he'd be happy running a successful bar in London. I mean, I love my bar in Bohemia, but it's not exactly the big city. He should have a healthy superiority complex."

I laughed. "But he has an inferiority complex because he knows you're better than he is."

"Possibly." Neil smiled.

"So we've talked to a lot of the Gold Toothers ..."

"Now there's an image."

"Golden-ticket holders? Anyway, we still haven't caught up with Arnold Preiss, the software guy, or Mr. Mixy, God help me. Or your friend Greer and her plus-one."

"I really don't know her well," he said, "but maybe the hotel can help me track her down."

"Let me know, will you? I'd like to meet her."

"Sure." He went to throw out the dregs of his cocktail, but I plucked the cool Dandy Tipple swizzle stick, with its top-hat topper, from it first. He raised his eyebrows.

"Craft project." I dropped it in my bag. "Don't ask."

"Uh-huh. OK. I'll let you know if I catch up with anyone. And it's entirely possible they'll catch us at the pool party this afternoon."

"Right. I'll see you in the kitchen thirty minutes ahead of time to help bring out all of our stuff."

We parted ways, and I headed over to Gina once again. After all this heat and testosterone and talk of murder, I missed my dog.

"Hey, Gina, I'd like to take Astra back to the room with me for a little while, OK?"

"Of course. She's your baby. She could probably use the cool-down." Plus Gina's suitors had dwindled down to one, Larry, in his little straw hat, and he looked pleased to have her to himself.

Astra did look hot. She was lying sideways on the concrete in the shade of Gina's lounge chair, panting, though she still had plenty of water.

"Astra, girl!" The dog perked up immediately at my voice, sat and barked. I ruffled the curls on her head and cooed before asking, "Want a treat?" She barked again, and I grabbed her leash and water bowl and waved to Gina. "See you later."

Astra watered a hibiscus on the way back to the room, where I gave her two treats just for being a good dog. I had enough time for a quick shower and a nap before I dressed for the pool-party gig. And naps with dogs counted double.

I was going to need my rest if I had to interview more suspects, especially since no one had leapt out as particularly skeevy yet. Though so far, not many of the collectors liked Fizz —and they all seemed to like rum a little too much.

Chapter Fourteen

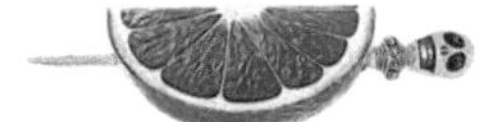

The bubbling clouds overhead eased the heat of mid-afternoon, but I was grateful for the shade of our cabana as we crafted cocktails for the afternoon pool crowd. The colorful shirts and vintage bathing suits had multiplied, the drinks were flowing, and a surf band played on a small stage by the cafe.

My little nap hadn't been quite enough for me and definitely not enough for Astra. I took pity on her and left her asleep on the bed before helping the rest of the Bohemia Bartenders wrangle our ingredients, props, signage and supplies for the pool party.

Our drink for this event was a Neil creation, The Eyewall, a variation on a traditional Hurricane. His was less sweet and quite potent (I limited myself to one "test" cocktail and still had a happy little buzz). Though it featured the traditional passionfruit syrup and two kinds of rum, it also had lemon and lime juice. We served it over crushed ice and garnished it with a cool light-blue Bohemia Bartenders swizzle stick and a lemon peel wrapped around a handcrafted rum-soaked cherry.

Melody had recommended I bring at least three outfits per day of Hookahakaha. I thought she was loopy until now, as I realized just how much sweat the human body could produce in South Florida in June.

She'd coordinated all of our pool-party outfits to go with a blue and yellow theme. The guys all had different aloha shirts with various blue backgrounds, and they looked great. Buoyed by Barclay's jokes and good spirits, even Luke was smiling, in spite of the ghastly events of yesterday.

Melody had found someone to make custom outfits for us gals, patterned with blue and white ocean waves and yellow hibiscus blossoms. Hers was a two-piece, with a wraparound skirt and an off-the shoulder midriff top. I went with funky short overalls over another scoop-neck white T-shirt. I also wore comfy sandals, since I was working, and had a new floral creation pinning up my hair on one side that featured a blue flower and a faux lemon. Not to mention lemon earrings and my leather bracelet with the beads and the gator tooth.

What I really needed was one of those bachelor-party guys to cool me down with a giant feathered fan.

We worked efficiently, with Neil shaking the drink over ice cubes and straining it over the crushed ice Melody scooped into the cups. I added garnishes. Behind us, Barclay crushed the ice old-school with a mallet and a canvas bag, and Luke batched the drink a gallon at a time. I'd just garnished enough cocktails to fill half the bartop when I looked up and saw a familiar face reaching for a drink.

"I know you!" I blurted.

The man stopped, cocktail in hand, a mischievous look on his face. It was a pale, clean-shaven, angular face with an elfin air brought out by his dimpled smile. Long neck. Longish, wavy brown hair. An open aloha shirt over a white tank top. Cute in a beanpole sort of way. He wore a light green straw hat adorned with a wooden tiki face. He held up his drink. "Does your knowing me mean I can't have this?"

"Oh, no. I mean, yes, you can have it," I said. "Mr. Preiss, isn't it?"

"Guilty. But please call me Arnold."

I glanced at Neil. He tipped his head to the side, indicating I could step out. Somehow his eyes were also saying *Be careful, Pepper.* But there was no way I could turn down a chance to talk to another Gold Tooth taster.

"I—I'm such a fan of your software!" I said as I came out from behind the bar. OK, that was less than genius, but in my defense, my brain was the temperature of a fried egg.

"Really?" He grinned. "Any particular one? Are you partial to the word processor, or"—he looked around like he was going to confide something really juicy—"are you into inventory management?"

I laughed. "Sorry. You caught me. I mean, yeah, I like the inventory management, but I'd rather have something specific to liquor and cocktails."

"Not a bad idea." He took a sip of the Eyewall and made a swoony face. "You want to talk about software? Or maybe how you made this fabulous drink?"

I touched his shoulder lightly, leading him away from the cabana, and lowered my voice. "Truth is, I want to talk about rum."

"Even better. And who are you, exactly?"

"Oh, sorry. Pepper Revelle. I'm with the Bohemia Bartenders, though when we're not doing events, I co-own a bar north of here, on Florida's east-central coast."

"Anywhere near Cape Canaveral? I'm working with NASA on a couple of projects and could stop by."

"Actually, yes! My bar is Nola, in Bohemia, a little south of the Cape. That's where Neil has a great bar, too, the Junction

Box—Neil is the leader of our little traveling circus of bartenders."

"Oh, I know his book well," Arnold said.

Neil really did know everybody. Or if he didn't, everybody knew his book. Of course, Arnold Preiss was a billionaire. He probably had every cocktail book there was.

"You have a ticket to the Gold Tooth Tasting, don't you?" I asked.

"I do. I was looking forward to chatting with Fizz face-to-face, but now that I can't ... Are you going?"

I shook my head. "Tickets are a little rich for my blood. But even without Fizz, there will be good rums there, you know."

Arnold shrugged. "I can get good rums anytime."

"I understand you're friendly with Conan Cray."

"That's true. He was very hospitable in New Orleans. Incredible collection. I learned a lot from him. Since he's stepping in as host, I'm sure the event won't be a waste of my time."

"But you had your heart set on tasting the London dock rum?"

He looked more closely at me. "Like I said, I can get good rum anytime."

"*That* rum?" I blurted out. *Real subtle, Pepper.*

"I didn't even know that rum existed, so it's not in my collection," he said coolly. "Not that I would mind having some. But no one has it now, do they? I hear the bottle vanished at Pau Hana."

Of course he knew. Everyone did. I lowered my voice even further. "The working theory is that *someone* has it. Would you know how to get such a bottle if you wanted to, Mr. Preiss?"

"Arnold." He looked me up and down, taking the measure

of my cute overalls. And maybe my legs. "I thought you couldn't afford the rum tasting. Surely you're not in the market for a bottle of London dock rum?"

"Mr. Preiss—Arnold. A good friend happened to be found at the crime scene, and he had nothing to do with the—with what happened to Fizz. Or the bottle. I'm just trying to find out what *did* happen so he doesn't get into any more trouble."

"Interesting." Arnold didn't seem very sympathetic.

"Can you let me know if you hear anything about that missing bottle? I know you're a big collector, and *you* can afford it. Chances are, somebody is going to come to you with it."

"What makes you think I won't just buy it and quietly drink it while watching *The Creature From the Black Lagoon* in my home theater?"

I remembered what Cray said. "Because you want to be legit. You want to be known as a collector. And hiding the biggest find of the century is no way to do that."

He narrowed his brown eyes at me, and after a few seconds, he smiled. "Pepper, you are absolutely correct. Anyway, I wouldn't waste a dime on buying anything connected to a crime. Not knowingly, anyway. I'll let you know if I hear anything, all right?"

"Thanks very much," I said, somehow feeling outmaneuvered. "Come by my bar in Bohemia when you're visiting NASA, and I'll make you something."

"I'll take you up on that, Pepper. Or if you'd like to let me make *you* a drink, my yacht is docked just outside in the marina." He smiled again, raised his cup in a mock toast and wandered off toward another cabana.

For real? His *yacht?* What was this, *Some Like It Hot?*

Though I'd never actually been on a yacht before. Maybe if I had an hour …

No, Pepper. Don't be an idiot. The idea of cocktails on a yacht might be kind of alluring, but there was something worrisome about Arnold Preiss.

Besides, I had to get back to the Bohemia booth. We were nearing the end of our shift, but the crowds kept coming.

I whirled to return and ran smack into a wall of hair. Sputtering, I stepped backward and straightened my glasses.

Oh, no. It was worse than just hair. It was a giant supernova of hair attached to the chin of Mr. Mixy.

Chapter Fifteen

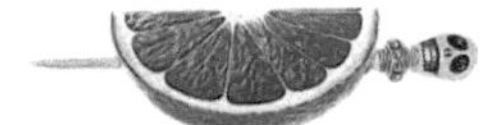

"Pepper!" shouted Mr. Mixy. He was a head taller than I was, hence my collision with his facial hair. His giant brown beard seemed to lead the rest of him around, but I vaguely deduced he wore an aloha shirt and shorts. His thick, dark eyebrows had risen in excitement, and his hazel eyes glittered. He leaned in to kiss my cheek, and I dodged him. Well, the beard. "Aren't you glad to see me?"

"I can see you anytime I want on Instagram."

"Oh, you always were my biggest fan." He smacked me on the shoulder, and I almost lost my balance. "What are you up to?"

"I'm here with the Bohemia Bartenders," I said in as dry a tone as I could manage. "I have to get back to the bar." *But I also had to ask him about the tasting and the rum. Rats.*

"What? You're still in Bohemia? You're not still working at that bar, are you?"

"I co-own that bar now, and it's been completely rebranded, thank you very much."

"Oh, Pepper. You should come to California. Great tiki scene. Great bar scene ..."

"I'm happy where I am, thanks." And it was true. Bohemia and Bohemia Beach became my safe haven after I left New Orleans and my parents told me not to come back, and I'd grown to love my coastal town. Plus I had really good friends there, and I could travel when I needed to stretch my wings, like I was doing now. Mr. Mixy could stuff it.

"So," he said, his voice a little softer. "Want to get a drink later? Or I could make you one."

"Look around, Stephan." His mouth pursed at hearing his real name. "Do you think I'm lacking for a drink?"

"It's not for the drink, baby. It's for the company."

"You lost the ticket to call me 'baby' a long time ago, furry face."

"You like it, huh? Want to pet it?" He grabbed a handful of beard and stroked it in an indecent manner.

I tried not to wince. "Speaking of tickets, you have one for the Gold Tooth Tasting, don't you?"

"Yeah. I thought it might be cool to talk Fizz into doing a video with me. So much for that idea."

"Have you heard anything about the London dock rum?" Might as well cut right to the point.

"Yeah, that we don't get to drink any of it and that it was stolen by the murderer. Sucks, man."

Yeah, man. Murder sucks. I almost burst a blood vessel trying to suppress my eye roll. "Have you heard any rumors about where it might've ended up?"

"No, and I'm not in the market, no matter how famous I might be now."

A slight headache blossomed as my brain wrestled with the captive eye roll. "Are you sure you wouldn't be interested in a bottle of that significance?"

He leaned over and whispered, "Pepper, babe. You know I'm a vodka guy. Only don't tell these tiki people that."

The eye roll ripped free and I blinked hard. "Craving vodka is a good way to end up dead around here."

"You think Fizz was a closet vodka drinker too?" He laughed. Not a nice laugh. "Look, if I could get it and taste that bottle on my Insta or YouTube channels, of course I'd be interested. But I'd turn it in as evidence. You know I'd never do anything else."

I wasn't so sure. He might broadcast it first. "Let me know if you hear anything, OK?"

"No problem. I've gotta go, but you can find me at the Tiki Skyliner if you want to take me up on my drink. I'm working with Tiger Tiki tonight."

Tiger Tiki was a well-regarded L.A. bar—in fact, one Fizz Martin had provided seed money for—and Mr. Mixy did some of his videos there.

"You work there now?" I asked.

"Only when they really need me. I'm pretty busy with my videos, and I gotta keep my sponsors happy. Not a lot of time to do real work." He laughed again, but something about his eyes told me he was lying. I'd learned the hard way how to tell when he was lying.

Maybe things weren't so great for Mr. Mixy after all. There was nothing bad about working at a bar—I literally did it every day of my life and loved it—but he always had the idea that he was better than everybody else. And if his escalating dreams of fame weren't working out, maybe he was looking for another way to be famous. An uglier one.

"I'm working tonight too. See you later," was all I said, and this time I managed to do one of those *Matrix*-style bullet dodges to avoid his beard as I headed back to our bar.

Melody looked tired, so we all did a shuffle so she and Barclay could take a break. Luke came up to the front with Neil and me, and we pumped out the drinks till we were out of deliciousness. Gina managed to snag one of the last of our cocktails. She wore a glazed, happy look.

"You feeling all right?" I asked her.

"Fine. I think I just got too much sun," she said, taking a sip. "Oh, this is delicious. I don't understand why I never drank before."

"I have no idea." Great. I was turning my business partner's sister into a boozehound. "What happened to Larry?"

"We're supposed to chat later. He was trying to get me tickets to some party. But I need to check on Astra."

"OK. I'll see you soon. Maybe you should lie down?"

"Good idea." She walked unsteadily toward our building at the back of the courtyard.

"What did you learn from Preiss?" Neil asked me as we started packing up our stuff. Barclay and Melody had returned, and everyone listened while we worked.

"He said he'd love to have a bottle of the rum but not illegally. Claimed he didn't know anything about it, though I have to say, he's a slippery one. I had the feeling he wasn't telling me everything. Same with Mr. Mixy."

"Ah, the infamous Mr. Mixy." Neil's expression was the equivalent of pulling my pigtail. If I had a pigtail. I was pretty sure it amused him terribly that I'd once had the Mixmeister as a boyfriend before I realized what a jerk he was, but that was a long time ago, when I first started working at the bar.

"Oh, his videos are really cool," Luke said.

I didn't have the heart to enlighten him about Mr. Mixy's vexatiousness. "At least we've told everyone we're looking for information. I don't know—maybe it would've been better if one of us pretended we wanted to buy the rum?"

"We don't fit the profile," Neil said. "I wouldn't be

surprised if an offer like that made its way to Cray, if someone tries to sell it. He'll let us know."

"Are you sure about that?" Cray had the collector's obsession. Nigel and Lottie detested Fizz. Mr. Mixy had a desire for fame. Mark Fairman and Arnold Preiss both had the money. And Greer was rich, too, but we hadn't talked to her yet.

We'd just loaded everything on a cart when a familiar figure strolled up to us. He stuck out like a redwood in a plumeria garden. He wore khakis and a white golf shirt, no jacket this time, and looked fresh as a daiquiri compared with the rest of us. But without the jacket, his gun and badge stood out on his hip.

"Hi, Dad," Barclay said.

"Detective Flores," Neil said. "How's it going?"

Luke and Melody and I didn't say anything.

"Just thought I'd check in with you and ask you the same thing," he said with a suggestion of a smile. Just enough to imply he was on our side, but not so much he couldn't withdraw his allegiance and change his mind.

"We're fine," I said. "Haven't heard anything about anything."

He turned to me. "What would you have heard?"

"I mean, you know, rumors about the rum or whatever."

"I've heard a little about you, Pepper," the detective said. "You're a curious soul. But don't get too curious about this case. There's still a killer out there. At least we think there is." His gaze turned to Luke, who visibly swallowed.

"Come on, Dad," Barclay intervened. "You know Luke's cool. What's the scoop? Can you give us any more details?"

Detective Flores looked thoughtful for a minute. "Since you were there, you saw what I'm about to tell you, right?" I nodded, wondering what was coming. "I've just had a preliminary forensics report. We feel sure that the club was the murder weapon."

"The muddler," I murmured.

The detective's mouth quirked. "Yes, the muddler. He was struck in the face with great force. We believe he might have been taking a sip out of that ceramic cup at the time—"

"The tiki mug," I said, not really intending to correct him. It just slipped out.

He looked at me sharply. "Yes, the *tiki mug*. There was an orange slice in his throat along with fragments of the cup."

My hand flew to my throat. "Did he choke on that?"

The detective shook his head. "I think he died of blunt force trauma, though the autopsy should reveal more details. Because even though he was hit very hard, it appears his head also hit the corner of the metal table on his way down to the tile floor."

"One, two, three, you're out," I whispered.

The detective glared at me. *Damn it!* I really hadn't meant to say that out loud.

"The point is," he said, "anybody who can kill somebody this way isn't afraid of doing violence."

"What about the phone call I heard him take?" Melody asked.

"Not a registered number. We think it was a burner." He turned to Barclay this time. "Be careful, OK?"

"We will," Barclay said.

The detective looked each one of us in the eye before strolling back down the path toward the parking lot.

We all exhaled at the same time. "Yikes," I said.

"He can be a little intense. But you were pushing his buttons, Pepper." Barclay looked like he was trying not to laugh.

"I didn't mean to."

"Doesn't matter. He's right," Neil said. "Pepper, don't do anything on your own. All of you, be careful."

Melody let out a comical groan. "Yes, boss!"

We all laughed. A little in relief, I think.

The guys volunteered to take stuff back to the kitchen and the staging room, so Melody and I each headed to our rooms. We had to undergo another transformation, and it would take us longer, anyway. Guys had it easy. They just pulled on a different shirt and were good to go. Though I was sure we all needed another shower before the Tiki Skyliner party.

When I got back to the room, Gina was passed out on her bed and Astra was contentedly chewing on the King James Bible I'd used to secure the gap in the curtains on the sliding doors. She looked to be about halfway through the Old Testament. My missionary mother would have fainted.

I rescued the book, put it on the nightstand and looked down at Astra. "Dog, you're going to give new meaning to the term holy shit. Come on, a quick walk, and then I'll give you your real dinner." She jumped up at the words "walk" and "dinner" and put her paws on me.

I picked her up and gave her a big hug, cradling her like a baby. I rubbed her belly and sniffed her floral-scented fur, fresh from a recent bath, and let her lick my nose. And thought about what Barclay's dad said.

Detective Flores had injected my esoteric rum search with cold-blooded reality. We weren't just looking for a rum thief. We were looking for a thief who wouldn't hesitate to kill to cover his tracks.

Chapter Sixteen

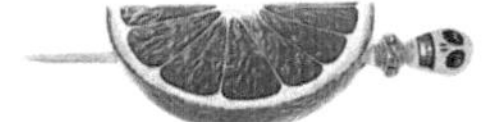

Imagine wavy video on your rabbit-ears console black-and-white TV set—the ripples that tell you you're going back in time. (I do that a lot. A hazard of being devoted to cocktail culture and the revival of its vintage glory.)

Anyway—*doo doo doo ... doo doo doo*—and it's 1965. The bar-restaurant at the top of the seventeen-story tower is spinning slowly, almost imperceptibly, but fast enough that if you leave your purse on the steady circle in the middle of the floor, it might escape you until the outer ring spins your table back around. There are floor-to-ceiling windows all around, the view framed on top by the space-age spokes sticking out horizontally from the round roof of the tower. The slow ride offers a fantastic spectacle: the sparkling blue of the Atlantic Ocean, the Intracoastal Waterway, pretty pink houses, passing yachts, and downtown Fort Lauderdale. If you're lucky, you'll see somebody famous. Frank Sinatra drinking a martini. Cary Grant giving you a wink.

I fantasize about Cary Grant giving me a wink.

This is the delicious history of the Wicker Wharf tower, and this evening, it was the home of the Tiki Skyliner party. Successors to the swingin' sixties crowd filled the circular room and formed lines at snack stations and at the half dozen highly decorated bars set up in a ring in the center. The outer doughnut of the floor slowly spun, disorienting the drunkest, and an exotica band played mellow tunes in what passed as a corner.

It was still light outside, so the glorious view was eclipsed only by the tikiphiles themselves, bursting with color like a tropical-flower explosion. Most of the men wore retro hats and snazzy aloha shirts or silly suits. Most of the women wore pinup-style dresses and floral confections in their hair.

We Bohemia Bartenders were dressed to the nines, too. Neil had asked for variations on red and black. Barclay and Luke had interesting aloha shirts that were half black, half printed—Barclay with big, red monstera leaves on one side, and Luke with a white and red and black pattern on half, complemented by a patterned sleeve on the other side. Melody had a Hawaiian-style long dress with ruffled sleeves and hem, more modest than her earlier attire. Neil wore a red Hawaiian-print vest over a black shirt rolled up to the elbows, with a red bow tie. Very Neil. Very tasty. And I went with a fifties-style halter dress that showed off my curves, with a flared skirt and another floral piece in my hair—and the same comfy flat sandals in black, because standing here for hours making cocktails was hard work. At least there was air-conditioning in the tower.

We were making a Neil concoction he called the Piña Pele, a fun attempt to update the much-maligned piña colada with classic tiki elements. It featured a dark rum and a boutique coconut rum; lime juice; pineapple puree; orgeat, the almond syrup so popular in tiki drinks; and large, painstakingly frozen coconut water cubes, with a sprinkling of toasted coconut on top—served in the actual pineapple with an orchid, a long paper straw and our groovy swizzle stick, which made our drink super popular for the Instagram crowd. And our drink did look fabulous.

Before the crowds came in, Neil called for a "family dinner." We poured shots of the thick, golden drink into five cups and made a toast to tiki, knocking them back to prepare us for the rush. And oh, man, was it good. The tangy-honey taste of fresh pineapple was cut by the tart lime juice and mellowed by the orgeat, all fortified by the sweet coconutty and molasses flavors of the excellent rums.

We made a production line to assemble and present the beautiful cocktails. Barclay and Luke prepped the cored pineapples, which had been in the freezer since this morning, and laid out the garnishes so Neil, Melody and I could put them together quickly for the thirsty crowd. Neil and I used a spindle blender to puree cold chunks of pineapple with the other ingredients, and Melody garnished the pineapples as fast as we could pour the mixture over the special cubes. Between batches, Neil posed for a few pictures with fans of his book, while a few of the guy drinkers insisted on posing with Melody and me and their princely pineapples for selfies.

The other bars were as slammed as we were. Mr. Mixy was hamming it up for the documentary crew that was making the rounds by setting limes on fire in Tiger Tiki's drinks. I was a little worried about the beard.

The Italians were stacking full glasses to the ceiling before serving them. And Alastair's London bar was pouring a very pretty drink they called Rum and the Lash, featuring the spiced rum from Mark Fairman's Fairyland Distillery, complete with miniature British flags.

Even Gina came by with her new pal Larry. She looked some-what refreshed after her nap, and she was wearing a vintage dress she'd found in the vendor hall. She had Astra with her, with a silk-flower lei wrapped around the dog's furry neck. My pup was quite the hit and barked when she saw me, so I had to take a thirty-second dog-petting break before I could get back to work. And grab a lime wedge out of her mouth that she'd found on the floor.

After a quick hand-wash, I was back to filling pineapples. As much as I would've liked to taste the cocktails made by other bars in the room, the pace was breathless. When I had five seconds, I wandered to the middle of the circle of bars with a cup of water over coconut-water ice and chilled for a moment.

It just so happened that Kim Martin was taking a break, bottle of water in hand, at the same time I was.

I know I wasn't the only one surprised when Kim showed up to take Fizz's place at the station for their flagship San Diego bar, Haku Mele. I'd watched them set up and stole glances their way as the onslaught of drinkers continued, and frankly, I was impressed. Fizz might've been the face of his tiki empire, but Kim was no slouch with a shaker. Mostly she seemed to stay in the back, probably to avoid any effusive expressions of sympathy from Fizz's fans, but she worked hard and had beautiful technique.

And now here we were, both taking refuge by the same pillar. She wore a black T-shirt and jeans—no tiki frippery, except one faux hibiscus flower pinning up her white-blond hair on one side. Kind of punk tiki. "I like the look," I said.

That drew a little smile. "Can't go wrong with black in the hospitality industry."

"Yeah, the standard uniform." I grinned. "Your drink looks amazing."

"Thanks. One of my recipes, actually."

Huh. Kim invented some of Haku Mele's drinks, too? "I didn't realize you were a mixologist."

Kim snorted. "That's how I started. That's what I was when I met Fizz at a club in New York. I wasn't working that night, but we were both seeing a band we loved. We stayed up all night talking about rum. And the rest is history." She narrowed her eyes. "Are you Melody?"

I couldn't expect her to keep everybody straight. "Pepper. I work with Melody." I cocked my head toward my friend.

"Oh, yeah. That's right."

"You doing OK?" I didn't want to upset her, but it seemed like I should say something. She looked tired.

Kim shrugged. "It's good to work. It helps me forget, you know? I haven't gotten much sleep. Lots of paperwork to go through. I hold up the business end of our business, but the accountant had a few surprises for me from Fizz's side."

"Fizz's side?"

"You know, the creative genius at work." She looked wistful. "He always had some project or other going, some bar in development, some wild promotion. It's what he was. Sometimes it was expensive, but his success tended to make up for it."

"He sure was popular." I swallowed another gulp of water from my cup. "I'm sorry."

"So am I," she said. "We had so many plans. The new Miami bar. The TV show. Everything's up in the air now. I guess time will tell." Her eyes unfocused for a minute, and I wondered if she was remembering back to that night at the New York club, being charmed by the brassy Aussie with big charisma and big plans. Then she focused again, shaking her head. "Anyway, he would want me to go on. That's why I'm here. Back to work."

"Work is one thing we can count on." I gave her an encouraging nod, moved back to our station and helped Melody assemble more cocktails. Barclay had moved up into the mixing position.

"Where's Neil?" I asked.

Melody leaned over and spoke softly into my ear so she wouldn't be overheard. "He saw some cute little old lady and jumped out to talk to her. Maybe you're not his type after all."

I pushed her away with my shoulder, and she giggled. It had to be Greer. Though Neil really did know everybody. I scanned the room as we worked. Demand for drinks was slowing down as the revelers reached their capacity and the event neared its end. Night was starting to fall, and a beautiful twilight painted purples and oranges behind the twinkling skyline outside the windows. Through the glass door that led to the observation deck, I thought I caught a glimpse of Neil.

"Do you think you can wrap it up?" I asked my colleagues. "I want to grab Neil."

"We know," Barclay said, and Melody and Luke burst out laughing.

"Oh, go suck a swizzle." Smart-asses.

"Go ahead," Luke said. "These are the last five pineapples anyway." He set them on the bar, and as the others fixed them up, I slipped out of the center ring of bars and headed through the crowd to the deck doors.

With the sun below the horizon, the air had cooled, and a pleasant breeze whisked around the top of the tower, ruffling hair and dresses as drinkers pooled by the railings and watched the winking lights of sailboats, cruise ships, airplanes and car traffic over the drawbridge that crossed the Intracoastal Waterway.

There was Neil, standing by the railing, chatting with a

pink-cheeked woman with short, white curls. She was probably in her eighties and was rocking a vivid muumuu. With her was a younger man in a de rigueur Hawaiian shirt. Well, relatively younger. Mid-fifties, I guessed, with silver streaks in his dark hair and goatee and a deep tan. Good-looking. *Good for Greer.*

Neil caught my eye as I approached. "Pepper! I'd like you to meet Greer Allighant, once of Bohemia Beach. Pepper has a New Orleans-themed bar in Bohemia."

"I'll have to try that sometime, if I ever get up there again. When I'm not on a cruise, I'm usually at my condo here," Greer said. "But I always liked popping into The Junction Box for a wonderful G&T now and again."

"Neil knows his way around a gin and tonic," I agreed. "Nice to meet you."

"And this is my friend Winston," Greer said. "Neil was just asking us about the fancy rum tasting. Winston is the one who talked me into getting us tickets. He knows quite a bit about it."

Ah, so Winston was the missing piece, the reason Greer was on the list.

"Winston Reckel," the man said, giving me a firm handshake and a friendly smile. "I met Greer on a cruise this winter during a distillery tour in Jamaica. We have similar sensibilities—she collects art, and I collect rum. I thought she might enjoy Hookahakaha."

"How do you like it?" I asked her.

"It's very nice so far. You don't pull punches on these drinks, do you? I remember coming here back in the day with my husband, bless his soul. And the Polynesian shows at the Yankee Clipper and Pau Hana. Those beautiful mystery girls bringing out the bowl and doing the slow hula and laying a lei on somebody, with the fella playing the gong and everyone just staring. So mesmerizing."

"They still do that at Pau Hana," I said, secretly jealous that Greer saw these venues in their heyday. "Are you planning to go there this weekend?"

"We'll be there Saturday. I hear the dining area opened late today because of what happened to that nice young man."

"Fizz Martin," I said. *Nice young man.* Perspective was every-thing. "That must've hurt, them opening late. These are the biggest crowds they get all year."

"Well, they opened just the same," Greer said.

"We might go over and get a drink in the bar later," added Winston. "We'll help them make up the bar tab."

We all shared a laugh. "Since you're a rum collector, you must know something about the rums Fizz was going to share at the Gold Tooth Tasting," Neil prompted.

Winston nodded. "I know what he told us about the London dock rum. And I've heard of the rum from the *Lord Archibald* and, of course, the Wray & Nephew. I'd love to get my hands on any of those."

"You haven't heard anything about the London dock rum, have you?" I asked.

Winston gave me a puzzled look. "I'm not sure what you mean."

"It disappeared from the crime scene," I told him. At this point, it didn't seem to matter who knew this nugget, since the rumor was rippling through the convention anyway.

"You kidding me? That's worth a fortune. I hope the thief doesn't damage it. Hey, Greer, would you like another drink?"

She looked thoughtful for a moment. "Maybe one more. I'd like another one of your pineapples, if you have one," she said to Neil.

"I'll get it," Winston said.

"Better hurry," I said. "There were only a couple left."

He headed inside, and I turned to Greer. "We wanted to ask you two to keep an eye out for the London dock rum. Can you let us know if you see the bottle anywhere? One of our friends is a bit tangled up in this mess, and we'd like to clear him."

"Oh, of course, honey. What did it look like?"

"Were you not at Fizz's presentation yesterday?" I asked.

"Winston went without me. Wednesday's my bridge day at my condo."

Neil and I exchanged a look. She really wasn't into rum if she skipped Fizz's presentation to play bridge, though apparently she could hold her liquor.

"The rum is in an old-looking bottle," Neil said, "kind of dark. When Fizz had it, it was in a wooden box. What else, Pepper?"

I thought back to seeing it in Fizz's hands in the Pau Hana kitchen. "The box had a picture of a ship burned into the side with the word 'JAMAICA.' Can you let us know if you see anything like that? And ask Winston, too?"

Greer tilted her head and looked at Neil intently. "That sounds really familiar." Her brow scrunched. "I know I've seen that very thing. A box just like that. Now where did I see it?"

Chapter Seventeen

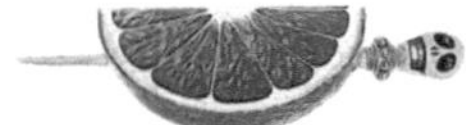

Well, holy Hemingway Daiquiri. We had a hit. A palpable hit.

If Greer could just remember where she saw the London dock rum.

"You saw a wooden box like that, with the ship and everything?" I asked her.

"Yes, I'm sure I did. Now don't look at me that way. I have an excellent memory, but I've seen an awful lot of stuff today. We went through the vendor hall. That's so impressive. Have you been? They were serving drinks in there, too, and they had a surf band that reminded me of that nice Dick Dale. I bought this muumuu there, in fact. They had some crafty wooden boxes at one table, but I don't think I saw your box there."

Neil's mouth quirked. "If they're selling London dock rum at the vendor hall, I definitely want to know about it."

"Now you're just pulling my leg." Greer smiled. "You know where I think I saw it? But that doesn't seem possible ..." She was lost in her thoughts again. She looked around as if she was looking for an answer, glancing through the windows and the glass door.

We followed her gaze. Winston was juggling one of our Piña Pele pineapples and another drink, but he'd been waylaid by the man I'd met that morning by the pool, Cap Calder.

Cap's captain's hat was pushed back on his head, and he was waving his hands around, obviously telling a hilarious story, because Winston was laughing hard.

Neil and I turned back to Greer. Something had changed. I could feel it. A little shock of anticipation shot through me before she said, "I do believe I might have seen that box in Winston's suite." Her tone suggested even she didn't believe what she was saying.

Neil's voice was cool, but I could tell by his body language that he was keen to hear more. "Are you sure that's where you saw it?"

Greer shook her head. "Well, now, I can't be *completely* sure. Winston brought all kinds of rum. He says he trades with other collectors. There was more than one wooden box in his room. He shuffled through them at one point, and they all looked different. So I'm not a hundred percent sure that's where I saw the one with the ship. We had a little cocktail and enjoyed the view on the balcony before we came up here, you see, so I didn't spend that much time in the room proper."

"You're not staying with him?" I asked, realizing too late that my question wasn't exactly delicate.

But Greer just laughed. "Oh, no, honey. I mean, I wouldn't push him out of bed, but we really are just friends. We both enjoy the thrill of the hunt when it comes to collecting. Only my art-collecting days are over, so maybe I'll pick up a bottle or two of good rum. He's teaching me what he knows."

"Back to the wooden box," Neil said. "Where was it in his suite?"

Greer had a mischievous look in her eye. "You think my friend had something to do with that murder?"

Neil looked caught out, so I spoke up, trying to set her at ease.

"I'm sure he didn't." *Of course he did!* "He's a collector, so maybe he just came across a similar bottle and knows where Fizz got his. Or there's an outside chance he bought it and didn't know what he was getting."

Greer smiled. "You don't need to pull any punches with me. I think I'd like to know the answers to all your questions myself before I invest any more time or money in Winston Reckel. So I suggest you two go have a look at his suite."

I looked between her and Neil. "Uh, do we just ask him if we can stop by?"

"We could ask to see his rum collection, I guess," Neil said.

Crap. Winston was coming out through the door and heading our way.

"Or you could take a look yourselves and not give him a chance to hide it." Greer reached out a pale white hand and I took it. And found a key card slipped into my palm. She winked. "Ten-oh-four. I'll give you a few minutes. Finally, my pineapple!" she said loudly as Winston arrived.

"Sorry," Winston said cheerfully. "Got talking to Cap Calder. Man, that guy has some stories. And he might be interested in some of my rum."

"Oh, really? I'd like to meet him," Greer said, making bug eyes at me.

I, in turn, made bug eyes at Neil and nodded at Greer and Winston. "Guess we better wrap up things. Great to meet you both."

"Mahalo," Winston said, raising up his drink with a smile.

"See you kids later." Greer toasted us with her pineapple.

I grabbed Neil by the elbow and hustled us back to the doors.

"No way," was the first thing he said when we got inside.

"She gave us the key! We have, what, ten, fifteen minutes. Solid window of opportunity."

"We have to clean up here," said Mr. Responsible.

"We can come back afterward. And look. It's practically done anyway."

It was true. With the last of the drinks gone, Barclay, Melody and Luke had worked their magic and practically erased any evidence we had ever been there. They were packing up Neil's bar bag.

"What's up?" Barclay said as we approached. "You look like you're going to pop, Pepper."

"I might. We have a lead. Somebody might have the ... *the nuclear football,*" I said as softly as I could.

"What? Details!" Melody demanded.

"Can't," I said. "No time. We have a key to the room. We have ten minutes. I'm going to go check it out."

Neil was no longer cool. "No, Pepper. It's too dangerous."

I got up in his face (on tiptoes, OK?) so I could be fierce and quiet at the same time. "I—am—going! This is for Luke, Neil. *For Luke.*"

Heat was firing off Neil as he stared me down, his nostrils flaring. He radiated anger. Resolve. *Something else.* It was sexy as hell. "We can tell Barclay's dad. He can go."

I stepped even closer, trying not to notice how good he smelled. Manly soap and a hint of rum. "Greer wasn't even sure about the box," I whispered. "Are we going to get the police involved if we're not sure? When it only takes a minute to find out?"

"It would be great if you found that rum," Luke said, anxiety in his eyes. "I'll go with you, Pepper."

"No!" Neil said. "You're in enough trouble already. None of you are going."

"Except me." I crossed my arms. "I have the key."

"Damn it." Neil looked at all of our faces, landing on Luke. Then me. "Damn it to hell, Pepper Revelle. I'll go with you, if only to keep you from getting killed. Barclay, can you grab my bag?"

"No problem."

"I want mine," I said, and they handed me my canvas messenger bag.

And then I was speed-walking toward the elevator, Neil huffing right behind me—in ire or exertion, I wasn't sure.

"Stairs," he hissed.

"What?"

"Fewer witnesses."

I shot him a look, appreciating his criminal mind, and headed for the stairs. The initial descent was kind of pretty, as a nice open staircase led to the bathrooms on the floor below. And then we got into a dim, utilitarian stairwell and clattered as fast we could toward the tenth floor and my first attempt at breaking and entering.

Chapter Eighteen

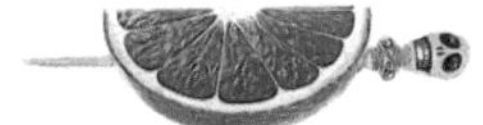

I don't love climbing stairs, but trotting down a half dozen flights in the tower was almost as bad. I was panting when we took the door for the tenth floor and popped out into a mini-balcony.

I pulled up short at the truncated view and the fresh air. "What the hell is this?"

"Access door." Neil pointed to a white door perpendicular to the one we'd just come out of. It took us into the small tenth-floor lobby by the elevators, and we headed down the hallway, looking for 1004. I ignored a group of four loud, happy drunks as they brushed past us on the way to the elevator.

"Take it easy," Neil said softly when they were out of range. "You look like you're hell-bent on breaking into somebody's room."

"Maybe because I'm about to break into somebody's room. Here!"

There was a short hallway off the main corridor, and we found 1004 at the end. I was about to plunge ahead when Neil held up a hand and then touched a finger to his lips in a silent *Shhh.* He leaned toward the door and listened for a moment.

He was always the cautious one. But he had a point. Suppose we walked in on something?

Finally, he nodded, and I slipped the key card into the lock. There was a click, and the green light flashed. I took a big breath and pushed open the door.

Just one light was on, a bedside lamp. I decided not to turn on anything else so as not to draw attention from—I didn't know. Someone with a telescope? A passing seagull? I was paranoid, OK?

The room was huge. Well, the suite. But it's not like it had multiple bedrooms. There was the bed, closet, dressing area and the bathroom, plus a living space with comfy furniture around a coffee table, next to a counter with a sink and a small fridge—a modest wet bar. All around the bar were a dozen or so liquor boxes of varying brands stacked against the wall.

I went over to look, lifting up a flap on one box. None of them appeared to be sealed. "All the bottles look different," I said to Neil. "Some of them look old. Collectible. Maybe the dock rum is in one of these?"

"Forget it. We don't have time to look through every one of these boxes. Look for the wooden boxes Greer was talking about."

While I tried to peer through the boxes crowded around the coffee table without moving anything, Neil headed to the closet. "More boxes," he said. "Is this guy moving in?"

Well, there was always the obvious place everyone hid everything. Under the bed. Though Greer said she saw the wooden box before they went to the Tiki Skyliner party, so that meant it wasn't hidden from sight.

I looked around again, scrutinizing every corner, and headed for the glass balcony doors, which were just beyond the king-size bed. The balcony was where Greer said they'd had their drink. The view was fantastic from here, just as it had been above, only this side of the tower faced the densely built barrier island and the Atlantic Ocean. In the last glimmer of twilight, the vast darkness of the water was relieved only by the lights of ships dotting the horizon.

I turned away from the windows, ready to resume my search of the liquor boxes, when I saw what Greer must have seen: maybe five wooden boxes stacked in the open bottom shelf of the nightstand.

"Neil!" I whispered sharply.

He came around the corner at a canter. "We have to hurry. It's already been ten minutes."

"If Cap Calder is talking, they might be there for another hour. Look."

I pointed out the wooden boxes. Truth was, I was afraid to touch them, mostly because I didn't want to be responsible for destroying a piece of rum history.

But Neil went right to work, kneeling next to the night-stand and deftly removing and checking each box. While they all had interesting markings and were made of different types or colors of wood, nothing looked like Fizz's rum.

Until the last one. Neil turned it around in his hands, and we froze as the ship mark came into view. The "JAMAICA" sealed it.

"I just realized my fingerprints are now all over this box," Neil said incredulously. "How do I let you talk me into this stuff?"

"Don't worry. You didn't touch the bottle, and the wood is rough. The prints won't be good." I had no idea if I was right, but what was done was done. "Look inside."

Neil opened the lid and closed it quickly. "Looks like it."

"Go ahead and put it back." Now I was getting nervous. "Let's get out of here and call Barclay's dad."

Neil hurriedly stacked the boxes in their original configuration, and we headed for the door.

And heard the lock click.

"Shit," I muttered as we both froze in full view of the opening door.

"I told you this was the wrong room!" Neil practically shouted.

My head snapped up to look at him. Was he delusional? Whatever he had in mind was not going to work.

And then Winston Reckel stepped into the room.

And, thank goodness, Greer was right behind him.

"No, see, it's the right room! Oh, Greer, I'm so glad we caught you!" My silly-sounding voice was almost as loud as Neil's. "You dropped your key card upstairs. We thought we'd drop it off on our way to Neil's room."

Winston's brown eyes shifted back and forth between us, and his jaw twitched. "You have Greer's key? How'd you know which room?"

Greer giggled. "I told them, silly. I suggested we all have a cocktail when they get a break this weekend. And aren't they lovely for bringing this back to me?" Greer took the key card from me in a move right out of community theater. Was Winston going to buy any of this? "Thank you so much, Pepper. Neil. I guess I had one pineapple too many."

Neil's voice resumed its almost-normal level of cool. "There's no such thing as too many pineapples."

I laughed. It was a real laugh, though it sprang more from nerves than humor.

"Well, since you're here, would you like a drink?" Winston still looked skeptical, but I had a feeling he wanted to know more about what was going on.

That worked, because I wanted to know more, too. Maybe we could use this unfortunate situation to our advantage.

"You have anything to drink around here?" Neil quipped.

Now we all laughed, because, hello. We were standing in the middle of rum central.

"Oh, I might have something interesting," Winston said, relaxing a fraction.

Greer winked at me as Winston flipped on more lights, rustled up a sleeve of clear plastic cups and set them on the wet bar. Then he started digging around in the boxes. "How about The Real McCoy 12-Year?"

"Sounds great," Neil said.

"Yum," I agreed.

I watched Winston closely as he poured the rum to make sure there was no funny business. We didn't know if he killed Fizz, but having the London dock rum didn't make him look like a saint. It didn't look good at all.

"Let's go out on the balcony!" I suggested. "It's such a nice night. I want to check out the view."

Neil gave me a *what the hell are you thinking?* look, but Greer's bubbly agreement had us all heading out to the balcony with our delicious rum. A couple of sniffs had me imagining a tropical beach in Barbados, where it was made, and it was spicy on the tongue. I drank it a little too fast. I blamed my nerves.

Focus, Pepper. If you're going to do this, you have to do it big.

Winston topped off our cups, and after a few minutes of chatter about what we could and couldn't see from the balcony, I turned casually around toward the room. "Oh, wow! Are those old rums? Are they part of your collection? I have to check them out!"

Neil made a strangled noise in his throat as I bounced into

the room, set down my cup and started moving around the wooden boxes under the nightstand.

"Don't!" Winston said, but it was too late. I'd pulled out the London dock rum box.

"This looks so familiar, doesn't it?" I said in a lilting, tipsy voice. I wasn't tipsy. Not really. But I didn't want to get all accusatory until we knew what we were dealing with. "I got a really good look at the rum Fizz had, and this sure looks like it."

I'm probably the only one who heard Neil sigh before he followed up. "Did you get ahold of a bottle of the London dock rum after all? I understand why you'd want to keep it a secret. Keep the riffraff out of your room."

"Like you, you mean?" Winston's voice was gruff and not at all polite now. "Unhand that box."

"That's what it is, isn't it?" I hugged the box. "I love the idea of holding a piece of history."

"Kind of like me." Greer launched into a peel of laughter. Greer didn't have to fake being tipsy. That ship had sailed a couple of pineapples ago.

"It's mine." Winston put down his drink on the nightstand and pulled the box from my arms.

"Are you sure it's yours?" Neil's voice had turned colder than Winston's, and we all sobered up at the sound of it.

Winston couldn't kill us all, and he was cornered. His furious look collapsed. "I told you, it's mine. Fizz never paid for it."

Holy crap on a cracker! "You stole it from Pau Hana?"

"You can't steal something that's already yours!" Winston put the box on the nightstand next to his cup and sat on the side of the bed. "I didn't steal it."

"Did you—" I started to ask.

"And I didn't kill Fizz," Winston said. "You have to understand. I deal in rare rums, OK? This came into my hands, and it was such a spectacular find, I knew Fizz would love it. He was a manic collector. He couldn't afford it, exactly, but I knew he had rums I wanted. He said he had another bottle of the Wray & Nephew 17, and I was willing to trade. But he was supposed to deliver it to me by noon, and he didn't. I wanted to talk to him."

Whoa. "You confronted him at Pau Hana?" I knocked back the rest of my rum.

"I did not. But I found my rum."

"You *found* the rum." Neil's deadpan skepticism made the hairs on my arms stand up.

Winston nodded. "I found it in back of Pau Hana. I swear. I couldn't believe it either. I was back there having a smoke and saw my box in a pile of discarded banana boxes."

"That really is bananas," Greer said merrily. "I'm going to get another drink."

While she headed back to the bar, Neil and I stared down Winston.

"This story isn't very convincing," I said.

"I know." Now Winston sounded miserable. "That's why I didn't tell the police. Of course they would think I killed him. But I never went in the kitchen. Ask anybody. And when I picked it up, I had no idea he'd been killed. But I would've picked it up anyway. I have no idea what this could go for at auction, but it could be significant."

Neil crossed his arms, drink still in one hand. "And you were going to trade it for one bottle of the Wray & Nephew?"

"Not just that," Winston said. "Fizz had some other good bottles, and he had connections. He was going to hook me up with other collectors."

I squinted at him. "Why would you leave something this valuable in your hotel room?"

"Too many questions otherwise. It blends in unless someone goes snooping." He glared at me. "I was going to tell the cops eventually."

I didn't believe him. But I didn't know if he was a killer. I also didn't want him to look too hard at why we were in his room in the first place.

"Would you like us to tell the lead detective on the case about your rum?" I asked. "We have kind of an 'in' with him." That might be exaggerating our relationship with Barclay's dad, but if Winston thought the police might take an extra interest in investigating the bodies of two mixologists like us, that was a good thing, right?

"I'll talk to them," Winston mumbled. "First thing in the morning. I want to call a lawyer first, all right? I didn't do anything wrong. I just reclaimed my own property. I'm saving history here!"

Precious history. "OK," Neil said. "We'll let Detective Flores know you're coming."

Winston opened his mouth and shut it again without saying anything. *Check.* It would look really bad if he killed us after we told the cops about him. But I'd rather not give him the chance.

"We've got to go. Big day tomorrow." Neil looped his arm in mine. "For all of us."

"Yeah." Winston scowled. "Thanks for that."

"I think I'll get a cab home," Greer said cheerfully. "Will you kids walk me out?"

Chapter Nineteen

We saw Greer off in a cab in front of the hotel, where an odd, boat-shaped car with tiki embellishments was parked. Ah. Cap Calder's ride.

"I don't believe for two seconds that Winston just found an invaluable bottle of rum in the trash behind Pau Hana," Neil said as we walked back in and headed for the lounge by the bar in the cavernous lobby.

"Winston's story seems ridiculous," I agreed. "But why would anyone make up a story like that?"

We took seats at one of the low tables. He sat next to me on the cushy bench, to my great pleasure.

I realized his choice of seating was probably not just because he got to sit next to me. He also had a view of the group of bartenders post-gaming closer to the bar proper, a few steps up from the level we were on.

Val was among them, her pink hair askew. "To the Hooka-hakaha bar bitches!" she shouted, holding up a shot, and the group around her laughed and shouted "Mahalo!" and downed the rum.

I mean, it had to be rum, right?

She looked around, flushed and happy, and spotted us. "Neil! Get over here! You too, Pepper!" At least she remembered my name, unlike Kim earlier today.

I tried to ignore the fact that all my muscles hurt from working all day and dragged myself up the few steps to the comfy chairs on the advanced drinkers' level.

"Tequila next!" Val shouted, and there were hearty hollers of agreement all around.

Tequila was efficient when one's quest was obliteration. Heck, maybe it would help me sleep.

"Line 'em up," I said.

Val grinned. "That's the spirit!" I wondered what she'd done with the tyrant who'd ruled the kitchen this morning.

While she rallied the rest of the crew, I spoke softly to Neil. "Do you think Winston killed Fizz?"

"Theft was the perfect motive," Neil murmured back. "He admitted to stealing that rum. He has it in his possession."

"I'm wondering if he's going to vanish tonight, rum and all."

"I doubt it. While we were in the elevator, I texted Barclay's dad about what we learned. He acknowledged my text, and my guess is he'll be heading over to the hotel soon, maybe with a search warrant for Winston's room."

"But Winston said he was going to talk to the police tomorrow."

Neil lifted an eyebrow. "Do you believe anything Winston says at this point?"

"Well, no. That's why I think he killed Fizz."

Val spun around from where she'd been chatting with the others and pointed at me. "That name shall not be spoken here!"

I resisted the urge to sink back in the chair. "Sorry. I didn't mean to bring down the crowd."

Val swayed a little as she grinned again. Slyly this time. "Do I look 'down' to you?" She took a couple of steps closer and plopped into a chair at our tiny table. "The world is infinitely better without that man in it."

Interesting. But what did she mean? "He wasn't very nice to you Wednesday, I noticed."

"He's only nice when he thinks he's going to get something. Well, he got all he could from me."

"What do you mean?" Neil asked.

She looked around. The others were busy counting down their tequila shots as the server set three more shot glasses on our table. "Drink first."

Oh, boy.

She raised her glass. And her eyes glazed over. "I can't think of a toast."

Neil smiled as we raised our glasses. "Will you take a quote instead? 'You're not drunk if you can lie on the floor without holding on.'"

"That's feckin' genius," Val said, and we all knocked back our tequila. "I guess I'm not drunk then."

"Dean Martin." Neil set his glass down like it was nothing.

Whereas the shot went through my brain like a log flume, splashing thoughts all over the place. Uh, what was I going to ask her?

"You were saying about He Who Shall Not Be Named?" Neil asked Val.

"You know my history, right? With the New York bar, I mean?"

"I know it was great. I had the pleasure of going there once."

Val's eyes, green with a splash of gold in the middle, widened behind the pink bangs. "I remember that night! We hit a few of Manhattan's finest establishments."

I tried not to let this revelation throw me. "What did—you

know, *he* have to do with the bar?" I asked before she strayed too far down memory lane. Though I was dying to know more about Neil's friendship with her. Sort of.

Val turned back to me as if she'd forgotten I was there. She blinked a couple of times, then starting talking low enough that we both leaned in. "I guess I should go back a little further." Her words were ever so slightly slurred. I hoped she didn't regret this in the morning. I hoped she didn't regret this and take it out on me and the rest of the prep staff in the morning.

"I met Fi ... *him* during my early days in New York. I was still working my way up. We had a ... few memorable evenings. I only found out later that he was already with Kim at that time. I felt like shit when I found out. I never would have hooked up with anybody who was spoken for. But he was good at omitting inconvenient facts, and he'd already started building his empire. So I knew who he was. I was young. I was easily seduced by dicks with cute accents." She turned and screamed "SHOT!" at the other bartenders, who whooped and ordered another bottle.

Then she was talking to us again as if she hadn't just yowled like a siren. "I think it pissed him off that I cut him dead from that moment on. Didn't talk to him. Didn't kiss his ass like everyone else. There were others in New York who knew I didn't like him, knew I must have a good reason and followed my lead. He didn't like that. He didn't like that at all. And I certainly didn't go to him when it was time for me to open my bar. I went to another investor who got me going with a newly renovated boutique hotel that was looking to install a classy craft cocktail experience. You know me. Classy." She winked, and we had to chuckle.

"But it was classy," Neil said. "Creative. Daring. Yet all built on classic technique. I mourned its passing."

"Listen to him!" Val said to me before turning back to Neil. "Silver-tongued devil. But I will grant you that you *are* correct. It was everything I'd ever wanted. I was so proud of it. It was my child." A tear teetered at the corner of her eye and slid down her cheek.

My heart went out to her. "What happened?"

"Fizzasshole happened. He bought the boutique hotel and kicked me out."

"But—you were successful," I said. As a bar owner, I knew success was nothing to sneeze at. You never killed the golden goose. Or even the Grey Goose, if it paid the bills.

"It didn't matter. I represented something he couldn't have. A thorn in his paw. Whatever." Val gave a thumbs-up to the server, who was back with a new tray and handing out shots. He plonked three more down in front of us. She held up her glass. "Let's do this."

I exchanged a look with Neil. Normally I was all in, but my head was already swimmy. He picked up his shot glass and dared me with his eyes. *Neil dared me.*

I held up my glass and returned his look. "To classy dames and Mai Tais."

"Hell, yeah." Val knocked back her tequila, and we followed.

The log flume in my brain derailed, and I had to take a minute to close my eyes. I heard Neil call over the server and say something. When I opened my eyes again, Neil was asking Val a question. "The consulting business going well?"

"Fantastic. No regrets. None. Especially now. Ding-dong, the dick is dead. Dead as a cheap bottle of champagne that's been left open overnight." She nodded at both of us. "I'll catch you later."

She moved over to the next table and its boisterous conversation.

A minute later, the server brought a big bowl of french fries to our table.

I inhaled deeply, and my mouth watered. "Truffle fries?"

"Damn, you have a great nose," Neil said.

"You are a god." I ate several before I looked up. He was watching me, a small smile on his lips. "Well, eat some. Don't act like you just threw a fish to a dolphin."

He laughed and joined me, and we both watched Val and friends as we polished off the fries.

"Do you think—?" he asked me.

"I'm trying not to think right now. Why don't you take me to your room?"

Chapter Twenty

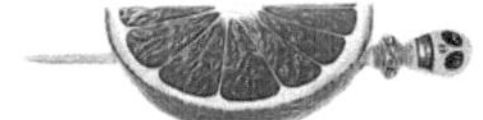

"Now, Pepper." Neil conveniently ignored my suggestion that he take me to his room and waved over the server. In a moment he was signing the bill, paying for the fries and one of the bottles of tequila. He was so nice. And yes, I looked. I'm nosy, OK?

He signed it to his room number.

I elbowed him. "You're on the same floor as Winston? For real?"

"It shouldn't be that surprising. They've blocked off a few of the floors for Hookahakaha guests."

"So you're going to show me your room?" I gave him what I hoped was a fetching smile.

"Why don't I show you to *your* room?" He offered a hand to help me up. An offer I couldn't refuse.

"What's the fun in that?" I used his grip to pull myself closer to him. "I have a roommate. You don't have a room-mate, do you, Neil?"

His eyes, with those wonderful gray irises ringed in dark blue, looked positively helpless. He couldn't blame me for any confusion he was feeling right now. He'd egged me on with those very eyes, didn't he?

"Let's walk and talk," he said. I grabbed my bag, and he tugged me along and guided me down the few steps to the main floor. Then he put his arm in mine and headed toward the tower. The tower! His room! "We'll just let you sober up a little, OK? Then I'm going to take you home."

"Home?"

"Your room."

"Whatever you say." I leaned into him as we walked. I admit, it was fun to tease him. But there was no doubt he did something to my wiring. It was that opposites-attract thing, his rock-steady to my tilt-a-whirl, and something else: his essential goodness. He was just a really good guy. Whereas Mark Fairman, for example, set off all my buzzers whenever we shared the same airspace, for all the wrong reasons, igniting all my worst impulses.

Maybe because it was late, we had the elevator to ourselves. "Val really didn't like Fizz," I said as we rode up.

"Understatement of the year."

"Could she have killed him?"

"He destroyed her dream. I'd say she had motive. If he'd done that to me, I don't know what I would have done."

It was hard to picture a vigilante Neil, but he was passionate about his bar and the art of the cocktail. And Fizz sure knew how to push people's buttons. Like Val's.

"So you knew her in New York?" I asked him. God, I was pathetic.

He looked down at me, a smile playing around his mouth. "She gave me a tour one evening." He wasn't telling me what I really wanted to know.

I leaned so hard into him, he bumped against the side wall of the elevator. "Did you have fun?"

He laughed. "It was fun. And no, nothing happened. I was dating someone else at the time."

I couldn't stop my frown. Of course he was. I mean, how

many guys had I gone through in the past ten years? But I'd never seen Neil with anybody since I'd met him. I faced him square on, pushed his back to the wall and pressed all five foot four of myself against his body. Which meant I had to look up at him. I reached up and cupped his cheek, the trim beard, and looked at him longingly with my big, gray-green eyes. I'd practiced this look. It was pretty good.

"Pepper, this isn't a good idea."

"What isn't? It almost was, in New Orleans."

"Almost. And then you fell asleep."

"Not because of you!"

"Nonetheless." Was he teasing me?

"You can't hold that against me." I kissed his neck and murmured in his ear. "Tell me you're not interested."

The elevator dinged and stopped. He gently pushed me away, but he still hooked his arm in mine and pulled me out and escorted me down the hall.

I let him guide me along. We passed Winston Reckel's room and all the others without running into anyone or hearing anything. Then he let me into his room.

It wasn't as big as Winston's but was still roomy. His blinds were closed, I guessed against the heat of the day. But it was nighttime now.

"Excuse me a minute." I found his bathroom, did my thing, touched up my lipstick.

When I came out, he went in, giving me a minute to look around the room. The bed was made and flawless. I guessed he hadn't grabbed a nap like I had. I set my bag on a chair and opened the closet. There was his suitcase, open but sitting on the folding trestle next to the safe, the clothes inside in perfect order. Trousers and Hawaiian shirts were lined up on the hangers. So neat. So Neil. I closed the closet, wandered to the glass balcony door and used the cord to pull the curtains open enough so I could slide the door open and slip outside.

It was cooler now, and a pleasant breeze ruffled my hair and the skirt of my dress. The Fort Lauderdale skyline twinkled in the not-quite-darkness of the city at night. The vehicles, ships and planes all looked like toys. Closer to Wicker Wharf, a big luxury boat glided along the Intracoastal Waterway, passing through the open drawbridge as cars waited on either end. Lights glittered, reflected in the water. There were yachts docked everywhere. One of them was Arnold Preiss's. I wondered which one. I could even see a little of the hotel's interior courtyard from here, the pools glowing blue in the night. Laughter and music carried up to me. The tikiphiles were still enjoying life.

"Too bad you're not in the tower," Neil said, coming up behind me. He leaned on the railing next to me. "You could enjoy this view all night long."

I turned toward him. "You're in the tower. And I'm available all night."

He didn't say anything for a second. Then he stood up straight and put his hands on my shoulders, letting them glide down my bare arms. I shivered.

"You cold?" he asked.

I shook my head and eased closer to him.

He slid his hands up my arms again, over my shoulders, my neck. He plucked my floral hair adornment and tossed it through the open door into the room. Then he ran his fingers through my hair. And looked into my eyes.

I reached up, pulled off my nerdy glasses and tossed them inside after the flowers. An open invitation if there ever was one. But he just stood there, looking at me. My body slowly caught fire, starting at where he touched me, tingling through my scalp, shooting down my spine and conflagrating all my lady parts.

It was like he was … afraid to do more?

I rammed my fingers into his nice, thick hair and pulled him close and pressed my mouth against his. He groaned softly, let his arms slip to my back and pulled me in for the kiss. I opened my mouth and tasted him and tequila. I was hot all over. But as our tongues touched, he pushed me away again.

"Why—why are you playing hard to get?" I sputtered.

"I'm easy to get. That's the problem. You don't want to have me. Trust me."

"Duh. I'm here."

"I've told you before. People who are close to me don't do so well. I can't take care of them. I can't take care of you."

I huffed. "I don't *need* anyone to take care of me. Plus, that's utter crap, and you know it. You take care of everyone."

"I worry about you, Pepper."

I stepped back, furious now. "Are you changing the subject?"

"It's the same subject." He looked embarrassed—and as riled up as I was. "It's too great a burden."

"I'm a *burden?*" My voice jumped higher. "Is that what you're saying?"

Neil looked around and lowered his voice, in the way that people do when they want you to be quiet, too. "No. The way I—it's me. I'm the burden."

"You're confusing. You're the king of mixed signals. I'm going home."

"Home?"

"Back to my room!"

"I'll take you."

"Forget it." I stomped inside, grabbed my glasses and my flower clip, stuffed them in my bag and headed for the door.

"Please, Pepper. I don't want you to go like this," Neil said, right behind me.

I turned again. "The point is, you want me to go. It doesn't really matter how." I pulled open the door and let it shut behind me. It's so difficult to slam good hotel doors. They're too quiet and take all the fun out of it.

My fury had burned out most of my buzz. I couldn't tell whether the heat I felt now was frustrated lust or plain old anger. This wasn't the first time Neil had implied he was somehow unworthy or incapable of getting involved with me. I needed to figure out why.

A cluster of five happy people were waiting for the elevator. I couldn't deal with people right now. I needed to cool off for a minute. There was a door off the foyer. Oh, yeah. The mini-balcony with access to the stairs. I opened the door, let it close behind me and took a deep breath, trying to settle my brain and my hormones. From here I could see a little of the ocean and a little of the port. My head was spinning a little. I needed water. I needed to hug my dog. But first I needed to get a grip. Literally. I held on to the railing and closed my eyes.

It took me half a second to register that the door behind me had opened. And that the person who opened it wasn't Neil.

By then it was too late.

An arm hooked around my neck. A man, I thought. He was strong. His other arm wrapped around my waist, locking me against him, and he slammed me up against the balcony railing. I couldn't see him, but I struggled like my life depended on it. Because as he pushed me, tipping me forward, I was pretty sure it did.

Chapter Twenty-One

I cried out, and that was a good thing, because the arm that was cutting off my air moved so he could slap a hand over my mouth.

"Do you want to be the second one to die?" the man said in my ear. I didn't recognize the voice. It was low and rough with an affected accent, like somebody doing a Batman imitation. It could've been anybody.

"Mmm-mm!" I hoped he knew I was saying "no."

"Then quit nosing around where you're not wanted." He pushed me harder against the railing as he held me up, and my feet actually left the ground, kicking, trying to find purchase on the guy. I grabbed for the railing and missed. The ground seemed to spin far below me. The tenth floor felt even higher when it looked like you were about to fly off it.

Then he dropped me to the floor and clocked me on the back of the head.

I crumpled to the concrete, covering my head, terrified, anticipating the next blow.

But in a few seconds, I realized he was gone. A door opened and closed. I looked up, shaking and nauseous. Which door? I grabbed a vertical on the railing, yanked myself to my feet and opened the door I'd come through. The hall was quiet. Could he have gone to a room? Grabbed an elevator?

I let the door close again and turned to the stairway door and pushed it. *That's the sound I heard.* This was the door he took, I was sure of it. I paused and listened. Were those footsteps? Maybe, deep in the tower. The sound was soft and echoey. Was it my attacker or someone else? I decided heading down those stairs wasn't such a great idea. I wasn't completely stupid.

I still wore my messenger bag, cross-body like I usually did. I had a cocktail knife in there. I had a ton of crap in there. But the chances of me finding anything quickly that I could've used as a weapon were zero to none. It would've taken me ten minutes, minimum. Maybe I needed to start carrying around my own giant muddler.

At least my phone buzzed and lit up like a beacon amid all my junk when it rang. And it was ringing. I eased inside the tenth-floor foyer before digging it out. I didn't want to be near a balcony right now.

I saw the caller ID and answered. "Neil?"

"I'm glad you're still talking to me. I wanted to make sure you made it home OK."

A little sob escaped me. "Somebody attacked me."

There was half a second's silence, and then he said, "I'll be right there."

The call ended, and my first thought was, *That's pretty dumb.* How did he know where I was? I could've been tied to the drawbridge by terrorists, for all he knew.

But it really didn't matter. When I saw him coming down the hallway at a run, I burst into tears and ran at him, too.

He looked shocked when I fell into his arms. "Why are you here?"

"I was getting my breath on that little balcony there by the stairs and someone came up behind me and grabbed me and told me I could die too," I said between sniffles.

"And you wonder why I worry about you," he whispered, but he held me tight. "Do you want to come to my room?"

"No!" I didn't want to repeat our earlier scene and get stuck in an infinity loop of sexual frustration and scary attacks. "But you can walk me back to my room."

"I can take you to a doctor."

"No." I disentangled myself, a little embarrassed now, and we walked to the elevator. He pressed the button, looking around as we waited, ready to head off any bad guys. I noticed he'd changed into jeans and a black Death & Co. T-shirt. One of the bars he'd visited during his tour of New York with Val, no doubt. On the back it showed a reclining skeleton holding a cocktail and said "Time Flies."

That could've been me. A drunk skeleton. Though with my diet, I had a long way to go before I became a skeleton.

"We should call the cops," Neil said.

"Please don't."

"Your attacker could attack someone else."

I fumed for a second. "I know. But I'm tired. I don't want to deal with it. I'll tell Barclay's dad tomorrow, OK?"

"I'll text him and let him know."

My reply was dry. "Great."

Once we were in the elevator, he turned to me. "Are you sure you're all right?"

"Yes. Maybe a little bruised. He pushed me around and hit me on the head. Not as hard as he wanted to, I'm guessing."

Neil looked furious. "Who was it? Can you describe him?"

"My back was to him the whole time, and he had this fake growly voice. He grabbed me. He could've dumped me right over the balcony if he wanted to. I guess he just wanted to threaten me."

"Exactly what did he say?"

"He said, 'Do you want to be the second one to die?'"

"Holy hell. Was it Winston?"

My eyebrows lifted. "I don't think so. I looked in the hallway right away. I assume he would've run back to his room. And it didn't sound like him. Whoever it was smelled like rum."

"That narrows it down," he quipped.

"My thoughts exactly." The elevator doors opened, and we stepped out and walked toward the lobby and the passage to the other buildings. The lobby bar still had a few hardy drinkers, but it was mostly empty now.

"I guess it could've been any of the people we talked to today," Neil said. "No accent?"

I thought back. "Like I said, it was a fake voice. It did almost sound like someone trying to do an accent. Like when actors who aren't American try to do an American accent."

"Could it have been English? Nigel Dashwood? Mark Fairman?" He smiled. "Alastair Markham?"

I laughed. "Thank you for that. Alastair couldn't knock down a feather pillow, and besides, he has no motive that we know about. Because I'm assuming that whoever did this also killed Fizz Martin."

Exiting the lobby, we went through the doors that led to the second-story outdoor hallway and began the long trek to my room.

"Could it have been Val?" Neil sounded troubled by his own question.

"I really thought it was a man. But she's tall enough. However, I don't think she was in any condition to play ninja."

"True. I don't think she attacked you, either. It's not like her. But I'm still wondering about the link to Fizz. I guess you could have been attacked by someone else—not the murderer, I mean—for some reason we haven't divined yet."

"Now there's a pleasant thought. Not one but two homicidal rum-swilling maniacs at Hookahakaha."

We turned the corner to my wing of the building. Neil put an arm around my shoulders. I knew I couldn't read anything into that, but I was grateful for the comfort just the same.

"Do you want me to stay with you?" he asked.

I rolled my eyes. "I have an innocent roommate who would think it was weird."

"It *would* be innocent."

"Ha," I said. "Not if I can help it." Neil looked amused, which was not necessarily the reaction I wanted. "And I don't want her complaining to her brother about me. Plus, Astra can protect me."

"I'm sure she'd happily intercept any threatening hamburgers."

"She's a good dog!" I objected, but his humor made me smile. Made me feel a little better.

We stopped outside my door. This was like that awkward moment after a terrible prom date. Was a kiss appropriate? Or would he file a restraining order?

After a moment, he leaned in and kissed me on the cheek, keeping his lips there for an extra second so I could be sure I didn't imagine it. "Call me if you need anything. And I'll see you in the morning."

I just stood there for a moment, feeling the burning impression of his lips on my skin. He nodded at the door. I nodded at him, pulled my key card out of the one inside pocket in my bag (I'm not a total disaster), and let myself in the room.

It was dark, and for a second, I had anxiety again, wondering what waited for me there. But then I registered the strangely comforting sound of Gina snoring. And a furry shape bounded out of the darkness and put her paws up on my legs.

"Oh, Astra," I whispered, picking up and hugging my dog. She licked my face. "Let's get some sleep, baby. At least I know you'll go to bed with me."

THE WICKER WHARF kitchen was even busier Friday morning, if that was possible. The pool bars would open at noon, plus there were cocktail seminars in the afternoon and room parties tonight. The only event the volunteers and bartenders didn't have to prep drinks for was the late-afternoon mermaid show at the Wreck Bar over on the beach.

There were more staggering numbers on the white board, and today the work seemed to center around bananas, strawberries and syrup-making—new batches of falernum and orgeat. Plus limes. Always limes.

Barclay, Luke and Melody showed up just after I did and took on halving, slicing and squeezing. Barclay seemed totally unfazed by the squeezer of death, so he cheerfully risked his digits.

Neil beat us all there, of course. He was working on sugar syrup and large batches of tea to use in the Planter's Punch we'd serve later at our room party, one of several hosted by select bars and teams in rooms that faced the courtyard.

I got stuck with trimming mint for garnishes, making sure we had manageable stems with the bottoms snipped and the lower leaves removed. Later, just before garnishing the drinks, we'd spank it—smack the mint to bring out the aroma of its oil, gently enough so we didn't break it and release the plant's bitter chlorophyll.

There wasn't a lot of chatter. Barclay, Luke and Melody talked a little about their adventure at a bar in Miami Beach the previous night, but I sensed a hangover hovering above them like a cloud. And it's not like Neil and I could go into detail about our evening, given all the ears around us.

Neil asked me how I was doing, and I repressed a whole lot of feelings and muscle aches and just said "fine."

We were ticking along when Val showed up, looking only slightly the worse for wear, her pink hair mostly hiding her weary eyes. She checked with her second-in-command, who brought her a hot mug of Earl Grey, and they spent a few minutes going through a thick, color-coded binder. And then she started working the room, commenting on technique, teasing a couple of guys about the night before and checking out everyone's ink. She came to us last.

"Neil."

"Val," he said.

"Pepper," she followed up.

"How you feeling?" I asked.

She scowled like I'd committed the most egregious sin. She leaned in close to me and spoke so softly, only Neil and I could hear her.

"I'm feeling nothing." Her eyes burned into mine. "I feel nothing, OK? And no one gets to think about me feeling anything. What I said last night? Forget it. I mean I never want to hear mention of it ever again. Anywhere. From anyone. You got me?"

This was scary Val. Not boisterous, drunk Val.

I tried to sound brave. "Cool."

Her eyes narrowed at me. She glanced at Neil, who just smiled and nodded sympathetically. Sympathy from Neil clearly wasn't as offensive as me asking how she felt.

She eyeballed me again, then walked away to yell at someone who was chattering while holding the cooler door open.

I glanced at Neil, who seemed amused. I wasn't. Val looked murderous enough talking to me. What if she'd gotten Fizz alone for five minutes at Pau Hana?

Chapter Twenty-Two

After the hard work of slicing and squeezing all morning, our team had the afternoon off. But not really. Like several other bar teams, we'd volunteered to do a room party that night. The parties let the tikiphiles liquor up before the big music event in the ballroom. Even though sponsors were kicking in the rum, we had a ton of decorating and prep to do.

My only respite was a dubious one, as Barclay's dad called me to get details on my attack the night before and asked if I wanted to file a report. I told him I didn't, but he said he'd keep notes in "the file," whatever that meant. Actually, I knew what it meant. He thought the attack was related to Fizz's murder. I tried to put the idea of a murderer hunting me down out of my mind and focused on the more pleasant job of party prep.

Since party rooms had to be accessible to the pool area, Barclay and Luke's room on the ground floor was volunteered for our party. Guests would come and go by the open patio door. Outside, we placed tiki torches and props to lure them into our themed room.

We were from a beach town, or at least the mainland town right across the Indian River Lagoon from Bohemia Beach, but at a tiki convention, a beach theme seemed trite. Instead, we went for a ghost ship theme, with shipwreck props and nets and coconuts and glass floats hanging from the ceiling. Luke and Barclay dressed up as pirates and spent a lot of time practicing their *Arrrrrs.* Maybe pirates were cheesy, too, but these were extremely sexy pirates.

Those rippling lights everyone used for the holidays—ours were in blue and green—made for a great underwater look, and we played an audio loop of crashing waves that complemented the surf band playing by the pool. Fake skeletons were draped here and there, some partially clad in pirate clothes.

We set up the bar—an ingenious folding thing made of teak that Neil assembled in ten minutes—in front of the beds, which were upended sideways and leaning against the wall. Melody camouflaged them with silver fabric, netting, fairy lights and fake crabs.

She was in the bathroom, preparing some sort of sea siren outfit. I couldn't resist dressing as a pirate with the corset and all, because it more than flattered my curves, and I really liked the hat. Neil, however, went minimal, in black pants and a blousy black shirt with a loosely laced deep V-neck. Speaking of deep, I was deeply appreciative of this opportunity to ogle his chest. It was only fair, as I noted with satisfaction that he was subtly ogling mine.

Five minutes to game time, I was helping him with the final preparation of our punch bowl, cups and swizzles. "How'd you get all this stuff in your car?"

"I shipped most of it," he said.

"Well, aren't you clever. And where'd you get the dive suit?" I pointed to the dummy antique diver set up in the corner wearing a grass skirt and a lei.

"My grandfather's garage. My parents thought it would be

OK, even though Gramps is ... anyway, we're checking on the house every few days just in case."

"I'm so sorry. You still haven't heard anything?"

He shook his head. "The police are hardly looking anymore, and there's been no communication. My dad paid a private investigator to see what she could find out, but there's no trail. It's like Gramps vanished into thin air."

"He's an adventurer, isn't he? You don't dive on shipwrecks for decades without being resourceful and clever. A survivor. He's got to come back to you."

"I don't know," Neil said. "I'm sorry Fizz is gone. I wanted to ask him about the shipwreck rum. You know, from the *Lord Archibald?* That was one of Gramps's ships. He worked on recovering that treasure. As far as I know, he never had any rum from the ship. I don't know if he had anything from the ship. He hardly ever mentioned it, which is weird."

"Why is that weird?"

"He loved to tell stories about all his dives—loves to tell, I mean." He looked chagrined about using the past tense. "He wrote books about them, and I've read them all, but he never discussed the *Lord Archibald* in any detail."

"You just have to keep hoping. Not to use up my cliché allowance for the day, but maybe no news is good news."

"There's that ... Oh my God."

"What?" I turned around to see what he was staring at. It was Melody. Or should I say the Sea Siren. She wore a bikini-style top in a shiny, scaly turquoise fabric adorned with shells, faux pearls and jewels, with an elaborate necklace and a matching maxi-skirt trimmed with gold accents. Her long, blond hair was loose and dripping with pearls and sea-green rhinestones. She had ear- and arm-pieces that looked like fins.

And her makeup shimmered in shades of turquoise and pink, accented by more bling.

"You like?" she asked, spinning.

I nodded, feeling inadequate, as I usually did when I saw Melody's fashions. "Damn, girl. You definitely have to go outside and lure people in."

"Yes." Neil cleared his throat. "Do that."

Note to self: Dress like a mermaid the next time I want to impress Neil.

"I'll go out there with her," Luke volunteered.

"So will I, matey!" Barclay declared as Luke frowned.

"Might as well," Neil said. "Open the gates. It's time."

I could hear the guys outside telling folks, "Welcome to our barrrrrr!" Their antics prompted laughter from the first wave of visitors as the onslaught began.

Dick and Dale's bachelor party was one of the first groups to enter our watery grave. They must've spent a fortune on matching tropical outfits.

"Hey, guys!" I called as Neil and I dipped Planter's Punch from the big bowl and garnished the souvenir cups with mint and swizzle sticks. "Any news?"

"Afraid not," Dick said. "There's a lot of buzzing about what happened, but nobody seems to have any real information. I've heard nothing about the London rum."

"Though apparently that shipwreck rum isn't all that unique," Dale said. "We were visiting Davy Jones's Locker Museum today, and the owner let Dick and I have a taste from his bottle."

"What?" Neil exclaimed. He and I exchanged a look. He looked even more stunned than when Melody had come out of the bathroom. "Shipwreck rum? From the *Lord Archibald?*"

"That's what he said," Dale said. "I wasn't that impressed. It was kind of sweet."

"Sweet" among rum connoisseurs was usually code for "sugared-up swill."

"OK, thanks," Neil said as they wandered off.

"How is that even possible?" I asked.

"I don't know. I'm confused."

I laughed. Neil was rarely confused.

Cap Calder came by in his captain's hat and an all-white outfit. "Well, you're quite the sassy lass, aren't you?" He took a thorough perusal of my cleavage. Then he took a sip of the drink Neil handed him. "Ah! Now that's what I'm talking about! I wondered when I'd get a real drink around here."

He grabbed a second one for the road and wandered off happy.

Nigel and Lottie buzzed through with nothing to report, and though I listened closely to Nigel's accent, I just couldn't hear Batman in it. More like Stephen Fry and the BBC.

Then Gina came by with Astra, and time stopped for five minutes while everyone petted the pooch as her tongue lolled in happiness.

"How's it going?" I asked Gina.

"OK." She picked up one of our drinks and peered into its depths. "I slept all day. I don't know what came over me."

"Bottle flu," I murmured as she took a deep sip of the Planter's Punch.

"Oh, but this is delicious!" Her eyelashes fluttered. It wasn't a weak drink. Did she realize that? "I feel better already!"

"Take it easy!" I called after her as she left with Astra. I shrugged at Neil. "She's doing pretty well for an amateur."

Arnold Preiss came through with one of the guest go-go

dancers on his arm. She'd been performing in the lobby outside the vendor hall earlier and wore the shortest skirt and the tallest white boots I'd ever seen.

"Any luck finding the rum?" he asked us.

"Well, *we* don't have it," I said. It wasn't a lie.

"Too bad. I'd still like a taste." The way he looked at me, I wasn't sure he was talking about the rum.

Then they were out the door, replaced by Mark Fairman. Was it lusty rich guy happy hour or something? But the thing about Mark, with his ginger rugby player good looks and English accent, is he always made me hotter than a sunspot, no matter how ridiculously naughty he was.

He looked me over. "Well, I've never wanted to have my ship boarded as badly as I do right now."

"You have a yacht here, too?" I asked, pretending not to get his meaning.

He chuckled, a low, gravelly sound. Not quite Batman, but ... "Would it be inappropriate to call you a saucy wench?"

"Yes," Neil said, handing me a cocktail to garnish.

I chuckled as I smacked a tuft of mint and tucked it into the top of the cup with the swizzle. My fingers brushed Mark's as I handed it over, and the steam subsequently exploding in my body almost popped my hat right off.

He stuck his nose into the garnish and took a deep whiff. "Mmm, that mint smells even better now that you've *spanked* it, Captain Pepper." He wiggled his rusty eyebrows at me. Oh, dear lord. Then he took a sip. "Well, blow me down."

I rolled my eyes at his bad double entendres. "Hear anything about what we discussed?"

"The dock rum? Not a word," Mark said. "Truth is, I have my nose out for another treasure. A collector here says he might have another bottle of the Wray & Nephew 17-Year for me. I've let him know I'm very interested."

I leaned closer to him and tried not to sniff his yummy aftershave, but my supernose couldn't help it. He smelled a lot more expensive than Batman.

I smiled up at him, hoping for more information. "If you don't mind me asking, what collector has the rum you want?"

"Winston Reckel. He's supposed to be at the tasting, so you'll get to meet him then," he said. "Cheers." And then he was gone.

Neil stared after him, then looked at me. "Winston is trying to sell Mark a bottle of the Wray & Nephew 17? I thought it was incredibly rare."

It took me a second to nail down what was really bugging me. "More to the point, why would Winston want to trade his London dock rum to Fizz for the Wray & Nephew, like he told us, if he already had some in his possession?"

Neil shrugged. "Trying to corner the market?"

This was weird. Maybe it was like when eBay came into being. Everyone realized that their collectibles weren't so unique anymore. Grandma's three-hundred-dollar figurine ended up being worth fifty cents. With all the rum collectors in the market and instant worldwide communication, maybe a lot more bottles were coming to light than ever before.

We were getting near the end of our punch supply when Mr. Mixy came in with a few other boisterous fellows. He leered at me. That was four guys in a row. I was starting to regret the pirate corset.

"Now," he said, "if you wore that for a series of YouTube videos, your audience would be as big as mine, Pepper!"

"That's my driving ambition," I said dryly, handing him a drink. "What's new?"

"I'm celebrating." His toothy grin flashed white through his beard. "I won't just be the king of social media anymore. I have a legit TV show."

"Really? That's great," I said with as much enthusiasm as I could muster.

"It's been my dream for a while. Maybe I'll do an episode at your bar, Pepper. Talk about how I came up from nowhere?"

Nowhere? My bar? If my eyes could shoot cocktail picks, he would've been dead on the spot.

"How'd you get the gig?" Neil asked.

"This production company was planning on doing a cocktail-focused show, but when their star fell through, I was next in line. And I'm sure I'll be much more awesome than they ever dreamed possible."

He can't mean ... I eyed the big-bearded one. "Their star fell through?"

"It's such a tragedy," Mr. Mixy said, not very convincingly. "Poor Fizz."

Chapter Twenty-Three

"So Mr. Mixy is getting the TV job that Fizz was supposed to do," I said after he and the others had left and we finally closed the door and started the cleanup. "It seems like an incredible coincidence."

"I thought Fizz doing the show was just a rumor?" Neil said.

"No, Kim mentioned the show. I think it was real. I mean, clearly it was, because now Mr. Mixy is Mr. TV Host."

"Would he kill to get that job?"

"Every day and twice on Sunday," I said without thinking.

"Tell me how you really feel," Neil joked. "But if you're right, you'd better be careful around your ex, too."

"Can we please not refer to him as my 'ex'? He doesn't notch high enough on the bedpost for that designation."

Neil chortled. "And who does?"

"There's a space open at the top," I said wryly.

Neil got that embarrassed look again, and I realized I'd probably said too much. It was like I'd told him "You're Number One!" when I was really just trying to let him know I had an opening. *Hint, hint.* I was never very good at hinting. My joke inadvertently put a lot of weight on my feelings for him just when I was trying to pretend I didn't have any.

Time to change the topic. "So ... I think we should check out that shipwreck museum and taste their rum."

"The *Lord Archibald* rum?"

"If that's what it is."

Neil rubbed his beard. "I'll ask Cray to come with us. He knows a lot more about it than I do."

"Tomorrow?"

"Right after we talk to Winston again."

I shot Neil a skeptical look. "You're kidding. He'll shoot us on the spot for touching his London dock rum. If it really is his. Hey, Barclay!" I called to our teammate, who was steadying a ladder as Luke, at the top, removed and handed down strings of lights.

Barclay left Luke up there and came over. "What's up?"

"Have you heard from your dad? Did he mention anything about visiting Winston Reckel?"

"Visiting is such a genteel way to put it," Barclay said with a grin. "He paid a call early this morning with Detective Cruz and crew, and they had a nice chat."

"About what?"

"My dad doesn't tell me everything. But apparently he threatened to charge Winston with tampering with evidence, tossed his closet looking for bloody clothes and generally scared the crap out of him."

"Does your dad think Winston killed Fizz?" I asked.

"The jury's still out, so to speak. But Dad seemed satisfied that the London dock rum really was Winston's, at least at some point. I guess Fizz had some emails on his phone that verified that he had an arrangement with Winston to obtain the rum, though the details weren't in the emails."

I chewed on this information. "So we don't know if

Winston was really trading the dock rum for a bottle of the Wray & Nephew 17."

"Did your father confiscate the dock rum?" Neil asked Barclay.

"In fact, he did, over Winston's strenuous objections. Forensics wants to have a look. If Winston's story is true and he found it in the trash, then somebody else must've handled it. They want to see if they can get anything else off it."

"That's not good," Neil said.

"Oh, it's fine," I said. "I told Detective Flores when he called earlier that we'd both touched the box."

Neil's eyes widened. "You did not!"

"We look more innocent that way, I figure. Because we *are* innocent. We're the ones who told him about the rum being in Winston's possession, remember?"

"I guess," Neil said.

Barclay looked puzzled. "If Winston was trading the London dock rum for a bottle of the super-rare Wray & Nephew like you say, maybe Winston has more of the dock rum stashed away. It's hard to imagine a high-end collector giving up his only bottle of it, no matter what the trade."

"Unless there was some financial advantage to doing so and he needed the money," Neil said.

"But it looks like he already had some Wray & Nephew 17, if he was going to sell a bottle to Mark Fairman," I said. "So he didn't need to give up the old London rum to get the Wray & Nephew from Fizz."

"Which is why we're going to talk to Winston again tomorrow before we go to the shipwreck museum," Neil said.

"A shipwreck museum?" Luke called from atop the ladder. "I want to go."

"Me too!" Melody called. She'd just emerged from the bath-room again, de-mermaided.

"Excellent!" Luke beamed at Melody.

"OK," Neil said. "I'm going to ask Cray to come with us too so he can try their shipwreck rum. I want to know every-thing I can about it."

Because it may link back to Neil's grandfather, I thought.

"Then I'm definitely going," Barclay said. "Nobody knows more about rum than Conan Cray."

WE PUT in our obligatory time in the hotel kitchen Saturday morning, though since our main events were over, the pressure was higher on other teams to pick up the slack. When Val came in, she announced to the room, "I got a couple of hours of sleep last night, so I'm feeling magnanimous. That won't last long, so if you have something stupid to say, get it out of your system now."

What little chatter there was in the kitchen died, at least until she got her tea.

To support the day's pool parties and seminars, the Bohemia team squeezed and sliced and diced until eleven. Then we stumbled out into the daylight like the hung-over vampires we were. I mean, we had to check out the bands last night, didn't we?

"Pepper and I will go see Winston," Neil told the others. "Can you pick us up a sandwich or something? I want to hit the museum and get back in plenty of time to get ready for the big bash at Pau Hana tonight."

"Why, are you dressing up?" Melody said.

"No," Neil replied, "but I know you girls are."

"Oh, yeah, we *girls* need a lot of time to get all *girly*," I mocked.

Melody looked at me funny. "Well, we do."

I scowled. "They don't need to know that."

"We have to get pretty, too," Barclay joked. "What do we look like, beach bums?"

"Luke does," Neil said to Melody's laugh.

"Hey!" Luke looked stricken, especially because Melody was laughing, though it was all in good humor. He surveyed his own mismatched and stained shorts and T-shirt. "I was squeezing limes, for God's sake."

The truth was, we were all wearing shorts and casual shirts (even if mine was a cute V-neck and Melody's was more of a wrap-around thing), but Luke did look more like a vagrant than the rest of us.

"I'll get him fixed up before the museum," Barclay said. "See you in the lobby in ..."

"Forty-five minutes should be plenty," Neil said.

A few minutes later, he and I were heading up the tower in the elevator. It was crowded this morning, with people getting off at nearly every floor, so it took a while.

Finally, we exited into the quiet corridor on the tenth floor. "You sure this is a good idea?" Neil asked.

"I thought you suggested this," I said.

"That was one of my more rash moments."

"You have rash moments?"

I followed Neil as we turned, entering the spur off the corridor just outside Winston's room.

I paused. "Is his door open?" A strange sound came to me, and I grabbed Neil's arm. "Do you hear that?"

He paused for a microsecond, glanced at me, then burst

forward, pushing the door wide to see Winston on the floor and a lean figure bent over him, kicking him in the stomach.

"Stop!" Neil called, but the figure, in jeans and a dark hoodie that concealed his—her—their face, made an unintelligible sound and jumped up. They hoisted a loaded backpack over their shoulder and ran for the balcony door.

I ran after them. OK, so I wasn't thinking clearly.

It was too late when I realized that when the attacker ran out of space to run, they were going to turn around and come right at me.

What I didn't expect was that they would hurl the sliding door open, dash sideways and leap right over the balcony.

Chapter Twenty-Four

I screamed, speaking of girly. I know. Circumstances warranted.

I reached the railing a second after the jumper went over and realized the Wicker Wharf tower's Jenga construction had served them well. The balconies were stacked with points sticking out in perpendicular directions. It meant a tiny triangle of the balcony below could be seen from above, and that's where the attacker jumped.

They never looked up, so I couldn't see their face, but they stumbled as they landed, and I could've sworn I heard breaking glass as their bag slipped and slammed into the concrete floor of the deck below. Sunlight hit the triangular reflective patch on the front pocket of the black bag, a brief iridescent flash. The jumper slung the backpack over one shoulder again and disappeared. They were heading for the room below us! From there, they could go anywhere.

I ran back into Winston's room. "They jumped onto the balcony below! They might be trapped out there! I'm going down to nine!"

"Pepper, no!" Neil said from where he knelt at Winston's side. "If he planned to jump over the balcony in the first place, he had a plan. Either that door was unlocked or easy to unlock."

"Or he'll just jump to the next one down," Winston said gruffly from where he lay on the floor. His arms were wrapped around his torso, and he grimaced as he tried to move.

"I should go," I said, but less emphatically. I flashed back to Batman, the guy who almost tossed me off the little balcony by the elevator, where there was nothing to catch me if I fell. Maybe it was the same guy. "But I'll stay if you think it's best."

The look of relief on Neil's face was priceless. "Thank you."

I hated being afraid. "Do I need to call 9-1-1?"

"No!" Winston managed to sit up, but not without a groan.

"Your ribs may be broken," Neil told him. "Plus, you need to report this."

"I can't report this!" Winston looked terrified. "He'll kill me!"

"Who will kill you?" I asked.

"Ah—that guy."

"Do you know who that person is?" Neil asked.

"No idea." Winston's eyes were wild with fear. I didn't believe a word.

"Did they take anything?" I asked, knowing they—he, probably—must have. There was something glass in that bag. Something that broke. "Bottles?"

"I'm not sure. I came into my room and there he was," Winston said. He looked from me to Neil. "Just like you did a couple of nights ago. Is he working with you?"

"Absolutely not," Neil said. Winston was struggling to get up, so Neil helped him to a chair.

I looked closely at the collector. "What about the London dock rum?"

"The police still have it," Winston said. "They're supposed to get it back to me tomorrow before I leave."

"And the Wray & Nephew 17?" I asked on a hunch.

"It's in the closet. He didn't—" Winston's eyes widened as he shut up.

I moved closer. "So you already have a bottle of the 17? The one you were going to sell to Mark Fairman? Then why were you going to trade the London dock rum for Fizz's bottle of the 17?"

Winston just sat there glaring at us.

"Maybe I should call an ambulance. And Detective Flores," Neil said. *Go, Neil!*

"No!" Winston looked terrified again. "Don't call him. I'm a collector, OK? But I also sell rum. I have a rich client who's obsessed with rare items, with having the last existing bottle of anything, if possible. Like owning the last dodo bird. If that means buying all the bottles of a particular liquor, he'll do it. And apparently, there was a whole case of the Wray & Nephew that had been found and sold piecemeal. Twelve bottles. I was trying to get them all back and sell them as a package for an extremely good price to this ultra-collector."

"Mark Fairman?" I asked.

"No." Winston stuck his tongue out a little, touching his lip where it bled. He'd really been beaten up. "I'm not telling you the name of my client, but since I'm not getting the Wray & Nephew 17 from Fizz or his wife, who has committed it to the tasting, there's no chance of me getting the 'complete set,' if you will. That's why I was also willing to sell a bottle to Mr. Fairman, to try to recoup my investment."

He stood suddenly, groaning again, holding on to the chair for support. Then he hobbled over to the stacks of rum boxes against the wall. One was sticking out, the flaps open. He took one look inside and swayed like he was going to faint. Neil and I leapt forward, grabbed his arms and helped him back to the chair.

"What is it?" Neil asked.

"He took my *Lord Archibald* rum," Winston croaked.

I gaped at him. "You had the shipwreck rum, too?"

"I don't know why you're so shocked," Winston said. "There were several bottles found on the ship. I managed to get ahold of a few of them."

"You and Fizz," I said.

Winston shrugged. "Collectors compete."

"Where'd you get the *Lord Archibald* rum?" There was a lot of emotion in Neil's question, and I knew he was thinking of his grandfather.

"I have a connection to the team that recovered the wreck."

"Tell me more."

Winston sneered. "Not on your life."

Neil's jaw tightened, and I wanted to hug him.

I turned to Winston instead. "You must be rich, buying all this collectible rum."

The side of Winston's mouth turned up. "Not so much. That's the problem with collecting. You may sell some, but you always want to buy more. The selling supports the buying. And around it goes."

Neil looked at me. He was clearly not amused with Winston Reckel's attitude. "We're leaving."

"That's best," Winston said. "I—thank you. He would've killed me."

"You should report this to the cops," I said.

Winston just glared again. "Yeah, that turned out real well last time."

There wasn't much more we could do, except maybe drop a hint to Barclay's dad about what was going on. The problem was, we had no idea what was going on.

"So," Neil said as we rode the elevator back down, "what do you think?"

"I think Winston Reckel is a one-man rum clearinghouse."

"I'm pissed he wouldn't tell me about his shipwreck connection."

"Yeah, I know. Maybe Detective Flores can get it out of him."

Neil shook his head. "He has bigger fish to fry. He still hasn't caught the killer."

"Who might've jumped off the balcony. But why? If the jumper killed Fizz and didn't steal the London dock rum from him then, why steal this rum now?"

"Maybe it's not the killer. Maybe it's just a thief who knows Winston has a pirate's treasure in his room."

The elevator dinged, and we got out at the first floor. I hitched my bag tighter against me as we walked toward the hotel lobby. It was kind of my security blanket, and all this violence made me nervous.

"If the jumping thief wanted to sell whatever he stole," I said, "he's not going to get as much as he wanted. I feel sure I heard something break when he landed."

"Good," Neil said. "Or bad. I'm torn. I hate to see precious old rums destroyed because somebody got too greedy."

"So now I guess we ask our contacts to look out for bottles of the shipwreck rum on the market, too?"

"Maybe we're going about this the wrong way. Maybe we shouldn't tip them off. We might catch somebody in the act. Let's just keep this on the down low until we figure out what's happening," he said. "And what Davy Jones's Locker Museum is doing with a bottle of rum from the *Lord Archibald*."

Chapter Twenty-Five

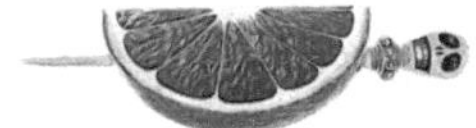

Barclay, Melody and Luke were sitting in the cushy
lobby chairs beyond the open-air bar, drinking water.
As we walked up to them, so did an old gentleman in
a full white suit and hat.

"Mr. Cray!" Barclay stood to greet him. "I'm stoked you're
coming with us today."

"I don't think I've ever stoked someone before. You may
call me Cray. We've met before, haven't we?"

"Yes, in New Orleans. I'm Barclay. I *love* rum."

"Don't we all." Cray smiled, his pale blue eyes twinkling.
Then he spotted us. "Neil. Kayanne Pepper." He touched the
brim of his hat in greeting. I had to admit, he had charm to
burn.

"I'll go get the car," Neil said.

In a few minutes, we all piled into the big SUV. Cray claimed
the front passenger seat, so Barclay volunteered to drive so he
could pick the old chemist/collector's brain during the twenty-
minute ride to the museum. That put Melody and a very happy
Luke, who'd changed his T-shirt, in the middle seat. Neil and I
took the back row, which everyone knows is the best place to be
on the school bus during an evening field trip if you want to make
out. Unfortunately, all we did was scarf down the tuna sandwiches
and potato chips Luke had brought us, along with a couple of

bottles of fancy fizzy water. It all really hit the spot. I hadn't realized how hungry and thirsty I was after all the work and drama.

Neil filled everyone in on what happened with Winston, so we were all more than ready to try the museum's rum. But it looked like we'd have to go through the exhibit first. We were told at the ticket window outside the squat, pink building that the owner only brought out the rum for special guests at the end of the tour.

"Go on into the lobby," said the friendly, white-haired woman selling tickets. "He'll be along in a minute. Feel free to shop at the Emporium while you wait."

I got her meaning once we entered. The store next to the museum was in fact part of it. There was a convenient door off the small foyer that led into Davy's Seashell and Swimsuit Emporium.

"Need any seashells?" Luke asked Melody.

"I've been wanting a conch I can use as a horn to wake up the drunks at the beach bar," she said. Poor Melody. She really wanted a craft-cocktail job instead of doling out frozen sugar bombs at a hotel bar.

"I don't know why we have to play games to get a taste of the rum," Barclay said. "Their visitors don't get much more special than an internationally known rum expert." He nodded at Cray. "Maybe we should tell them that."

Cray shook his head. "My dear, I believe we should tell them no such thing."

"Why?" Luke asked. "Do you think he'll charge you more to taste the rum?"

"I think he might not bring it out at all," Neil said. "Play it cool. If Dick and Dale are right, he'll hit us up sooner or later."

At that moment, a side door opened, and we were greeted

by a wiry man barely taller than me, with a few wisps of brown hair and the kind of elephant wrinkles and deep tan that came from years spent in the tropical sun. He wore weathered leather sandals, cargo pants the same color as his skin, and a loose, white shirt buttoned only halfway up, revealing wiry gray chest hairs and a gold necklace with an old-looking gold coin hanging from it.

"Good afternoon. I'm Thor Roberts. Welcome to my museum!"

"Not Davy Jones?" Luke asked.

Thor, who probably couldn't even lift a hammer, laughed heartily. "Haven't you heard of Davy Jones's locker, young man? Well, look here." He pointed to a large painting on the foyer wall. Or a reproduction, as it was peeling in a couple of places. It depicted a hazy green underwater scene, with fish swimming above wreckage and skulls on a sea floor, and the ghostly form of a sunken sailing ship in the background. "This is Davy Jones's locker, named for 'the fiend that presides over all the evil spirits of the deep,' as Tobias Smollett wrote. If a sailor spotted Davy Jones clambering up his rigging, he knew doom would follow. And that I might find his remains centuries later, because I am a *treasure hunter!*"

Thor regarded us all with a broad smile that faltered slightly when he realized we weren't "oohing" and "aaahing" as expected.

"That's really interesting," I said, just to keep him going. "Are some of your treasures in the museum?"

Thor's smile returned to full wattage. "Yes, they are, young lady. I'm so glad you asked. Right this way."

The museum was just OK. Davy Jones's Locker seemed like one of those typical old Florida roadside attractions that had probably been irresistible to tourists before they all started worshipping The Mouse.

The exhibits looked a little raggedy, and some displays consisted only of yellowed newspaper articles in frames and theatrical-looking props instead of real antiques. Thor Roberts pointed out a few glass cases stuffed with artifacts he said he'd found—tools, coins, vases, cannonballs. There were a lot of model ships. He told tales of shipwrecks and cited wild figures for how much everything was worth.

"Here we are at the captain's cabin. How are you liking the tour so far?" Thor said about half an hour in, in front of a mockup of a pretty room—er, cabin in an old sailing ship. Slanted "windows" on three sides showed backlit images of the sea and sky. There was a table with maps and a scope and other props, along with ornate wooden cabinets and a round chandelier with flickering electric candles hanging above.

I was pretty sure we'd covered most of the museum. And I was pretty sure Thor was hinting, because he was standing next to what looked like a big brass spittoon labeled "TIPS."

"Fantastic tour," I said, digging out five bucks and dropping it into the bucket. Neil and Cray and the others followed with varying contributions, and it must have been enough.

"Excellent," Thor said. "Then I think you'll appreciate a find that I consider my time machine, because it brings me right back to the middle of the eighteenth century, when America was still a British colony. That's when a British ship of the line turned pirate marauder went down in a terrible hurricane in the Caribbean. And just twenty-five years ago, a bold crew discovered it and all of its treasures." He looked around at all of us. "My friends, who would like to taste rum pulled up from Davy Jones's Locker? From the same rum the ship's officers must've enjoyed, as it was found in pristine bottles ... rum from the *Lord Archibald* itself?"

Now we didn't have to fake our enthusiasm, and he reached behind him and opened a small cabinet in the display and pulled out a squat glass bottle.

My first impression was that the bottle did not look like the one Fizz had presented at Pau Hana. My second was ... how in the hell could he afford to pour all of us a drink from it based on our measly tips?

But he did. He got out small shot glasses and poured scant drams in each one, telling us that we were each about to taste hundreds of dollars' worth of rum because he could tell we were special guests or some such nonsense.

"Now don't just knock it back," he said. "Sniff it. Let it sit on your tongue. Then swirl it around and really taste it before you swallow."

"You're so good at this," Cray said in his dulcet Southern accent as Barclay tried not to laugh.

The scent was the first thing I locked onto, and it was ... unremarkable. Not unpleasant, but not interesting. I mean, it's not like I'd ever had rum this old, rum that had been in the ocean for hundreds of years, but I would've expected a certain funk, and there was none of that. When I sipped, it was smooth. Pleasant. Like sucking on a caramel. It didn't change my life, that's for sure.

The others made appreciative noises as Neil asked, "So you helped recover the treasure of the *Lord Archibald*?"

Thor shook his head. "Alas, no. I wish I'd been on that crew. The booty was enormous!" He laughed at his own use of the word "booty," and I caught Melody's smirk.

"Then where did you get this rum?" Neil pressed.

"I have a connection," Thor said. "Well, a connection to a

connection to someone on the crew. He's found me a few bottles."

A few. Ha.

"Do you think he'd sell me a bottle?" Cray asked, his eyes twinkling again. "Wonderful stuff."

"I doubt it. It's very, very rare," Thor said, looking pleased. "But since you're such a nice group, I'll give you his name. OK?" He pulled a business card from one of the pockets in his cargo pants, scribbled something on it and handed it to Cray.

"Thank you so much," Cray said, slipping the card into a pocket in his white jacket.

Five minutes later, we were back in the SUV, heading for Wicker Wharf. Neil drove, with Cray as co-pilot. I sat in the second row with Barclay so I wouldn't miss anything, while Melody and Luke chattered in the back.

"So what did you think?" Neil said.

Cray smiled. "Oh, my."

"Don't keep us in suspense," I pleaded.

"Well, I thought it sucked," Barclay said, and we all laughed.

"I'm afraid it did," Cray said. "The problem is, it did not suck *enough*."

"It seemed sweet to me," I said. "Too smooth. It smelled too ... nice. Not that I've ever tried three-hundred-year-old rum before."

"You still haven't," Cray said. "A rum that old, that's been buried at sea, frankly wouldn't taste that pleasant. Don't get me wrong—it would be a thrill to taste the real thing. I don't know what he has there, but it's not from the *Lord Archibald.* I'm fairly certain it's not even from the top shelf at the liquor store."

Neil sighed—in relief or frustration, I wasn't sure.

"Can I see the card he gave you?" I asked Cray.

"Oh, yes. You're going to like this." Cray pulled it out and handed it to me.

On one side was Thor's contact info. On the other, he'd scribbled a name.

"Winston Reckel!" I exclaimed.

"Of course," Neil said. "The man is supplying rum to every collector in Florida."

"That may be concerning to several people, possibly even him," Cray said, "given that this rum, at least, is not what it seems."

Chapter Twenty-Six

Back at Wicker Wharf, Cray excused himself to take a nap, and Luke and Barclay and Melody headed for the vendor hall. I talked Neil into taking a walk around the pool bars so I could learn what he thought about the shipwreck rum.

"You OK?" I asked him as we stood under a palm tree on the fringes of the revelry and sipped delicious Mai Tais by Chicago's Lost Lake, featuring macadamia nut orgeat.

"I don't know why I thought that charlatan might have a lead on the *Lord Archibald,* but I'm disappointed," he said.

"You don't even know if that shipwreck is connected to your grandfather's disappearance, do you?"

"You're right. I'm grasping at straws. Anyway, the more interesting point is that Winston Reckel is supplying the guy with fake rum."

"Well, real rum. Just not shipwreck rum. Maybe Winston doesn't even know it's fake."

"Possibly," he said.

"Then again, the bottle didn't even look like the one Fizz had. Do you think Winston is trading the real stuff for himself and the knowledgeable collectors and putting one over on guys like Thor the treasure hunter?"

"Thor?" came a familiar voice from right behind us.

I spun around to see Val, a drink in her hand.

She stepped closer. "You two weren't at that stupid treasure museum, were you?"

"A little field trip," Neil said. "You know the guy?"

She laughed. "I know he's as genuine as a three-dollar bill. He might've flirted with treasure hunting here and there, but most of the stuff in that museum is a joke, including the rum. He actually bought the museum from another guy, thinking it was full of gold coins and other valuable stuff. When he had it appraised, the insurance people told him it was ninety percent fake. The real stuff had been sold right out from under him."

"Sucks for him," I said.

"Yes, it does," she said. "It's too bad, too, because I was hoping to learn more about the *Lord Archibald* from him."

I raised my eyebrows at Neil.

"What's your interest in the shipwreck?" Neil asked in his calm way. Which was good, because I would've done something embarrassing, like jump and squeal.

Val looked around and lowered her voice. "I heard a story when I was in Ireland consulting, helping a tiki bar launch in Dublin. There were some drunk guys who came in one night talking about lost treasure. They looked and sounded like money men, a little bit dangerous. I know it sounds fanciful, but it was a slow night, and I found a reason to sit in the booth behind theirs. I love a good story. And they were talking about rum from the *Lord Archibald*. Some kind of special rum in a special bottle, extraordinarily valuable."

"The rum Fizz had is extraordinarily valuable, isn't it?" Neil asked.

"Sure, but this sounded like something ... unusual. Anyway, since then, researching the ship has been kind of a hobby for me. Honestly, I'm no treasure hunter. But if a bottle of that stuff will give me the coin to open another bar in New York, I'd be very interested."

"Have you had any luck?" I asked.

She gave me one of her hard stares. "Not much. I found an antique dealer in London who said he had a letter from the captain. You know, the one who turned pirate? The dealer said it was in code and wouldn't let me look at it unless I showed him I had the money to buy it. Of course, I didn't. The next time I asked him about it, he said it was stolen."

"Stolen! Sounds like somebody is on the same trail you are," I said.

"Maybe. Or he was bullshitting me." She took another sip of her cocktail. "I think he wanted to be paid in something other than money, if you know what I mean. And I've had it with that kind of crap from men. They're either trying to seduce me or rumsplaining. No offense," she said to Neil.

He chuckled. "None taken. I don't deal in crap, myself. And I wouldn't presume to rumsplain any rums to you."

She nodded at him. "I can buy that." She tossed her head, flipping her pink bangs out of her eyes for a second. "Later."

"You like her, don't you?" I asked Neil. *Argh*. It was the rum talking.

"I do like her." His tone was innocent. Amused. "Don't you?"

"Yeah. I think I do. Though she can be scary sometimes."

He laughed. "That's part of her charm. And now I'm going to keep my eye out for a letter from the captain of the *Lord Archibald*."

"Pepper!" I looked up to see Gina coming toward me in a fabulous tropical dress (I *really* needed to check out the vendors), Larry trailing after her like a puppy, and my real puppy straining at her leash to get to me.

"Hey, Gina! Hey, Astra!" I leaned down and with one arm, scooped up the pup, who licked my face and stole the lime wheel off my drink. Astra swallowed it before I could snatch it back.

I sighed and handed my cup to Neil. "You're such a sweetie," I cooed to the dog as she panted in my face. "Yes, you are. Dumb, but incredibly cute."

"She's having fun. Everybody loves her," Gina said as Neil and Larry greeted each other. "Though she kicked up a fuss earlier that had me kind of worried."

I scratched behind Astra's ears. "What do you mean?"

"When we were walking down the sidewalk over there, we almost got mowed down by some guy in a hoodie. Astra acted like she wanted to take a bite out of him. But he was gone too fast. Headed toward the parking lot."

Neil and I exchanged a glance. "When was this?" Neil asked.

"About lunchtime?"

"Did he have a backpack?" I asked Gina.

"Maybe. I was too busy trying to keep Astra in check to notice. She's so sweet to everybody, I thought it was weird."

"Yeah, that's not like her at all. Why don't you take a break?" I told Gina. "I've got to get ready for tonight. I'll give Astra a little walk before I head for the room."

"That would be awesome," Gina said. "Um ... Larry asked me to go with him to Pau Hana tonight. Would that be OK? I mean, will Astra be all right?"

I looked at the hot, happy dog. "She'll be exhausted after all this partying. I'm sure she'll just want to sleep. She'll be OK in the room for a few hours." I put her on the ground and grabbed the leash from Gina.

On impulse, I turned to Neil. "Want to go for a walk?"

"Sure," he said. "It's not like I've had any time for the weight room."

Huh. Neil used weights? I thought he mainly lifted bags of ice. This explained a lot about his hidden muscles.

"Let's walk by the marina," I said. "I want to see the water." I also wanted to see if I could get a sense of where hoodie guy might've been going—assuming it was the same guy who beat up Winston Reckel. If he was headed to a getaway car, then he probably wasn't even attending Hookahakaha. We'd never find him.

Neil dropped our empty cups in a bin. With Astra trotting ahead of us, we strolled out of the hotel courtyard, through the parking lot and to the walkway that bordered the marina. The docks were lined with shiny boats, chrome glinting in the sun. A breeze from the east hinted of the ocean. The water glittered, suggesting refreshment, even if we were sweating.

Astra seemed thrilled to have new things to smell and pee on as we gawked at the boats, which got bigger and bigger as we headed toward the Intracoastal Waterway.

"Too bad I'm not into boats," I said. "These are gorgeous."

"Beautiful. I have nothing in common with these people," Neil said to my chuckle. "You know, this quote keeps coming back to me."

"When don't you have a quote rattling around in that head of yours?"

"I don't think they rattle. It's not like it's empty in there."

I laughed. "Definitely not. The quote?"

"Well, you know I have this thing for reading old temperance literature."

I quirked my mouth at him. "No, I don't know this. Why would you put yourself through that?"

"It's interesting," Neil said. "And sometimes it has a point.

That movement arose out of suffering. I mean, Prohibition was a disaster, but I get it. Not everyone has the good relationship with alcohol that we do."

"Granted," I said. "I guess that's a good perspective for a bartender to have, especially when you have to '86' someone."

"At The Junction Box, I inform them they've been cut off with a pre-printed coaster laid over a glass of water so they can leave quietly with their dignity intact."

"Oooo, I might have to steal that idea. But wait ... what's the quote?"

"Oh, right. It's from a temperance poem called 'The Rumseller's Dream' I found in an 1887 education journal. I memorized the first stanza because it was so, I don't know, melodramatic." Neil took a breath as I looked at him expectantly and launched into the verse:

The Rumseller dozed in his easy chair,
At the close of a busy day.
And before him passed in dreams, as he slept,
A long and sad array
Of those whose lives had been wrecked by rum,
'Till scorched by its fiery breath,—
They had gone to their graves in untimely haste,
Or worse—to a living death.

I remembered to close my mouth after a second of processing the words. "That's eerie."

"I know," Neil agreed. "It's not about murder, obviously, but it's creepy. It's about all the lives the rum seller has ruined. He sees a parade of them and mends his ways."

"Well, I'm not mending my ways anytime soon."

"I should hope not. Not in the middle of Hookahakaha."

And then I almost fell over when Astra dug in her feet at a cluster of bushes by the hotel's ballroom building, straining against the leash, refusing to move as she barked at the bushes.

"Come on, Astra. Do you have to poo?" I asked as Neil snickered.

Astra whined and surged forward. The leash snapped right out of my hands.

"Damn it!" She scrambled under the bushes as I tried to grab the leash, afraid she'd run off and be attacked by an iguana or something. "Astra! Get out here!"

Neil headed farther down the sidewalk to try to head her off.

A minute later, a triumphant Astra emerged from the bushes, her face covered in tiny sand spurs, which are these horrible, thorny little things that adored dog hair. And she had something unwieldy, dark and smelly in her mouth. Something made of fabric.

"Rum," I murmured as I got a whiff. I grabbed her leash and tugged the object out of her teeth. "Good girl."

"What is it?" Neil asked, taking it from me.

"It's a bag. It smells like rum."

"That must be why she wanted it." He grinned. "As a present for you."

"Smart-ass." I took it back and turned it over. It was a backpack. A backpack with a small, iridescent triangle on the front pocket that flashed in the sun. "Oh my God, Neil. This is the backpack the jumping thief had when he stole those bottles from Winston Reckel."

"No way." He looked closely at the bag. *"EO.* Does that mean something to you?"

The letters were in the little triangular patch. A line

seemed to encircle the O, like a plane orbiting the Earth. "Orbiting the Earth," I murmured. *"EO*. ErthOrbyt."

"Wait," Neil said. "You mean Arnold Preiss's company? They don't make bags, do they?"

"But they do promo items, right? All companies do. Just the sort of thing an employee might carry around. Or a CEO."

Neil looked skeptical. "See what's inside."

I gingerly opened the bag. An alcoholic vapor wafted out of its depths. I angled the inside toward the sun. Something reflected the light. Fragments. "Broken glass," I said. "Thick, old glass. This has to be the bag."

"Maybe. Probably. But the chances of it being Arnold Preiss's bag are pretty astronomical."

"Are they?" Astra sensed my excitement and barked. "It fits, sort of. He's an obsessive collector. And how many people at Hookahakaha would have this bag?"

"Why would he dump it?"

"Evidence. If he got searched, no one would find it on his yacht if he left it behind in the bushes."

"His yacht?" Neil looked around. "His yacht is here?"

"Yeah, that's what he told me. We should go see him."

He shook his head. "There's no way a billionaire tech CEO is stupid enough to use his own branded bag to rob a rum collector."

"He didn't expect to screw up and break the bottles," I said. "And maybe he's not cut out for crime."

"Ha," Neil said. "Or jumping over balconies?"

"He climbs mountains, doesn't he?" I asked.

"That doesn't mean he jumps off them. At least, not without a rope."

"Up. Down. It's all the same. He won't hurt us. He's into computers, not kung fu."

"And yet he might've beaten the hell out of Winston."

I couldn't fault his logic, but I smiled up at him. "Come on. Let's take a look around. You can protect me."

Neil rolled his eyes. "Astra will protect us. Let's stow that bag somewhere. Let him think we have it safe, not give it to him outright."

"These bushes worked pretty well before."

"OK." I put it back where Astra had found it and noted where it was in case we wanted to pick it up again later. Sensing adventure, the dog didn't seem to mind me re-burying her treasure. "Now let's see if we can spot the yacht."

Neil was already doing a three-sixty. "I spotted it."

I followed his gaze and swallowed hard. There was no mistaking it. At the far end of the walkway, where the biggest boats were docked, a sleek, silver-gray yacht dominated the view. It was easily half the length of a football field, with multiple decks and a bunch of antennas and domes on the top. It looked like a supervillain's battleship. And on its bow, it featured the exact same logo that was on the rum-soaked bag.

As we walked in that direction, I carried Astra and used a comb from my bottomless bag to get the sand spurs out of her fur. She was very patient and happy to be held, but my mind was humming.

As we got closer, I saw a couple of uniformed crew moving around the big boat. A guy on the top deck in some kind of paramilitary uniform cradled an assault rifle as he scanned the horizon.

"What the hell does Preiss need a goon for?" I asked.

"Prestige?" Neil suggested. "Also, he really is worth a bazillion dollars. Security is probably something he worries about."

"He invited me to come check out his yacht," I said. "It should be no problem getting on board."

"Pepper, think for a minute. He just saw you and me in Winston Reckel's suite—I mean, if it *was* Preiss. Or maybe it wasn't. What if the jumper was the guy with the big gun or some other 'security'? Whoever it is could identify us and realize we know something. Are you sure getting on the billionaire battleship with a man who almost killed Winston Reckel is the best plan?"

I was torn. One, I hated boats. They made me barf. But a big boat standing still wouldn't be so bad.

Two, I'd always wanted to see inside a yacht.

Three, I didn't want to die.

"You may have a point," I said. "Maybe it's better if he doesn't know we're on to him."

"And if he doesn't, he'll probably come to Pau Hana tonight for the big bash and act like everything's normal. He might even get drunk, let his guard down."

"And I can corner him in the bar and make him talk."

A corner of Neil's mouth twitched. "Right."

"But we're going to go get that bag Astra found and save it for Detective Flores, OK?"

Astra barked in agreement as Neil nodded.

Time to get all tiki'd up and ready for battle.

Chapter Twenty-Seven

Pau Hana had an entirely different feel tonight. First, our team wasn't working, and the freedom felt delicious. We could just drink and have fun. And maybe interrogate potential killers.

Second, it seemed ten times as crowded as it had been for Fizz Martin's seminar three days before. We had to wait in line to get in the door for happy hour, and the bar was jammed with slightly sweaty but beautifully dressed revelers in all their tiki finery.

It's times like these when it's handy to know a costume designer. I'd called on my friend Penelope to create a dress for me. It was strapless, patterned in monstera leaves in various shades of green and cream against a lichen background to match my gray-green eyes (yes, my eyes have been compared to a symbiotic fungus-algae life form, but lichen is a *pretty* fungus, and you would do well to remember that). The skirt was puffy, made more so by a pink crinoline. The neckline was scandalously low, accented by a floral necklace. My dramatic décolletage was softened slightly by a big green fabric monstera leaf ruched over the front of the bodice and held in place by a showy pink silk orchid. I even had a matching monstera-leaf purse. And I wore my convention wristband and my alligator-tooth bracelet for good luck.

The crowning touch really was a crowning touch. I'd used silk tropical flowers and leaves to create a headpiece that was reminiscent of the crown on the Statue of Liberty—only all the spikes were made with various bars' swizzle sticks in green and pink and yellow. It was obnoxious. It was beautiful. And at least, with the chunky-soled sandals I wore, it made me taller.

Luke and Barclay wore attractive Hawaiian shirts and matching straw hats. Neil's was more of a bowling shirt in black with a wide stripe of pineapple fabric down one side and pocket trim in the same fabric on the other, and his subtlety made him stand out all the more. Melody, whose blond hair was pinned back on one side with a big floral clip, went with a one-shoulder maxi dress made of yards of colorful, floaty, translucent floral fabric.

At any other event, we would have shone like beacons. At Hookahakaha, we were but tiny sparks in a tropical fireworks show.

While I scanned the crowd for Arnold Preiss, part of me wanted to forget all the craziness with Fizz and Winston. I just wanted to drink Mai Tais and flirt with Neil. But then I'd catch Luke in an unguarded moment, a haunted look in his eye, and I knew we needed to figure out what happened. Apparently Barclay's dad had paid him another visit this afternoon, looking for answers, and Luke was more nervous than ever about ending up in jail.

We all partook heartily of the excellent happy hour. After just two of Pau Hana's legendary cocktails, a kick-ass Jet Pilot and a Special Reserve Daiquiri with its pretty shell of crushed ice, I was loose and happy in spite of consuming my weight in crab rangoons. Gold Dust Lounge was rocking the bar, with all its nautical, below-decks decor, and the crowd was fluid and merry. And despite a couple of trips through the lobby to the bathroom, where I paid a dollar to pee, I hadn't seen Arnold Preiss. Nor Winston Reckel, for that matter.

I saw a lot of other folks—the jolly Nigel and Lottie; Dick and Dale and their wedding entourage (looking delicious again in their matchy-matchy finery); Mr. Mixy, who winked and shot his finger gun at me like he owned me (which, given the circumstances, was not comforting); Cap Calder, who was double-fisted drinking again in his captain's hat and white outfit; and Mark Fairman, who blew me a kiss and bought me a third drink. I was drunk enough to catch the kiss and stuff it down the front of my dress. Maybe it wasn't the wisest move on my part, but he *loved* it. Neil, to my delight, positively glowered.

I decided to be patient in my quest to find Preiss. There would be another floor show after our dinner seating and a second wave of the crowd, plus maybe I'd sober up a little by then. At least I hoped so, Mai Tai in hand, as we were escorted into the main dining room by a white-jacketed usher.

Conan Cray joined us at our table in the elevated back area of the main dining room. As we ordered Asian-inspired dishes, there were tunes on stage from the ukulele man in the grass skirt and slightly drunken speeches by the organizers. And then the event honcho gave a brief and heartfelt speech about Fizz Martin, calling Kim up on the stage to present her with flowers. She wore a black dress with a simple orchid corsage, and she was crying, and the crowd roared in appreciation, and there were many tears. Maybe not from *all* the people who knew him, but still. Even I got a little choked up.

And then there were fantastic musicians and dancers performing entrancing pieces from the South Pacific, culminating in a fire dance with torches that brought down the house. It was easy to get caught up in the escapism and yummy food and drinks and forget about all the bad things in the world outside.

Or in Fizz's case, in the kitchen.

Our group split up as we left the dining room so the busy servers could turn the room over for the second seating. Barclay and Luke and Cray went to the front bar, Neil to the restroom, Melody to the gift shop. I headed toward the garden in back of the restaurant but pulled up short by the fish tank near the Chinese ovens when I heard the name "Fizz Martin" whispered. I hid behind a column for a second, then peeked around the corner to see who was talking.

It was a couple of the female dancers, now in matching bikini tops and short sarong-style skirts, flowers in their hair. "So that tribute was for the guy from Wednesday night? The one who got killed in the kitchen?" one of them said.

"Yeah. He owns a bunch of tiki bars. Well, owned. There was a rumor he wanted to invest in this place."

"Too bad he didn't. They could've fixed the air-conditioning."

The second dancer chuckled. "Can you believe he slipped me his number when I took him his mystery bowl?"

"Before the slide show?"

"Yeah. I'd put the drink on the table and was doing the dance and slipping the lei over his head, and he tucked a napkin with his number on it right into my waistband. A lot of nerve."

"And his wife gave you a dirty look, I bet."

"She wouldn't be the first wife to give me a dirty look. You know that. Uh-oh, Pip is waving at us."

"More mystery bowls ready to go, no doubt. I think we're setting a record tonight."

"As long as we all get a taste of the tips, I'm fine with it."

They both laughed and brushed past me, heading for the manager I'd seen the first night.

Those women didn't seem too upset about Fizz dying, but they also didn't seem angry enough to help him transition to that big tiki bar in the sky. Though they suggested Kim was ticked off. Still, I was sure they were right—I could totally see wives getting a little jealous of these perfectly fit island maidens in their skimpy attire, especially when they were doing the hypnotic mystery bowl dance to the slow thrum of the gong. I mean, I'd seen how the guys in my crew reacted when the mermaid troupe came through the dining room earlier. They practically had to pick their eyeballs out of their drinks and return them to their sockets. Men were simple creatures, and a wise woman learned that just because they were looking didn't mean they were touching. If they were good guys, that is.

Fizz apparently didn't qualify as a truly good guy, but did Kim know that? She might not have even seen Fizz slip the dancer the number. She might've just been jealous on principle. I certainly wasn't going to enlighten her to his shenanigans. Besides, the point was moot. Once his show started, she was running the projector the whole time.

I wandered out to the garden, which was lovely in the twilight—the waterfall rushing, the torches flaring, recorded bird and monkey calls piercing the chatter. There were a lot of people out here, some eating and drinking at the tables on the back patio, others catching a smoke or wandering through and taking pictures. I got my phone out and snapped a photo of a squat, pot-bellied tiki half-hidden in the jungle vegetation along the circular path. Something like that might be cute by the pool I shared with my aunt at home.

And that's when I spotted Arnold Preiss. He was a few feet

beyond the tiki, half-hidden by a bushy palm, nibbling on the neck of the go-go dancer he'd escorted through our room party.

Well, this was awkward. But I didn't have a lot of time, and I'd been searching for him all evening. I stepped off the path, moved toward them and paused, waiting until they were aware I was there. She looked bored as they noticed me and broke apart. He looked annoyed.

I addressed myself to the dancer, pretending like I hadn't interrupted their canoodling. "I'm so sorry to bother you, but I have to ask, where did you get those fantastic boots?"

"Oh, these?" Her eyes lit up. Perhaps fashion was more appealing than techy billionaires. She showed off her towering boots and went on to tell me all about a great vintage clothing website, and I noted it in my phone. I was more interested in talking to Arnold, but I could definitely benefit from being four inches taller.

"Arnold," I said when she took a breath. "How are you doing? After your workout today, I wasn't sure if you'd make it here tonight."

"My workout?" In a moment, I saw his annoyance transform into something else. Something uncomfortable. Maybe even worried. I just stared at him, willing him to realize I was on to him. Or at least, I thought I was on to him. He kissed the dancer's cheek. "Ruby, honey, I need to talk to Pepper for a minute."

The go-go gal actually looked relieved. "No problem. I want to hit the gift shop anyway."

She was gone in a twinkle, and I crossed my arms, clutching my leaf-shaped purse, missing my messenger bag. Arnold Preiss made me nervous.

His tone belied his impish smile. "You should stay out of matters that don't concern you."

"What matters would those be?"

"I think you know very well. You have no idea what you're in the middle of."

"Here's what I do know." Or hoped I knew. "You beat up Winston Reckel and stole priceless rums from his room today, then took a flying leap to escape like some kind of Batman." I realized what I'd said. *Batman? Could he be the Batman-voiced guy who threatened me?*

Arnold stepped closer to me, leaning in so he was talking in my ear. "Pepper, little bartender, go back to your little bar and don't interfere. Even if I'd done the ridiculous thing you say, I have more money and lawyers than Pau Hana has tiny cocktail parasols. And you have zero evidence."

Now he was starting to piss me off, maybe because he called me "little." Short jokes always pissed me off. Though I had to admit, he didn't sound like Batman.

I whispered in his ear, too. "I have a rum-soaked Erth-Orbyt backpack with fragments of a stolen rum bottle and your fingerprints."

I had no idea if it had his fingerprints, but it sounded good. And Arnold jumped back as if he'd been stung.

"Pepper?" came a voice from behind me. "I've been looking for you."

Chapter Twenty-Eight

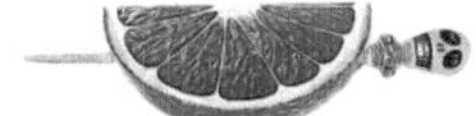

Neil pushed aside the palm fronds and stood next to me, and I exhaled in relief. He'd freaked me out for a second, surprising me like that, but maybe it was good to have backup, especially since we had Arnold Preiss cornered. I wondered if the CEO had one of his security guys lurking behind a palm tree. Better make this quick.

"Why would you attack Winston?" I asked Arnold. "Did he have a bottle you wanted? Just couldn't wait to get your hands on it?"

He shook his head and laughed a bitter laugh. "God, you're clueless."

"So make us less clueless," Neil said. "I'm sure the police would be very interested in why you attacked Winston and stole his rum. We can just pass the evidence on to them."

Oooo, *evidence* sounded good. Like it was more than a stinky backpack my dog had pulled out of the bushes.

Arnold shook his head. "I don't particularly want the world to know about my private dealings with Reckel. You or the police. I'd appreciate it if you keep this fairy tale to yourself."

"But we know everyone in the tiki world." I pointed to the swizzle sticks in my crown, and Arnold smirked. "Even if the police don't get involved, we could tell everyone we know in two seconds in the right online forum that you're a thief."

Arnold really looked smug now. "Have you ever heard of libel, little Pepper?"

"Hey!" I poked him in the chest. "That's enough of that, Mr. Supercomputer. We have an 'in' with the cops. We have a personal interest in what's happening here, and we are not taking *no* for an answer."

Neil had placed a hand on my shoulder, like he was trying to pull me back to sanity, but I was already over the edge.

Arnold seemed to respond well to me in bitch mode, because his smirk softened and his shoulders slumped. "Believe me, you would've wanted to beat up Winston, too. Not that I'm saying I did it."

"What's the deal with you and Winston?" Neil asked.

"He ripped me off."

"How?" I asked.

Arnold looked around, but no one was interested in our conversation. "He sold me bad rum."

My brow furrowed. "You mean like collectible rum? Isn't it expected that some of the antique stuff doesn't taste very good?"

Arnold lowered his voice even more. "If it were actually antique, I would've been perfectly fine with it tasting like muck. But it wasn't. Almost everything he's sold me is fake—at least the most expensive stuff. Hundreds of thousands of dollars' worth of counterfeit bottles. He owes me."

Well, damn Dionysus. Winston was dealing in counterfeit rum on a grand scale. Not just a case of bad bottles to Davy Jones's Locker or an innocent error. Big-ticket rum to big-ticket guys like Arnold Preiss.

"Are you the only one who's been ripped off?" I asked.

Arnold smiled ruefully. "I have no way of knowing. I was particularly eager and particularly rich, so I was probably a lush target. But I wouldn't be surprised if he had other victims. Reckel seems to have an awful lot of rare rums, doesn't he?"

"But why did you steal bottles from him if they're fake?" Neil asked.

"Leverage." Arnold had apparently given up denying he was the thief. "I want my money back or the real rum. I feel sure he's had some of the real stuff at some point. He had to base the forgeries on something, right? I've threatened to go to the police with what he's sold me, so I needed some of that shipwreck rum he's hawking to every dork with a hard-on for collecting pirate treasure."

"You didn't have any of the *Lord Archibald* rum before today?" I asked.

"I hadn't bought any of it yet, though I was thinking about it before an expert told me a couple of my other bottles were fake. After that, I went to an appraiser who knew about forgery and was very disappointed to learn that more than a dozen different 'rare' rums I'd bought from Reckel were knockoffs."

"Why not just go to the cops for real instead of blackmailing Winston Reckel?" I asked.

"Because it's embarrassing, OK?" Arnold kicked at a lime slice someone had left in the grass. "First, in the tiki community, I'm trying to get some traction as a rum collector. I'll look like a fool. And can you imagine the headlines? If I look like an idiot, my company looks stupid, too. My stock dives. This is serious stuff for me. And Winston doesn't know I don't want to go to the cops. Like I said, I just want him to make it right. He stays out of jail, and I stay out of *Inside Edition*."

"But it wasn't exactly smart to beat up Winston either, was it?" Neil pointed out.

"I wasn't planning on it. I was just going to duck in, take

what I wanted and leave. But then he showed up, and I was so angry, I lost control. And then you showed up, and I ended up losing one of the three bottles when I jumped. So, thanks." Arnold oozed sarcasm.

"I have to admit, that jump was impressive," I said. "How'd you get into his room?"

"Hacking a hotel key? Ha," Arnold scoffed, but he looked a little bit proud too. "Child's play. And I worked out escape routes in case I got caught. Unfortunate I had to use the most extreme one."

I looked him in the eye. "Are you smart enough to create an untraceable burner phone?"

"Please. That's easy. But you can go down to the corner store and buy one right now if you want." He crossed his arms. "And we're done here."

I couldn't agree more. But I had other questions. A lot of other questions. And he needed to know he couldn't mess with us, either.

"OK, here's the deal," I said. "We'll keep your secret until we have a reason not to. Don't give us that reason, OK?"

Arnold looked from me to Neil and back to me again. "Pepper, I have the power to make your *little, tiny* life evaporate. But that's not who I am. I'm just a guy who wants justice. Justice is what I was imparting today. If you can accept that, I'm willing to keep this civil."

I was about to object to his not-so-veiled threat, but Neil cut in first. "Watch your manners, Preiss. Or the tiki gods will burn down your grass hut."

Neil grabbed me by the hand and pulled me away as Arnold stared after us. He didn't seem like much of a threat just then. More like an outcast who'd had a "kick me" note taped to his back at school and wanted revenge on the bully who put it there. In this case, the bully was Winston Reckel. I had to hope he wouldn't go after us.

Anyway, given what we'd learned, we had another barrel of rum to uncork, so to speak.

Neil and I headed through the jungle to the shady end of the path, just outside the stage door, where no one was around. He let go of my hand, which made me a little sad, but I liked how close he was to me as we leaned against the windows of the back dining area. Inside, a surf band wearing black suits with skinny ties, surrounded by a densely packed crowd, tore into a song that made the glass vibrate.

"The Intoxicators," Neil remarked.

"They rock! They make me want to dance." I looked from the scene behind the glass back to Neil. "So if Winston Reckel was selling or trading rum to Fizz, as he said ..."

"Given what Arnold Preiss just told us, I wonder how much of Fizz's rum was fake."

"Exactly. Kim has the bottles now, right?"

"Yes. The shipwreck rum and the Wray & Nephew 17 are slated for the tasting tomorrow."

I winced. "It wouldn't look good if the world's most avid rum fans realized that the headliner bottles for their Gold Tooth Tasting were all swill like that stuff at Davy Jones's Locker."

"Will they know?"

"They'll know it's not real. That's all that matters. It won't look good for Hookahakaha or the charity."

Neil rubbed his beard. "You know what we have to do ..."

"Taste it," we said at the same time.

"Right now," I added.

He nodded. "I'm going to find Cray."

Chapter Twenty-Nine

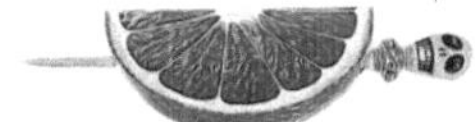

Neil, Cray and I showed up at Kim Martin's hotel room door an hour later, after confirming she wasn't still among the party crowd at the restaurant. I wasn't exactly surprised she'd left. That Fizz tribute was emotionally overwhelming even for me. I couldn't imagine what it must have been like for his wife.

Kim's room was in same wing as mine, but at the far end and across the corridor. It took two soft knocks from Neil, but she finally opened the door, wearing one of her black T-shirts and what looked like soft jammy shorts. Her eyes were red, and her pale blond hair was mussed. An old movie was playing on the TV—*The Breakfast Club.* You could do worse for '80s comfort food.

"What's up?" Her gaze took in all three of us, lingering an extra moment on my swizzle-stick crown with an expression somewhere between curious and irked. I realized it had at least one of her and Fizz's bars represented on it.

"Can we come in for a few minutes?" Neil asked. "We need to ask you about the rum for the tasting."

She sighed. "I guess so."

As we entered, I took off the crown and stuck it in my messenger bag, which I'd retrieved from my room in the five minutes I had before we gathered for this little meeting. I'd also taken Astra out for a pee and left her happily snoozing on my bed. She was one partied-out dog.

There were two queen beds in the room. Kim sat cross-legged on the unmade one and used the remote to turn off the TV. The sliding doors were open. They faced a canal, where a big boat was sliding by, all lit up.

"Pretty," I said.

"It's kinda cool," Kim agreed. "I like boats. I've ridden the water shuttle a couple of times already. It helps me think."

"The water shuttle?" I asked as I sat on the edge of the second bed with Neil. Cray took the desk chair.

"It can get you to downtown and some other places," Neil said, "but really, it's just cool to ride it around and see how the other half lives. All the big houses on the canals. Maybe we can go beachside for lunch and take a ride after the big tasting."

"That sounds fun," I lied. I didn't want to be barfing on a water shuttle tomorrow. Then again, if it meant being with Neil, I'd consider it. Because I was piteous.

"So, what do you need?" Kim asked, ending the small talk. "I have the bottles. I'm happy to give them to you now, if you want. To be honest, I could use the money I'd get from selling them, but Fizz would've wanted the tasting to go on."

I looked at Neil, who looked at Cray, who shrugged slightly. Nobody wanted to tell Kim the bad news.

Might as well get this over with. "Cray needs to taste your rum," I said.

Kim seemed puzzled. "He'll taste it tomorrow, right?"

Neil shook his head. "We need to taste it now, because it might not be what we think it is."

Kim cocked her head at us, her mouth slightly open. "Spit it out."

"There's some fake shipwreck rum circulating," I said. "Fizz may have bought some of it."

"The Wray & Nephew, too," Neil said.

"What do you know about this?" Kim asked Cray. Made sense. He was the guru.

"I know the same thing these two lovely people are telling you. And it so happens that someone they talked to tonight also talked to me some months ago and had me try rum they got from the same source. He'd been hoodwinked as well."

"Wait!" I turned to Cray. "You were the expert that—"

Neil cut me off before I could blurt out Arnold's name. "The only way to be sure is to taste the rums. I think we can all agree that presenting fraudulent rum at this kind of tasting won't look good for anybody."

What he wasn't saying was that it would tarnish Fizz's reputation and, by association, Kim's.

She got it right away. With obvious reluctance, she unfolded her legs and rolled off the bed, went to the closet, rummaged around and came back with the kooky hula-girl bag Barclay and I had bought to put the rum bottles in. She extracted the open-face box with the Wray & Nephew and the burlap-wrapped shipwreck rum and set them on the desk, tossing the bag aside in the process.

Kim unwrapped the squat, pitted ship's bottle, its dark green glass almost iridescent from its presumed stay under the sea. Then she unboxed the other one. Its plain label was mostly white with red accents and tiny type that said "J. Wray & Nephew Ltd." at the top.

She looked at Cray. "So do we need to sacrifice a pigeon or something?"

Neil snorted and Cray smiled. I respected her sense of humor, given the horrendous week she'd had.

"Allow me," Cray said. "Tools?"

I pulled my mini-kit out of my bag and handed it to him. He took out the sharp cocktail knife—a new one, since I lost my other one to circumstances in New Orleans—and went to work on the red wax that had been poured over the top of the shipwreck rum.

I stood to get a better look. "Shouldn't you be preserving that for history or something?" I asked as he dug into the wax with little fanfare.

"The wax is new?" Neil proffered.

"Correct." Cray dropped a chunk on the desk and kept working. "Standard practice to protect an ancient cork when one is buying and selling these little treasures."

"If it is ancient," I muttered and caught Kim giving me a dirty look.

The cork offered less resistance than the wax, but it also crumbled coming out. I extracted a tiny strainer with a handle from my bag, which Cray regarded with amusement. He used it to strain out the cork bits as he poured a minuscule amount of the shipwreck rum into one of the hotel glasses.

"You first." He held the glass up to Neil, who shook his head.

"You're taking all the fun out of it." Cray turned to me. "Pepper?"

I couldn't help myself. I took the glass reverently, not sure what I held. The fakery was excellent, if it was fakery. Who wouldn't fall for the elaborate packaging, the promise of owning—tasting—history? I rolled the glass around, observing the legs, the way the rum clung to the glass. Hardly conclusive. And it was dark enough to speak of age, I supposed.

Then I pushed my nose into the glass and breathed deeply of the fumes. A tiny twinge of disappointment vibrated through me. I barely wet my lips with the stuff, but I thought I had my answer. I handed it to Neil, who gave me a funny look and took a tiny sip. Then he handed it to Cray.

Cray took his time sniffing, looking, tasting, sloshing, tasting again. He smiled at me, his eyebrows lifted in question.

I grimaced. "Davy Jones's Locker."

"I'm afraid so," Cray said as Neil nodded.

"What does that mean?" Kim asked.

"This is not antique rum, though it's very nicely presented," Cray said. "And it tastes very much like a fraudulent rum we tasted earlier today at a local museum. It's possible it's from the same source."

Kim's eyes were flashing. "How can you be sure?" But beneath her anger, I heard the regret. She knew he was right.

"I'm sure, my dear," was all Cray said. He offered her the glass, and she shook her head. He pointed to the red and white label. "Shall we try the other?"

The Wray & Nephew was easier. There were a few words typed in the middle of the white on the label: *17 Year Old*. Of course. The red seal on top was wrapped in protective plastic.

The fact that this bottle wasn't fancy gave it more credence, kind of like the holy grail in the third Indiana Jones movie. The analogy was appropriate, because this Jamaican rum was legendary, the holy grail of tiki mixology.

After a couple of minutes' work—Cray was more careful this time—he poured a small amount into a clean glass. "I'll go first, if you don't mind. I've tasted this rum before."

He wore a poker face as he handed it to Neil. I was the last to taste it. I went through the same ritual as with the previous rum. This one didn't have the cloying caramel sweetness of the other, but it lacked the kind of complexity and funk I'd expect of a blend that included rums that were now a hundred years old. But what did I know? I'd never tasted anything like this before.

Kim took the glass from me this time and sipped. She looked at Cray. "Too easy on the tongue."

Cray nodded. "I'm afraid so. It's actually not a bad rum. Jamaican, I think. They've taken something quite good, perhaps darkened it a bit, though it's supposed to be golden in color."

I sat back on the bed next to Neil. "It didn't seem right to me, but I wasn't sure why. How did you know?"

Cray looked off into the distance. Into the past, maybe, when he tried the real thing. "Do you know how this rum got to be a seventeen? It was supposed to be a fifteen-year-old rum, but the company couldn't get it off the island in the middle of World War II. They didn't want it blown up by U-boats. So it aged longer than it was supposed to. Eventually, they shipped it out. It was immensely popular. Trader Vic used it in his first Mai Tai. But it disappeared, sold out. I've only heard of a few bottles sold in the past few years, and they were recent discoveries, labeled like this, not with the romantic old label with the dagger. And there aren't many people left who would recognize the real thing. The authentic Wray & Nephew 17-Year-Old includes rum from a particular pot still. Even it was just a small percentage of the overall blend, that pot still element is so distinctive, an old hand like me notices its absence."

There was a moment when we all sat in silence, mourning the original Mai Tai we would never taste. Or at least, those of us who weren't Cray.

"You said the fake rum you had earlier today might be from the same source," Kim said. "What source?"

Neil and I exchanged a glance, and I spoke. "Did Fizz ever have dealings with a collector named Winston Reckel?"

Kim's nostrils flared. "That bastard."

"You know him?" Neil asked.

"Yes, I know him. He and Fizz were best buddies. He was like a drug dealer, always ready to feed the addiction, finding Fizz what he wanted for more and more money. So many bottles. So much rum. And none of it is any good?" Her eyes widened. "I was counting on selling some of it. Damn it. Damn him to hell."

"Could Fizz have found out that the rum wasn't authentic?" Neil asked.

She shook her head. "Not that I know of. He never gave me any indication."

I sat up straighter. "The phone call."

Kim looked at me sharply. "What? What phone call?"

"Somebody called Fizz right before ... anyway, maybe it was Winston Reckel. He admitted he'd been trying to get ahold of Fizz. And he took the London dock rum from Pau Hana." Wow, Reckel was a counterfeiter *and* a killer? "Maybe Fizz *had* found out, and Reckel wanted to contain the damage. So Reckel arranged to meet him."

"Reckel wanted to silence him before he told anyone else!" Kim shook her head. "Evil. Pure evil."

"But why would Mr. Reckel have stolen just one bottle if he committed the crime?" Cray asked.

"Fizz only had one bottle on him. The London dock rum," Neil said.

"Maybe Winston figured once he got rid of Fizz, no one would find out about the counterfeit bottles. Sorry," I said to Kim's look of anguish. "But Ar— at least one other person knew about the fakes. Only Winston couldn't get to him, and it wasn't in that victim's interest to make it public. Which made Fizz the loose end."

"Fizz was not a loose end. He was my husband!" Kim turned angry eyes on all of us. "You all need to leave now. Take your crap rum with you. I need to figure out what to do."

"We can tell the police, if you like," Neil said gently as Cray neatly corked and packaged the bottles.

After a second, Kim nodded. "Yes, that would be best. Thank you. I'm sorry. I know you're just trying to do the right thing. I thought I was figuring things out, what to do with the company going forward. I could've used that rum money. This throws a wrench into the barrel."

"You of all people shouldn't be sorry," Neil said, "but we're sorry for disturbing you."

I nodded in sympathy, afraid to say anything else. Cray placed the packaged bottles in the hula girl bag and gave it to Neil, and we murmured our goodbyes and left Kim's room.

By unspoken agreement, we didn't say anything until we'd gone downstairs and taken a few chairs by the empty pools. All the partiers were still at Pau Hana, so the adjoining rectangles of shimmering water, lit blue in the night under the palm trees, resembled a tranquil, geometric island lagoon. Above us, the tower glowed with changing colored lights. A welcome breeze made the air almost cool.

"We have to tell the police about Winston Reckel," I said.

Neil nodded. "I'll text the detective."

"What about Arnold Preiss? Oh, and *you*—" I turned to Cray. "You were the one who enlightened him about his bad rum."

Cray put out his hands, palms up, and lifted his eyebrows. "You have me, my dear. I consulted with Mr. Preiss in confidence. How did you find out about his woes?"

"We happened upon him attacking Winston and stealing some of the fake rum to use as evidence," Neil said.

"That must have been exciting," Cray drawled.

A laugh bubbled up from my throat. "That's one way to put it. Later, Arnold told us an expert had told him his rum was fake. And you said you'd met with a victim of the fraud, so ..." I pulled my little tin of licorice jelly beans from my bag and popped one in my mouth. Their comforting flavor reminded me of absinthe. "Anyone?"

Both of the men took a couple, and we all chewed contentedly for a minute.

Then Neil looked at me. "Why did you ask Arnold about a burner phone?"

"Detective Flores said a burner phone or at least an untraceable phone called Fizz before the murder. Remember, Melody heard Fizz answering the phone? I wondered if maybe it was Arnold who called. But now I don't know."

"From what Melody said, Fizz was pretty friendly to whoever called," Neil mused. "Did Fizz even know Arnold?"

Cray nodded. "Quite possible, given the world of high-end rum collectors is so small, but I never observed them together."

I nodded. "So it was most likely his so-called 'best buddy,' Winston Reckel."

Chapter Thirty

It was one of those nights when my dreams spun all of my anxieties together in a blender to make an absurd cocktail. The setting: Pau Hana's dining room. I wore a muumuu that I kept tripping over as I tried to get to the bar, but all of our suspects kept stopping me. Nigel and Lottie wanted to interview me for their blog. Mr. Mixy wanted to film his show at my bar and tell everyone how happy he was to get out of Bohemia Beach. His dream beard undulated like a magic carpet as it waved to all the women passing by. Arnold Preiss kept calling me "little girl" and threatened to shrink me with some ray gun he invented. Val smacked him on the back of the head and kept on walking. Cap Calder used a giant muddler to row a boat through the dining room, where a river of rum had materialized, and toasted me with a full tiki mug. Winston Reckel wanted to sell me fake rum for my bar. Mark Fairman came up behind me and kissed my neck, but when I turned, it was Neil, and he was shaking his head in disappointment. The whole time, Fizz Martin sat on the stage, staring at me with a dark, grim gaze ... until he burst out laughing.

That's what woke me up at dawn, sweating, partly from the creeps and partly because there was a hot, hairy dog curled up against my hip. I took a quick shower, the first of what would no doubt be many today. Gina was still asleep. I hadn't even heard her come in.

I hooked up Astra to her harness, and she led me outside into the muggy morning. The sun had barely cracked the horizon, and there were still streaks of pink in the lavender sky.

We headed to the marina sidewalk first, with Astra walking me, as usual. Maybe she wanted to see if there were any other interesting items in the bushes.

She sniffed and peed as we went. A big iguana sat on the edge of the concrete walkway from which the docks branched out, scaly and gray and green and magnificent. One eyeball twitched and his dewlap wiggled as Astra neared, but he didn't move, and my dog was oblivious, even though the thing was as big as she was.

Almost no one was stirring on the boats, except for one loaded with fishing poles heading out to the Intracoastal. One man sat on his deck in just his shorts, reading a newspaper as he sipped a cup of coffee. Aboard a sleek but modest yacht, a radio played salsa as a woman polished the shiny railings.

I supposed any yacht was modest compared with Arnold Preiss's, and we were heading that way. I'd just been too wrapped up in Astra and the other boats and my own groggy mind to think about him. I looked down the walkway toward the Intracoastal Waterway and saw ... nothing. There was a big, wide berth where the huge yacht had been docked yesterday, and I had a clear view to the other side of the water.

It was gone.

Arnold Preiss had left the scene of the crime.

Or at least his boat had.

I let out a breath. I was glad he was gone. I hadn't liked his threats. Especially because he had the bucks to carry them out. Anyway, he was probably headed for his place in West

Palm. The police could catch up with him there if they wanted to.

"Come on, Astra." I tugged her back around and texted Neil as we walked: "Arnold's yacht is gone." I was pretty sure Neil was going to let the cops sort out the Arnold connection, partly to protect us from any hijinks he might decide to pull, but I wanted him to know the latest.

As we reentered the big courtyard with the pools and the palms, green and lush and peaceful, Astra found a spot to make her morning deposit under a hibiscus. I bagged it and looked around for a trash can, did my doody duty and saw Dick and Dale sitting by the pool. Their entourage was nowhere in sight.

I wandered over. "Hey, guys." Astra put her paws on Dick's knees and got a smile and some good petting for her trouble. "How's it going?"

"Fantastic." Dale's smile was broad. Almost as broad as his shoulders. "It's the big day."

"Oh my gosh! Your ceremony—at the Pau Hana gardens, right?"

"This afternoon," Dick said. "But we're doing the tasting first."

"That'll be fun," I said, hoping I sounded convincing. I'd left Neil and Cray by the pool last night figuring out what they were going to do to make up for the missing big-ticket rums.

"We're having a wedding after-party out here later," Dick said. "Why don't you come?"

"To make drinks?" I asked.

They both laughed. "No," Dale said. "To eat, drink and be merry. Though Barclay and Luke volunteered to make drinks for us."

"Thank God." They laughed again. "I mean, yeah, I'd love

to be there to congratulate you. And you can't go wrong with Barclay and Luke's cocktails. Have a great day!" I pulled Astra away, but not before she licked the remains off Dale's empty plate. An early breakfast sounded like a good idea.

I got a pricey egg sandwich from the pool cafe and charged it to the room. I stood under a palm tree and ate it, dropping a few bites to Astra, while watching a handsome man doing laps. The water glistened on his muscular back as he moved. His physique was mesmerizing, so much so, I didn't realize who it was until he stood up. Rivulets of gleaming water slid off his broad chest, and his red hair was dark and wet and slicked back. It was a real James Bond moment as he walked out of the pool and grinned at me.

"Hot Pepper," he said in that yummy gravelly voice with the yummier English accent. "Want to take a dip?"

I wanted to take a lick, but instead I swallowed my last bite of sandwich and shook my head. "Gotta work."

"Too bad. Maybe I'll see you later?"

"Maybe," I squeaked, and then I fled with Astra, who also seemed interested in licking Mark Fairman. Then again, Astra wanted to lick everyone.

I delivered her back to the room, where Gina was awake but still in her jammies on the bed, scrolling through a tablet screen and looking hung over. "Oh, hi. I'm sorry I didn't walk her this morning."

"No problem. It was—interesting. I've got to check in at the kitchen anyway."

"Go ahead. I'll feed her," she said as the coffee machine gurgled. She nodded to it. "I need a lot of coffee before I can face the world again—or Larry."

"Uh-oh. Did something happen?"

"I tried to do a hula dance with one of the bands. I think it was hula. Though I don't actually *know* the hula. He said it was awesome, but I don't remember a whole lot."

Whoa no. I'd completely corrupted my business partner's sister. "As long as you got back here safe and sound."

"Yeah, I was too drunk to do anything else, and he was a gentleman. Mostly. He's a pretty good kisser."

La la la la. TMI. Too much information. I didn't want to know the details because I didn't want to lie to her brother later. "OK, then. Uh ... see you later. Can you survive one more night of this?"

"Sure! This is fun! Come here, girl," Gina said to Astra as my roomie got up and grabbed the magic food container. The elated dog didn't even notice me leave.

I walked down the corridor and through the doors that took me into the lobby.

And what a commotion there was in the lobby!

As a half dozen tiki folk gawked, Detectives Flores and Cruz and a couple of uniformed police escorted Winston Reckel toward the doors. He was in handcuffs and looked as if someone had just woken him up. Plus he looked like he'd had the hell beaten out of him, which he had, thanks to Arnold Preiss.

Winston saw me and halted, and his stare made my blood run cold.

"Guess I won't get to teach you how to fly," he said in a low, grating voice as the uniforms who gripped him by the arms yanked him toward the door.

I gaped as they went out the doors and pushed the collector into the back seat of a police car, its lights flashing blue.

Batman!

Holy Dionysus. I knew that voice. I *knew* it. It was

Winston Reckel who'd almost thrown me off the tiny balcony! Something else to tell Detective Flores, though he'd already left with the troops.

The good news was, they had him in custody. We could all drink a little easier tonight.

When I got to the Hookahakaha stations in the kitchen, almost no one was there. Val drank tea at her spot while she sliced limes, and her second-in-command trimmed mint across the room. Val regarded me with a cool stare. Then she nodded, and I put my bag down and settled in near her at the Bohemia table.

"What do you need?" I asked.

"While we wait for the drunks to show up?" She almost smiled. "We need nine hundred basil leaves and three hundred cucumber slices."

"Peel on?"

"Of course."

Easy enough. Given how sleepy I was, it was best I didn't have any complex knife tricks to execute today.

I found boxes of cucumbers, washed them and started slicing. After several minutes, I said, "Looks like they caught Fizz's killer."

"Is that right?" Val looked up, and we both stopped slicing for a moment.

"A rum collector who was selling fake rum and hoping to cover it up, apparently."

"Very interesting," she said. "Who's the collector?"

"Winston Reckel. Know him?"

"I've seen him around. Collecting isn't my thing. Life's too short to hang on to stuff just because. I have to admit, I've been mighty curious about who did it. Maybe because I wished it had been me." Val's laugh was low and dark. "When I went back to the kitchen, I saw your friend Melody there, making him a cocktail, so I backed out nice and slow."

What? *Wait a minute.* "You were in the kitchen when—"

"Briefly. I was going to make sure you guys cleaned up after preparing the drink for his talk. Which you did. Not that it mattered much, given what happened later."

She was checking up on us? That sounded like Val. But how could she tell we'd cleaned up the kitchen when she wasn't even around long enough for Melody to see her?

"Melody didn't mention seeing you," I said, turning back to slicing cucumbers, trying not to sound too curious.

Val snorted. She was slicing again, too. With a nice, sharp knife. We both had nice, sharp knives.

Oh, stop it, Pepper. No way you're going to win a knife fight with cocktail ninja chick.

"She had her hands full," Val was saying, "pouring a drink for poor, helpless Fizz."

"You never saw him after that?" I snuck another look at her.

Val raised an eyebrow. "What are you asking, Pepper?"

"Just wondering. You know, how Winston Reckel got back there and out again with no one seeing him." At least, I hadn't heard of anyone seeing him.

"There are a million ways in and out of that place. That door in the back of that nook—"

"The one that went to the storeroom?"

"Yeah," she said. "The storeroom also exits to the outside for easy loading in of stuff. That's how we got the supplies in. He might've walked in one way and scooted out the back, no problem."

Holy shit. Did Detective Flores know that? He had to. They processed that scene for hours. No wonder he had trouble pinning down the killer. Anybody could've gotten in and out of there.

"That explains it," was all I said as I finished the cucumbers and moved on to the basil.

"Kim's got to be relieved they caught the guy. And now that her darling husband is gone, who knows—maybe I'll actually go into one of her bars now." Val chuckled.

The bartenders and volunteers started trickling in, including Barclay, Luke and Melody. Melody had a story about a drinking contest she had with a guitarist from one of the surf bands, and Luke didn't look too happy about it. But he looked a lot happier after I told him about Winston's arrest. And after about an hour, I figured I'd better check in and see if Neil needed anything for the tasting. I said goodbye to everyone, cleaned up my space, grabbed my bag and left, thinking.

Truth was, I thought a little too much, all the time. I had a rich fantasy life. But if Winston could've gotten back there into our corner of the Pau Hana kitchen and out so easily, maybe Val could have, too. Twice.

Chapter Thirty-One

"They say it's five o'clock somewhere, and though it's only four o'clock in London, I say that's close enough for our evil purposes today," Mark Fairman said to laughter.

It was II a.m., South Florida time. Mark stood at the center of a long executive table in a deluxe meeting room the hotel had provided for the Gold Tooth Tasting. And I was in the seat next to his.

I felt a little like Cinderella at the ball, with Mark as my fairy godmother. Even if I couldn't get the image of him as Wet James Bond out of my head. He was playing fairy godmother—OK, godfather—to the whole event.

When Neil had requested I wheel a cart of glassware up from the kitchens for the tasting, I found him and Cray and Mark in the meeting room, which was partway up the tower and had a great view of the grounds and Intracoastal and skyline. They were going over last-minute details. And since at least two of the seats were empty—Arnold's and Winston's— Mark offered one of them to me. As the last-minute sponsor, it was totally within his rights to do so, and I could hardly say no, could I? So I rushed back to my room, put on a fetching trop- ical frock and lipstick and my new rhinestone-accented cat's-eye glasses (for special occasions), and came back for the tasting.

"When our friend Cray here told me there'd been a mishap with a couple of the rums you were going to taste today, we had a bit of a chat," Mark was telling the Gold Tooth tasters. "You see, I'd brought some very nice bottles from my estate outside London that Cray was going to take off my hands. But he suggested I donate them instead to this event, and I was only too glad to do so."

He went on to explain his generous donations, which went over my head but made those in the room clap and ooh and aah.

On my other side, Greer Allighant leaned over to whisper in my ear. "Do you know what he's talking about?"

"Not nearly enough," I whispered back. I made a note to myself to do more research into rum.

"Winston would've explained it to me," she murmured, "but he's not here, and I couldn't get ahold of him this morning."

I raised my finger to tell her to hold on for a second, as Mark finished up his speech and everyone applauded.

Neil, at the head of the table with Cray, stood and addressed the crowd. "Now, if you'll just enjoy the food while I finish the first pour, we'll get started."

Nigel and Lottie, Mr. Mixy, Dick and Dale and Cray headed for the table loaded with fancy cheeses and appetizers. Mark bent down to me. "Can I get you something, love?"

My brain turned to Jell-O. "That would be lovely," I said breathlessly. He grinned.

"Would you get me a plate, too, dear?" Greer called out.

Mark's mouth hung open for a second. "Uh, of course."

I had to smile as he walked away. Plus I got to watch him walk away, if you know what I mean.

"Oh, he's a cutie, isn't he?" Greer said. "You were going to tell me something about Winston?"

I nodded and took a long draft from my fancy FIJI water bottle. They'd been provided to everyone at the tasting. It's always good to hydrate when getting blotto on thousands of dollars' worth of rum, though one doesn't necessarily have to do so with water from seven thousand miles away.

"About Winston—it's not good news," I told Greer.

"He's not dead too, is he?" She looked horrified.

"No. At least he shouldn't be. He got arrested this morning."

"Oh, my. Well, everyone should be arrested at least once in their life. Drunk and disorderly?"

I almost choked on my water. "Not exactly. I think they're charging him with fraud and maybe worse." I kept my voice low so the others wouldn't hear. "He was selling fake rum to collectors, and he killed Fizz to cover it up."

Her eyes widened. "But they were such good friends. I—I mean, I can't say I'm surprised about the rum. Really. He just had so much of it and never seemed to have all that much money. He was always happy to have me pay for everything. I'm a liberated woman and all, but I don't really trust that quality in a man, you know?"

I nodded, trying not to smile. I believed in an equal division of the bill. Unless Mark Fairman was paying.

"But he and Fizz were just so chummy," Greer continued. "They were always chatting on that message board they had, all the rum people. Most of the people here, I believe. I can't believe he would hurt him like that." Greer shuddered and sipped her water. "I could use some of that rum."

"They were in an internet group? Like on Facebook?"

"Not there. On some other site. They all had cute little nicknames, but they all knew who was who. He let me see their chat one evening. He was Smoking Barrels. Fizz was Dr. Funk, even though he already had a silly name. Then there was Mr. Mixy"—leave it to my ex to keep his name. "That one rich fellow was Kokomo. That cutie you're sitting next to was Lord of Scoundrels. That fellow Nigel over there—"

"Wait. Who was Kokomo?" Why did that ring a bell?

"That techy billionaire fellow. What's his name?"

"Arnold Preiss?"

"That's him!" Greer said. "Oh, good, here comes the rum."

Arnold Preiss was Kokomo ... *Oh my God!* Melody mentioned Kokomo when she recounted Fizz's phone call, the one he got just as she was leaving him. Fizz called the caller *Kokomo.* It was Preiss who called Fizz just before he was murdered. Preiss, who could have easily arranged a last-minute meeting and killed him.

Only problem was, I wasn't sure why he would. Did Fizz owe him money? Kim kept talking about finances and wanting to sell off the rum before she knew it was fake. Maybe things were so bad, Fizz borrowed from his super-rich rum collector friend. Or did Fizz know about the faked rum and threaten to expose Arnold being duped, maybe for blackmail? But if that wild notion were true, why would Fizz be so excited about showing off his fake rum?

I was more confused than ever—and about more than Fizz. Neil moved around the room, arranging three glasses of rum in front of each taster. He placed a trio in front of me and gave me a funny look, just as Mark sat down, sliding loaded plates in front of Greer and me.

"Thanks, guys," I said to both of them, forgetting my

worries in the presence of four of my favorite things: Neil, good cheese, better liquor, and Mark Fairman.

The rums were either outstanding or interesting and often, both. As Neil distributed a few glasses at a time and Cray spoke, we tasted a dozen of them, ranging from upscale modern rums to a few rare collectibles, including a 1904 bottle of *rhum agricole* from Martinique. A couple were from Pau Hana's precious coffers—Lightbourn's Barbados Rum and some very old Lemon Hart—fascinating, given the restaurant's collection went back to the 1940s and 1950s.

As the event wrapped up, most of our small group drifted over to the food and chatted happily. Mr. Mixy described how awesome his TV show was going to be to Nigel and Lottie. Greer and Cray got along like a grass hut on fire. Dick and Dale made their goodbyes so they could go get married.

The quantities might have been small and the snacks hearty, but after twelve healthy doses of strong spirits, plus a cocktail Neil made from one of the newer rums (excellent, of course), I was beyond happy and perfectly content sitting at the table and listening to Mark Fairman. I didn't give a flying fig about the more stressful events of the weekend. I was three sheets to the wind of Mark's breath in my ear as he told me about his excellent wine cellar in England and how much he'd like to show it to me.

"Does your hotel room have a wine cellar?" I asked him.

"It's a suite. No cellar, but it has a superb bar and an even better bed," he whispered in my ear.

"Pepper." Another voice. Another voice I liked, though it sounded firm and commanding and no-nonsense. I looked up. Neil was standing on the other side of me, looking authoritative in his vest and bow tie, his bar bag over his shoulder. "Can I take you to lunch?"

Neil. Lunch. We'd talked about lunch. "But there's still cheese left," I said.

"I can order in whatever you want," Mark rumbled in that rough whiskey voice.

"We have things to do," Neil said.

Did we? Maybe we didn't, but Neil's eyes were so earnest ... and I started to realize that being seduced by Mark Fairman might not be the wisest way to spend my afternoon. Especially when I had stuff to tell Neil.

"All right," I said to Neil, trying not to sound like I was sad about leaving Mark, though maybe I was, a little. I turned to the redhead, remembering the nickname he gave himself on the rum board. "I can't thank you enough for today, and I hope I can return the favor sometime ... Lord of Scoundrels."

Mark laughed. "You're always surprising, Hot Pepper. I like that about you. And you can bet I'll take you up on your offer ... but today was my pleasure." He scanned my clingy, low-cut tropical dress and leaned in to whisper again. "But you have no idea how much pleasure you'll be missing."

Chapter Thirty-Two

I practically jumped out of my chair. It was either that or jump Mark's bones. I slung my bag over my head, cross-body, and hung on to the strap so I wouldn't fall over.

"Bye, then!" I grabbed Neil by the arm and practically dragged him out the door.

"What did he say to you?" Neil sounded furious. "Did he insult you?"

"No, no. It was just time to go. Hey, slow down."

"You're the one running."

He was right. I slowed just as we got to the elevator and released his arm.

Neil pressed the button. "Do you—like him?"

"Mark? Oh, he's fun. You know."

"I don't know." His gray eyes looked darker than usual. Neil had once told me people thought he was boring. Certainly he was a contrast to the gregarious English distiller. Was he feeling inadequate? Hurt? Considering he made a hobby out of pushing me away, what was I supposed to do with that insight?

The elevator dinged and opened. I waved him in. "Come on. I have stuff to tell you."

"Let's go get some lunch. It might make you feel better," he said as the car moved.

"But I feel *fantastic!*"

"That's what I'm afraid of."

"Nothing to be afraid of. The murderer is caught, probably ..."

"What do you mean by that?"

"Shhh," I said as the elevator door opened to a few people waiting to get in. I stepped out and looked around. "This isn't the lobby."

"It's my floor. Give me a sec. I have to stow my bag. I'll be right back." He looked at me as if he expected me to insist on coming along, but why would I? The last time didn't end so well.

Neil came right back, as promised, though now he was wearing a medium-loud tropical shirt. We headed to the lobby and caught a cab outside.

"Should we invite the others?" I asked as the cab rolled out of the gate and caught the green light that let it turn left toward the beach.

"Barclay was volunteering at a seminar with the rum ambassador from London, and Luke and Melody were helping the bars at the final pool party this afternoon."

"Well, that's nice. Now I feel guilty."

Neil chuckled. "Do you really? About what?"

"That should be obvious. About not working."

"You've worked enough. Do you feel guilty about anything else?"

"Whatever do you mean?" I tried to look innocent. "At least I'm not guilty of murder. But I'm still not sure who is."

The cab driver glanced at us in the mirror. Neil gave me a small head shake, telling me to be quiet as the car navigated the beach road lined with big hotels, condos and restaurants. It was thronged with people. The wide beach was busy, too, and the sun shone hot on the sand and sparkling blue ocean.

A few minutes later, we were being shown to an outdoor table on a shaded deck, overlooking a west-facing marina filled with huge boats. Yachts. Whatever. These people probably ate money for lunch.

We, however, were going to have seafood. Neil ordered the crab claws as an appetizer, which came to us already shelled, luscious and buttery and garlicky, and we both ordered fresh tuna sandwiches with nice, salty fries. And fizzy, sweet, blessedly caffeinated Cokes.

"Man, I needed this," I said when I was halfway through my meal. The sandwich and sobriety had cut through my drunken fog, and I could almost think again. And my first thought was that I would have been extremely reckless with Mark Fairman if not for Neil. I couldn't resent Neil for his intervention, even if my id was still thinking about redheads with excellent wine cellars.

Neil looked more relaxed, too. "Now can you explain what you meant back there?"

"You weren't even drunk after that tasting, were you?"

"I was working. I tried a couple of the rums, though. Wonderful selection. We owe a lot to Cray."

"And Mark Fairman?"

"I guess." Neil's eyes narrowed. "What were you saying about the killer?"

"When Barclay's dad arrested Winston Reckel this morning—I assume for the murder, but maybe for the fraud too?—Winston said something on the way out that convinced me he was the one who almost pushed me over the balcony."

"That bastard. Why do you have doubts about him killing Fizz?"

I told Neil about the online rum club and that Arnold was known as Kokomo, so he must have been the one who called

Fizz right before the impresario was killed. "So Arnold could've been setting Fizz up."

"Why?"

"You *would* have to ask why." I grinned. I shared some of my theories about money and blackmail, but they didn't sound that plausible in the light of sobriety. "I guess I don't know. Why do you think he called Fizz?"

"I don't know, either."

"Plus Val saw Fizz with Melody right before it happened— and she also said there was another exit through the storeroom. So that means she could have been in play."

"It was like Grand Central Station back there."

"Apparently. And Val hated Fizz. She knew her way around the kitchen. No one saw her pop in the first time, right? Not even Melody. Val could've snuck back and killed him, too."

Neil took a sip of his soda. "You found all this out this morning?"

"I was busy." I finished my last fry with a big gulp of Coke and sighed in contentment.

Neil shook his head. "I don't know about Val. I'd hate to think she'd do it, but it sounds like we might want to share some of this information with Detective Flores."

"At least about the phone call. Do you want to do it, since you're his mole on the inside?"

A corner of Neil's mouth lifted. "Ha ha." But he got out his phone and texted the detective about Arnold being the mystery caller. And about Winston likely being the one who attacked me.

"Maybe Winston will confess and that will be that." Having a full stomach made me hopeful.

"They might make him a deal," he said, picking up the bill the waitress left. "The detective was very interested in the fraud stuff I texted to him. Protecting Winston's secret, the bottle forgeries, was a pretty good motive for murder."

"Can I pay for some of that?"

"Business expense." He smiled. I was being treated all over the place today.

"Oh, and we're invited to the wedding after-party tonight," I said.

"Dick and Dale mentioned that at the tasting. Sounds fun. Our work will be over. Actually, it's over now. We have the afternoon to ourselves." He smiled even wider, and my heart went gooey. "You still want to do that water shuttle ride?"

Gah. I didn't like boats, it was true, but taking a ride with Neil might be a good way to make sure I hadn't messed up our friendship back there. And now that I'd left Mark's orbit and reclaimed my sanity, I still liked the idea of being more than friends with Neil.

"Sure, let's do it," I said.

We walked south for a bit, past the big Bahia Mar hotel to the marina where the water shuttle stopped. We bought tickets at the kiosk and waited for the next boat to arrive. The usual clouds that formed on the sea breeze were percolating and darkening inland. Looked like storms were in the offing.

But the shuttle boats were running as usual, not to be cowed by South Florida's daily summer maelstroms. A modest double-decker arrived in a few minutes, and we boarded, heading for the top deck and the best view.

The boat waited for a few minutes, taking on late arrivals. I sat on the bench at the back of the top deck with Neil, close to the railing on the water side. I swapped my clear cat's-eye glasses for sunglasses I had in my bag. We were in the sun, unlike the folks under the upstairs awning or in the party room below, but I enjoyed watching the sky and the building clouds.

Fishing boats and yachts chugged through the marina, heading to and from the river and canals.

"Travis McGee's boat docked here, you know," Neil said.

"Oh, I love those books! *The Busted Flush,* right? What a great character."

"He liked his gin. And the Bahia Cabana used to be there," Neil said, gesturing to the south.

"This is significant?"

"It was funky but kind of cool. Hookahakaha held a few events there in the past. And I once tried and failed to extract my brother from a minor spring break disaster there."

Neil had told me he had a brother who died, but he rarely mentioned him. "What happened?" I asked.

"Story for another time." Neil smiled as he reached for his pocket and pulled out his buzzing phone. "Saved by the bell. Uh-oh. It's Barclay's dad." He answered the call, and judging by Neil's brief responses and questions, the detective did most of the talking.

Neil ended the call with a thank-you after a couple of minutes, pocketed his phone and looked at me. "They intercepted Arnold Preiss disembarking from his yacht in West Palm and pulled him in for questioning this morning after Winston told them he thought it was Arnold who beat him up. So Winston acting all shocked when we were there right after the attack was just a big lie."

"Everything about that guy is a lie."

"True. The London dock rum is fake, too. Forensics suggested it, and Winston admitted it."

"Wow." I don't know why I was shocked—and a little sad, too. Maybe because so many dreams and stories had been pinned on that rum.

"Barclay's dad wanted to warn us to be careful," Neil

continued. "Keep an eye out for Arnold. They let him go, and he was pissed. Asked if we'd turned him in."

"Great," I said dryly.

"He's capable of violence, obviously, but at least it looks like he didn't kill Fizz. They have to check out his alibi, but he says he wasn't even at Pau Hana on Wednesday."

"What did Arnold tell the police?"

"After making them wait an hour for his lawyer? Apparently Arnold told them he called Fizz that day to warn him about the rums being fake. Seems pretty plausible, since they were friends through the online rum club."

"Yeah, it does. He could've just told us that."

"He's probably still scared to death it'll get out that the billionaire tech genius was duped by a rum forger."

The boat lurched just then as it got under way, and my tummy did a pirouette, accompanied by a symphonic gurgle. "Whoa no."

"You OK, Pepper?"

"Fine," I huffed out, working on my breathing. Nice and slow. I was fine. So what if I'd had a barrel's worth of rum and a giant lunch and I was on a medium-small boat and—

It lurched again, leaning a little as it circled out toward the canal. Exhaust fumes wafted up to me, and I shut my eyes tight and held on. This samba in my stomach would pass. Surely it would pass.

"Just keep talking," I told Neil.

"Are you sure? You look kind of green."

"Talk!" I opened my eyes to see a few other passengers glance my way. "Sorry. I'll be OK."

Neil covered up a chuckle. "OK. Detective Flores also said Arnold told him he called Kim, too."

Chapter Thirty-Three

I scrunched my eyebrows. "What? Arnold called Kim? When?"

Neil nodded. "I'm not sure when, but he said he wanted to warn her about the fake rums. They were all friendly, I guess, because of the online rum club. He wanted to ease the blow. He called Fizz next."

My stomach felt better. The chatter was helping. But I was confused. "Wouldn't we have noticed Kim taking a phone call? She was running the projector."

"I don't know. It was dark. Arnold's a liar, anyway. He's probably trying to cover his ass."

"Hey, look at that!" The freshening breeze made me feel slightly better, plus the view was impressive. We were motoring west down a wide river with the skyline in the distance—the clouds looked darker and closer—and huge, stunning houses glided by on either side of us. Canals branched off with more zillionaire houses, more extreme boats docked next to them. Coconut and royal palms rippled in the wind. Occasional iguanas appeared, sunning themselves on the concrete walls and wooden docks that bordered the waterway.

We enjoyed the view for several minutes. And then my tummy did another roll, just as the captain's voice boomed over the speaker, telling us about some celebrity not being able to find a place to dock his massive boat and that Fort Lauderdale was the superyacht capital of the world and we'd get to Las Olas soon. I closed my eyes again, trying to shut it all out. And keep it all down.

"Pepper?" Neil's hand landed on my shoulder, and he squeezed, warm and comforting. "We'll get off at Las Olas, OK? Walk around a little. We can take a car back to the hotel."

"Ergh." I put my hand over my mouth. Even being in a car didn't sound good right now. And I really didn't want to lose my lunch all over Neil. "I'll be right back. *Please* stay here." I didn't want him to forever remember me chumming the waters of Fort Lauderdale.

I dashed forward to the stairs and headed down to the lower deck. Everything around me was a blur as I rushed from the front of the boat toward the stern through the crowded enclosed lower section and outside again to the back railing, at the edge of another small seating area.

I gripped the rail and leaned over, closing my eyes behind my sunglasses, gulping air. I held on and willed all of my systems to go from red to yellow to green.

Except for the engines, it was mostly quiet back here, just under where Neil and I had been sitting. Behind me, people laughed and music blared in the enclosed section, but the sounds of the party were muted, as the cabin was closed up tight to keep in the air-conditioning. The idea of air-conditioning was appealing, but I didn't trust what my tummy might do if I saw any kind of food.

As the wind picked up, I breathed a little easier and my stomach switched from the samba to a relaxed slow dance. Not perfect, but I didn't feel like an explosion was imminent.

Thunder rumbled, and I stood up straight and blinked. I

turned to get a look at the storms in the west. I took off my sunglasses, stuffed them in my bag and rubbed my eyes.

And saw a familiar face in the shadows, a lone figure in jeans and a black T-shirt on one of the white benches, white-blond hair blowing in the wind.

"Pepper. You feeling OK?" Kim Martin asked.

I nodded. "Better." *Kim.* How long had she been there? There was something I wanted to ask her. What was it? "Back on the water shuttle again, eh?"

"Like I said, it helps me think. How did the tasting go?"

"Pretty well, considering we had to substitute the big-ticket rums. I think everyone was happy. I might've been a little too happy."

She chuckled. "I know how that is."

"I'm sorry we surprised you last night. I know you have a lot to deal with right now."

She shrugged. "That's OK. I had to learn about the bad bottles sooner or later. At least I know now."

I remembered what I wanted to ask Kim. "What's funny is I just heard that Arnold Preiss warned Fizz about the rums and that he called you, too."

Kim looked to the side, out over the water. "Storms are coming. You can set your watch by them down here."

I leaned back against the railing, trying to get everything straight in my head. "Arnold must have called you during the presentation. Do you remember that?"

She turned back to me. "Yeah, I guess he did. It would've been rude to talk in the dining room, so I ducked out to the lobby to take the call while the movie was playing."

"So you knew about the rums being fake?"

She snorted. "Am I supposed to believe a liar like Arnold

Preiss? Total social climber. He just wanted to be the next Fizz Martin."

Now my mind was racing, but I didn't want to push too hard. I kept my voice even. "I mean, you had to wonder, right? Wonder if Arnold might have been correct about the rums? They were worth a lot. Maybe you went to the kitchen to talk to Fizz about it. Only maybe you saw something there you didn't want to see."

Kim nodded slowly as if she was entertaining my theory but not buying much of it. "Like what? My dead husband?"

"He wasn't dead yet." I took a leap. "You saw him with Melody."

She stood and stretched and walked over to stand next to me, her back to the railing like mine.

I did a quick look around. We really were alone. The party people were oblivious in their closed compartment. Neil was on the deck above me with a handful of other tourists. Would he hear me yell if I needed to? Would he come looking for me?

Kim leaned a little closer. "There's something you need to understand, and maybe you do, since you're a woman. All men are horny bastards and the star of their own movie. Everyone else, especially if she's a woman, is just a bit player. And Fizz was not only horny and self-centered. He was blind, and he was stupid. I just wanted to talk to him about the rum. About all the money he spent on that goddamn rum. Real or fake. It didn't matter. Well, it might've mattered a little, since I couldn't resell fake rum once the word was out."

"You weren't upset about Melody?"

"Not about her. The women pissed me off in general, but the money was the worst, because it symbolized how little respect he had for me. *I* made the money, and he spent it. I put my soul into building that empire. I managed the business.

Most of the drink recipes are mine. Did you know that? The women were just an insult, lemon juice in the wound. At least Melody slapped him. I enjoyed that." She chuckled again, her eyes going soft as she remembered. I recalled how she asked me at the Tiki Skyliner party if I was Melody. Kim knew very well that I wasn't.

"Fizz was stupid," I said, repeating her thought. "But you aren't, are you?" *Don't accuse her. Not yet. We're just two women having a conversation.*

"I like to think I'm reasonably intelligent."

"So that afternoon at Pau Hana, in the kitchen, you—talked to him?" I flashed back to the kitchen myself. "Did you leave through the storeroom?"

"That door back there? It was locked. I walked right out through the kitchen. I was wearing almost what I'm wearing now. You called it, back at the tower party. It's the hospitality uniform. There's nothing more invisible than a kitchen drudge wearing black."

"But whoever killed him was covered in blood, right? That's why they thought Luke didn't do it. He wasn't bloody enough."

"Think, Pepper. You're pretty smart, too, aren't you?" There was the slightest edge in her tone, but I didn't want to retreat. Not yet.

I saw the scene again in my mind. Me getting out my kit. *Mise en place.* Getting directions from Kim and Val. Donning the apron and the gloves.

When I found Fizz, the other apron was missing from the rack.

I spoke softly. "You wore an apron?"

"Of course. Threw it in a laundry bin on the way out. Stuffed it under a big pile of tablecloths. I got lucky there. But I always have spare T-shirts. I changed in the van just to be sure and got back to the projector just before the movie ended."

She did it. Kim killed her husband. Kim killed Fizz Martin.

"Did you take the London dock rum?" I asked.

"Don't call it that." Anger edged her tone, and the sky answered with thunder, closer, now. "It was fake. Just another symptom of Fizz's disease. I figured the cops would be chasing a thief if it disappeared, so I took it out back and tossed it into the garbage."

"And Winston found it."

"He makes a good fall guy, doesn't he?" Kim smiled. "You're OK with that, aren't you, Pepper? Especially since you tracked him down. I thought maybe Melody ... but Winston Reckel will do."

She was creeping me out, but I had to know more. "Sure. He almost killed me. He's perfect," I said. "I'd still like to know how it went down. How did Melody not see you?"

"I hid behind a rack of plates. She was in a hurry to get out of there. Can't say I blame her. And then Fizz was yukking it up on the phone with Arnold. Didn't believe him. Hung up, and I confronted him about the bad rum. He blew it off."

She paused, watching a string of pelicans glide by. "You know, he still had her lipstick on his mouth. Watermelon pink, I'd call it. Just a smear from his disgusting come-on. Maybe that's what did it. What tripped me. It's like my mind knew what I was doing before my body did. As we were talking, I put on the apron, the gloves, and he didn't even notice. He hardly ever noticed me." Kim's voice was quiet, curious, as if she was trying to figure out how she lost a game of solitaire instead of losing her mind. She looked down the river, past the frothy wake. "He told me I was a wet blanket. Paranoid. He was laughing at me. *At me.* When he closed his eyes to take a big sip of his drink, I grabbed the muddler and swung. Did a Babe Ruth right into his face, shattered the mug, shattered him. Home run first time. He went down, *bam, bam,* hit the table, hit the floor. I watched him breathe his last breath and got out of there."

I was so transfixed by her icy delivery that I hadn't realized she was edging closer until her hip touched mine. She reached across me slowly and caressed the strap of the messenger bag I wore across my body.

"Nice bag," she said.

Just before she grasped the strap and yanked.

Twisted.

Looped it around my neck and pushed me hard against the railing.

It all happened in a split second, and I was too daft to see it coming. Kim was taller than I was, and her high-heeled boots gave her even more leverage as she did her best to crush my throat. I grabbed at the strap, pulling, flailing, trying to get my fingers under it.

"I don't think you get it," she said, her eyes drilling into mine. "Relax. It'll go easy. Nobody can see you. You'll take a quick dunk, and that will be that."

She was right. It would be easy—for her. She was leaning over me, pushing me backward against the railing. A casual observer might think they were looking at a couple, or one person bending over the rail.

"We're approaching the Las Olas shuttle stop," the speaker boomed. "Disembark for downtown Fort Lauderdale, River-walk and the shopping district."

I wriggled and gasped, but she had an iron grip. I had to breathe for just a few more seconds. Surely someone would see me. But all of a sudden Kim was wrestling me to a small gate in the back railing and down a couple of steep steps, onto one of the twin platforms that hung off the back of the boat at water level. At least I sucked in a gulp of air as the noose momentarily loosened, but now there was no way anyone could see me as she bore down, tightening her stranglehold. I desperately thrust a few fingers under the strap to fight her off, to keep her from crushing my windpipe. She was strong. Stronger than I was.

As I struggled, another part of my brain pictured the few tourists who were disembarking moving to the lower level, to the gangplank access. It was on the side of the boat, accessible from the stern seating area, right next to the enclosed middle compartment. They wouldn't have any reason to look over the back railing.

The partiers were singing "Happy Birthday." I dimly heard the voices.

Neil will look for me. This is our stop.

Or my stop, forever.

I looked up as I fought her, saw fluttering flags hanging off the top deck and the sky roiling above them as lightning flashed and thunder roared a few seconds later. No one looked over the railing. I tried to call out for Neil, for anyone, but the only sound that leaked out was a sad croak, lost in the drone of the engines. Fat raindrops started to fall on my face as I wrestled Kim and the boat slowed.

Dizziness seized me as I ran out of air. She was killing me *right now*.

Chapter Thirty-Four

Kim ratcheted my bag strap one more twist, choking out the last of my oxygen.

And praise Dionysus and Mark Fairman and all the rum and seafood I'd had earlier, because in one violent explosion, I broke Kim's grip and barfed it all up.

"Argh!" she cried, jumping back from the eruption.

It was all I needed. I slammed my shoulder into her as I clambered back up to the main deck, just as the boat was sidling up to the platform. I hurled myself past the crewman who was holding open the little gate in the side of the boat and leapt the three feet separating ship from shore without even waiting for the gangplank.

"Pepper!" I heard a voice shout. *Neil?*

It didn't matter. I'd been in fight mode. Now I was in flight mode.

And the skies opened up. It was a crashing rain, a frog-strangler, an instant soaker, the kind of summer storm that only South Florida could produce.

I gathered my wits and took off down the curving sidewalk that bordered the water. When I looked back, Kim was jumping off the boat, sprinting through the deluge, following in my footsteps, gaining on me.

Still running, I looked forward again too late to realize what was right in front of me.

An iguana. A big, fat, stationary, disgruntled iguana.

He might as well have been a fire-breathing dragon. He bobbed his head and swatted his tail at me to no avail as I tripped over him and slammed into the brick walkway with a cry.

Pain shot up my knees. I reflexively cursed yet another ruined party dress and hurriedly stuck a hand in my bag, searching around for something, anything I could use as a weapon. The cocktail knife was wrapped in too many layers. *No time.*

Still huddled on the ground, practically drowning in the downpour, I looked back. Kim was too close, wild-eyed, heedless of the fact that she was now about to attempt murder in public, in the middle of a daylight deluge, not in a cozy back corner of the Pau Hana kitchen.

I froze. Should I roll? Run? The indignant iguana had no such issue and scampered away, its tail swishing.

I clambered to my feet, untangled my bag from my body and poised to swing it at her head. But as Kim got ten feet away from me, her hair stood straight up and she stumbled, her eyes surprised and confused.

And in a biblical blast right out of my missionary parents' playbook, a bolt of lightning lit her up like a nuclear bomb.

The instantaneous flash-bang shattered the sky. I threw up an arm to shield my eyes and myself from the concussion, dropping to the sidewalk again. A little zip of electricity shot through me, just enough to freak me the hell out—a side flash from the bolt that knocked Kim to the ground.

Everyone was screaming—the people on the boat, the

people who got off. It was mayhem. I just hugged my bag and stayed curled up on the brick sidewalk and let the scene unravel like a monkey jailbreak at the zoo until I felt strong arms around me and let Neil enfold me.

"My God. What happened to you? Are you OK? Oh, my God. Your neck." He touched it, and I batted his hand away. "Shhh. It's OK. The captain called 9-1-1. There'll be police here soon and an ambulance."

"Kim," I managed to croak.

"I know. I'm sorry. I should have come looking for you. But I was on the phone with Luke, filling him in, and I just didn't realize—"

"OK," I whispered. "It's OK."

There was no shelter, and the storm raged. People were running for it, some to the boat, others to whatever they could find off the Riverwalk. A uniformed mate from the boat leaned over Kim, and the sound of approaching sirens split the air, competing with the rain and thunder.

"Here," Neil said. "Come with me. Can you walk?"

I didn't say anything, just let him help me up some steps and under a rain-free overhang outside the doors of a nearby high-rise condo. We sat dripping on the ground and waited as Neil wrapped an arm around my shoulders and my heart slowed down.

"Water," I finally croaked, pointing to my bag.

He rummaged around in the messenger bag and pulled out a small metal bottle, uncapped it and handed it to me. I swished and drank, getting rid of the bad taste, soothing my sore throat.

And then I attempted a smile. "At least we're not on the boat anymore."

"So you're the one who messed up my case?"

I looked up to see Detective Flores smiling at me. Really smiling, this time.

Neil and I were sitting at an empty outdoor table at a closed restaurant in the small brick plaza between the boat access and Las Olas Boulevard. The rain had passed, as it does, and weak sunshine filtered through the clouds. I was plying my knees with ice packs given to me by the EMTs, who'd already checked me out and left in an ambulance with Kim and a police escort. Somehow, she'd survived the lightning strike.

I returned only half a smile to the detective. "I'd have been just as happy not doing it the hard way." My voice was raspy, and my throat hurt.

"I have to agree with you there," the detective said. "What is it about you that makes people want to kill you?"

"Not funny," Neil said.

"I have to agree with you there," I echoed the detective.

"Can you talk?" Detective Flores said, sitting next to us and setting a small audio recorder on the table.

And so I did, telling him about my conversation with Kim and everything that followed.

"We'll check out her room and her van," he said. "A rental, probably, right? Since they came from California? The shirt might still be in there. Even if it isn't, there should be traces."

Of blood. Traces of blood. He didn't say it, but abruptly I was pulled back into that moment, that terrible scene when I found Fizz dead. I blinked it away and felt Neil's hand rubbing my back again.

"We might need you back down here to testify," the detective said. "If she survives."

"She was talking to the EMTs," Neil said. "But she didn't look great."

"Sometimes it's worse surviving a lightning strike than it is being killed by one," Flores said. "It might be worse for Mrs. Martin, anyway. This isn't going to be pretty."

"I'd really like to get back to the hotel, if you don't mind," I said. "And not by boat."

Neil chuckled, and I glared at him.

"Do you need a ride?" the detective asked.

"We've got one." Neil nodded at the road, where his own big black SUV turned the corner and pulled up next to the plaza. Barclay was driving, and he and Luke and Melody popped out and ran over.

"Oh, my poor dear Pepper," Melody gushed, jumping in to hug me.

"Ouch."

"Sorry," she said. "What happened to you?"

"Just a little beaten up."

"Hi, Dad," Barclay said to his father, and they exchanged a manly handshake I figured was code for "Glad to see you're alive."

"You coming over for dinner?" the detective asked him. "Your mom is making dumplings."

Barclay smiled broadly. "Absolutely."

Neil was quickly relating the story to Luke, whose face broke out in a grin like the sun after a storm.

"I'm sorry," Luke said, looking at me and then at the detective. "I know I shouldn't be happy, but this means you have the killer. And it's not me!"

We laughed. Even me. "That's OK," I said, "but you owe me a drink. Later." My tummy actually felt tons better after losing my lunch, but I still needed some rest and water before

I could think about a cocktail.

Luke nodded happily. "Good thing we have a party tonight, then."

Chapter Thirty-Five

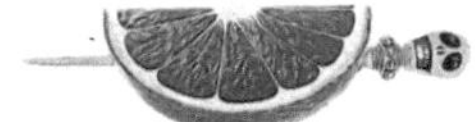

Cocktail people knew how to celebrate. Drinking good cocktails wasn't about getting drunk. It was about tasting the best in life—the best liquor and ingredients and creativity in a glass—and enjoying those happy moments that were often all too fleeting.

And maybe getting a little tipsy as a byproduct.

Dick and Dale's after-wedding party was lovely. They'd taken a small area of the green lawn under the palms, near the pools, and strung up white lights and paper lanterns. It was just outside Luke and Barclay's room, so the boys set up Neil's portable bar on the edge of their patio and served Mai Tais, Rongorongos and whatever else the crowd requested as a vibes player gently hammered out relaxing tunes.

After the nightmare with Kim, I'd gone back to the hotel and showered and taken most of the afternoon to nap with Astra, punctuated by drinking large amounts of water until I felt darn close to human again. Gina and Melody and I visited the vendors just before they closed, so I found a few deliciously wild outfits at good prices, and then we had a light room-service dinner in the room. Astra managed to sneak a shrimp from my shrimp cocktail, tail and all, and was delighted with the idea of eating in bed, an experience I hoped she wouldn't want to bring home.

The food and hydration and comforting girl talk fortified me, so I was ready to join the party in one of my new clothing finds once it got dark.

Gina joined Larry for a late swim, and Melody went looking for her sailor beau. I walked Astra around and chatted with friends new and old, avoiding any conversation that brought up what happened that afternoon. The tiki rumor mill hadn't quite caught up with events, but it churned hard and fast.

I found myself alone in front of the heavily laden table in the small food tent, contemplating whether I could face cheese again, when Neil came up to me with a frosty glass.

"Is that for me?" I asked, feeding a bit of cheddar to a grateful Astra.

"Depends. Are you ready to drink again?"

"Depends. Did you make it?"

Neil smiled. "Yes. I gave Luke a break and made this just before he came back to the bar."

"Then I'm ready to drink again." I took the pinkish drink from him, sniffed its fluffy mint garnish and took a sip from the paper straw. "Oh, this is good."

"Reverb Crash. The Florida version—pink grapefruit instead of white."

"And ... passionfruit? Orgeat?"

"You're good. And rum, of course."

I nodded. "I might need a break from rum when this is all over. At least for a couple of days. But this is fabulous. Refreshing. I could use some refreshment right now."

"You look ... fresh." He scanned my new-to-me, riotously tropical caftan in greens with cream accents. It wrapped gently across my breasts, allowing a little of my curves to show in the V, eased in at the waist and flowed all the way to the ground, where my softest sandals coddled my toes. I wore my sparkly dress-up geek glasses. A lei of fresh white orchids, which had arrived at my room earlier with a card that said "Looking forward to our tour of the wine cellar ~ M.," adorned my neck and helped hide the welts that I didn't want to think about. And I carried no bag at all, just my key card in my pocket.

"I may wear caftans from now on," I told Neil. "It's all so loosey-goosey under here, you know?"

He took a step closer. Interest sparked in his eyes. "It is?"

"Oh, yeah. After what happened today, I wanted to wear as little as possible for maximum comfort."

I could see him resisting the urge to scan me again. He was such an adorable nerd, and he was so fun to tease. Sure, I had panties on. But no bra. *Ahhh.*

"So," Neil said, "I ran into Val earlier while you were resting. She said she got a strange message from Kim through her lawyer asking Val to take over all of the bar operations for her tiki empire for the near future. Val kind of joked about it, but it sounded like she was giving it some thought, especially if she can get what she wants in writing. The lawyer told her Kim was awake and doing well. Apparently well enough to realize she's going away for a while. She hinted in the note that she might sell everything if she can find a buyer. I guess she needs a manager who knows cocktails in the meantime."

"Good for Val," I said. "She deserves to have some dreams come true. But I'm sure the irony of stepping into Fizz's shoes isn't lost on her."

"That might even be part of the appeal."

A *tink-tink-tink* sounded from outside, and we went out to see Dick and Dale up near the bar, still in their beautiful Hawaiian wedding shirts, white imbued with a silver-gray tropical pattern. Dick was clinking his glass with a spoon, and they were both beaming, surrounded by their handsome groomsmen in bright matching aloha shirts.

"We'd just like to thank you all for being here for our wonderful, happy day," Dick said. "We'll be retiring to our room now"—whistles and clapping met this announcement, to his endearing blush—"and the bar is about to shut down, but we just wanted to say ... Mahalo!"

"Mahalo!" everyone echoed, toasting to their future. And to the excellent party.

As the crowd began to drift apart, Neil and I approached the bar, where Luke and Barclay were shutting down. I hooked Astra's leash to the desk chair inside, and we helped move everything back into their room. We were just about finished when Melody showed up, entering the sliding glass doors in a slim-fitting Hawaiian-print dress, her blond hair partially up in a loose bun held together by a red hibiscus adornment.

"Your timing is impeccable," I said.

"Thank you." She made a little bow, not minding my teasing at all. "My quest was unsuccessful, so I'm ready for the next stage of the evening. What are we drinking now?"

The guys laughed.

My cocktail was gone, and I was ready for more. "Just say it's not rum."

Barclay cocked his head. "What if it were a very special rum?"

"Like top shelf at ABC special?" Luke asked.

"More special than that," Barclay said.

I resisted the urge to run. "Barclay, buddy, I'm not sure I can take another tall tale about a very special rum."

"Pepper, dude, I totally get it. But I think—I think I might actually have something *really* interesting."

Barclay was not given to wild speculation or showmanship like a certain departed bar impresario, but still.

Neil apparently couldn't resist. "How interesting?"

Melody, Luke and I groaned, but Barclay just smiled. "Hang on a sec." He went around the corner to the closet, and we heard him rummaging. And then we heard, "Shit!"

"Whoa no," I said, and Astra barked.

Barclay came out looking frazzled. "It's gone."

"What's gone?" Luke asked.

"The rum. THE rum."

"What do you mean, THE rum?" Neil asked. "What is it?"

Barclay looked apologetic and anxious at the same time. "It's ... something I got in London."

"Don't tell me ..." I said.

"It might be," Barclay said. "It *just might be.* I had it before the party. I put it in a vodka box so no one would take it."

I laughed. This was such a snobby mixologist thing to do.

"OK, if it is something *very special,*" Neil said, "we need to figure out where it went, and fast."

"Cap!" Luke shouted.

"What do you mean, cap?" Melody said. "It had a cap?"

"No, Cap Calder was in here earlier," Luke said. "He was pretty much obliterated and said he needed to use the head. I told him to go to our bathroom. I didn't see him leave."

"But he obviously left," Neil said. "Maybe with the rum?"

"It's a place to start." I hoped we weren't about to climb on the merry-go-round again. "I remember him telling me he had a room that faced the pool, over on the other side of the courtyard. Let's see if we can find it."

The guys shut up their room, and we all trouped around the courtyard under the waving palms, Astra in tow. It was darker on the far side, with fewer lights and I was starting to think we'd have to ask the front desk to connect us with Cap when I saw a figure in white sitting at a table on a patio outside a room half-obscured by a giant bird of paradise plant.

I pointed, and we headed that way to find Cap, his captain's hat pushed back, sitting comfortably in a chair and sipping from a plain hotel glass. A bottle with a yellowed, unremarkable label sat by him on the table. Next to a cardboard vodka box.

"I guess we found it." Barclay sounded a little sad.

"Hiya, Cap," I said.

He looked up at me and blinked. "Pepper? Hey, lady. Nice dress."

"Thanks. You know everyone?"

He looked around. "Neil, I know."

Neil nodded and introduced the others. "Barclay thinks you might've accidentally picked up a bottle from his room earlier."

Cap's eyes did their best to focus on Neil before they wandered to the bottle on the table. "This? Damnedest thing. I was looking for a little something to take to the room, you know? And I figured no one would miss a bottle of vodka. And I opened the box and found the most extraordinary bottle. There's plenty. Do you want some?"

Luke made a funny sound. I looked over to see him with a knuckle stuffed in his mouth, stifling a giggle. Melody joined him, and in a moment, they were both snickering while Barclay glared at them.

Finally, Barclay looked back at Cap and sighed. "We might as well all have a drink."

"You sure?" Neil asked him.

Barclay nodded. "That's what it's for, right? And I'll tell you a little story, and you can judge for yourselves."

Neil nodded. "You know who else might want to be here for this?"

"And who would be a great judge of what you've got here," I added, seeing where Neil was going.

"Cray?" Barclay's face lit up. "Definitely. Call him. To be honest, that's why I brought the bottle to Hookahakaha to begin with. I wanted him to taste it and tell me what he thought."

As Neil made the call, the rest of us gathered up chairs; Luke borrowed some from the neighboring patios so we could all sit.

Cray appeared in under five minutes, wearing a muted light-blue guayabera shirt and a look of excitement. His eyes were immediately drawn to the bottle on the table. "Is that it?"

Barclay nodded. "It just might be a real bottle of long-lost London dock rum from 1933."

Chapter Thirty-Six

"Why do you think this is a bottle of London dock rum?" Cray asked, settling into a chair next to the table and examining the bottle as the rest of us took a seat and Astra hopped into my lap.

Barclay clasped his hands together, rested his elbows on his knees and leaned forward. "A series of coincidences and lucky meetings led me to the woman I got this bottle from when I visited London last summer. I visited a lot of bars—"

"No kidding," Luke joked.

"Obviously." Barclay smiled. "Even Alastair's bar. It's really pretty good. We'll have to check it out when we go to the gin festival."

My ears perked up at this. *Us? Going to London? OMG!* Then I focused on Barclay's story.

"I met these guys at Trailer Happiness in Notting Hill—oh, wow, the drinks there—anyway, they were real rum history nuts, talking about odd places and people they'd talked to, and they said one of the craziest was Louisa. 'Just goes to show you can't believe everyone with a story,' one of them said."

"The currency of the liquor trade is outrageous stories," Neil noted.

Barclay nodded. "I know, but I was curious. I asked them who this Louisa was, and they said it was an odd old lady they'd met at a fundraiser for the London zoo where they were tending bar. She was a volunteer there, and she told them she grew up with a really interesting rum and still had a few bottles left. When they asked her what it was, she claimed it was rum that survived the dock fire in 1933. They thought that was hysterically funny."

"Age and eccentricity are not to be trifled with," Cray said, and we all laughed.

"Too true." Barclay leaned back and looked around. "You guys know how obsessed I am with rum. I decided I wanted to talk to Louisa myself. I went to the zoo office three times asking for a volunteer named Louisa before I found someone who knew who I was talking about and told me she actually volunteered at the Zoological Society library. So I went there and got lucky. She was working. I told her I was interested in rum, and she told me she had a story—"

"Get on with the story, already!" Melody said to our chuckles.

Barclay smiled. "OK. I took her out for tea, and it turned into a whole afternoon thing. She invited me back to her flat for homemade scones—"

"Oh, for God's sake," Melody said.

"I'm getting to it! She told me her father worked at the No. 2 Rum Warehouse at the West India Docks in 1933 and was there that night, playing cards with friends, when the fire broke out. His first thought was apparently to save a barrel that was a particular prize of his supervisor's—partly, I think, because he saw that the inevitable was going to happen. The fire spread quickly, and the whole place was going to burn down. And he thought it would be 'cheeky,' in her words, if he stole it right out from under his boss's nose. Though he referred to it as a 'rescue,' she said.

"The barrels were pretty unwieldy. What made me suspicious of Fizz's bottle was that I couldn't connect how he got a vintage bottle from what was essentially a barrel operation. The barrels were measured and tested in a long shed that ran alongside the warehouse and then transferred into the warehouse. Later they were blended and bottled and moved out.

"Anyway, Louisa said her father convinced his *mates* to roll this barrel out of the warehouse and into a *lorry* one of the guys had nearby during the confusion surrounding the fire." Barclay threw in little bits of droll English accent as he talked. "She learned all this later, as she wasn't born until 1941."

"Sounds a bit suspicious," Cray said.

"Maybe so. But it was all so interesting and specific. She said the rum was from Guyana and had been aging in the warehouse for thirty years. Thirty years! It must have been fantastic then. Imagine what it tastes like now!"

"And what do *you* think of it?" I asked Cap before realizing that he was asleep, his empty glass in his lap. He might've been drinking the rarest rum any of us had ever tasted and fell asleep doing it.

Cray looked upon him with pity and held up the bottle, which he'd been cradling while Barclay spoke. "The bottle has no formal label. It's handwritten. 'Father's rum, 1903, Guyana, West India Docks.' Implying it was made in 1903 and aged in the warehouse until the fire. Louisa's work, I take it?"

Barclay nodded. "She said he and his friends hid the barrel until they could find bottles for the rum and never told anyone they took it. So there's a slim chance there might be more out there. He never labeled his for fear he might get caught someday. She took it upon herself to label the last few bottles after he died."

"And she gave a bottle to you?" Luke asked Barclay in disbelief.

"The last one!" Barclay shrugged. "I think she liked me. She said she was old and alone and didn't have anyone to leave it to. And I think she liked that I believed her."

"Provenance is damned difficult to prove," Cray said. "This probably wouldn't be worth much at auction just for that reason, though the story is fairly irresistible."

"Well, I don't want to sell it," Barclay said. "I don't even want to keep it, if it means some fanatic is going to kill me for it. I want to drink it. With all of you."

I nodded toward the open sliding doors that led into Cap's room. "Think he'd mind if we borrowed a glass?"

"I'll look," said Melody, not waiting for an answer. She came back in a moment with a sleeve of plastic cups. "Even better!"

As she set out the clear cups, a hush fell over us all. We were about to taste history—maybe. It was natural to be skeptical. But like Barclay, I had a feeling Louisa might have been telling him the truth, or at least the truth as she knew it.

Cray did the honors, pouring a small amount of the dark gold liquid in each cup. We passed them around until we each had one. We watched Cray first as he went through his ritual of sniffing and rolling the cup, eyeing how the rum clung to the sides.

He looked up at us. "Someone should make a toast."

"Not me," Barclay said.

"I will." Neil raised up his cup. "To good stories, good rum and great friends."

I caught his eye and smiled as I raised my cup as well. Then I took a deep whiff of the rum's wonderful, darkly sweet aroma.

Astra's nostrils flared, and she nudged the hand that held my cup. "Not for you, girl," I told her and took a small sip. The rum was complex and smooth at the same time, mellow sweetness tinged with heat and wood and just a hint of smoke—not from the fire, I guessed, but from its aging.

A sigh moved through the group like the wind in the palm trees.

"It's excellent," Luke said. "Not that I'm an expert."

"It *is* excellent," Barclay said reverently.

"Yes," I breathed, prompting a raised eyebrow from Neil.

Melody murmured her approval, and we all looked at Cray.

He was still holding the elixir in his mouth; he swallowed as he felt our collective gaze. And his eyes sparkled. "This is very fine. And very old. And I'd like to believe this is just what Louisa said it was."

"Like to believe?" Barclay asked. "But you don't?

"Actually, my dear, *I think I do.*" Cray took another sip, and his eyes closed in happiness.

We all exchanged a glance. Cray thought it was the real thing!

I sipped even more slowly after that.

The rum might have been a treasure, but it was also an opportunity to experience history, a beautiful moment to share with friends. Soon our chatter picked up as we enjoyed our drink and the evening and one another's company. Cap even woke up and gladly accepted another small pour in his glass, accompanied by the short version of the story. This time he was alert enough to appreciate it and drank as reverently as we did.

When we'd finished, a few fingers' worth of rum remained in the bottle.

"You take it, Cray," Barclay said.

"Oh, I couldn't," he said, but he perked up like a kid at Christmas.

"It should go to someone like you. You'll appreciate it and take care of it."

"And maybe drink it," Cray said to our laughs.

"I hope you do. Otherwise, what good is it?" Barclay said.

I nodded. "It's like a tree falling in the forest with no one there to hear it."

"Agreed, Kayanne Pepper," Cray said. "I can't thank all of you enough for a most memorable evening. And Barclay? I owe you one." The collector stood, cradled the bottle in his arm and moved slowly across the grass into the shadows as Barclay beamed.

"Should he have an armed escort?" I asked.

"There's no one who knows what he's carrying except us," Neil said.

"About that—I'm sorry I took your bottle." Cap seemed almost sober now. His catnap did wonders. "I had no idea."

"Maybe it was for the best." Barclay sighed. "I'm actually really happy. And tired. I'm going to have sweet dreams tonight." He got up, as did Luke. They returned the borrowed chairs, and we all said goodbye to Cap and started back toward the pool. Melody peeled off to her room, and the boys headed to theirs while Neil and I paused in the shadows to let Astra water a bush.

She did her business, then sniffed the ground and barked once and started tugging on her leash, trying to get under the branches.

"Oh, no, you don't," I said, bending over and peering into the leaves without success. "You have a light?" I asked Neil.

Neil pulled out his phone and shone the light under the bush. I had a moment of dread as I looked. What if it was more evidence? Or, heaven forbid, the London dock rum? Or a severed limb covered with mystifying tattoos?

Like I said, rich fantasy life.

But it was nothing more scary than a discarded piece of pizza. I firmly pulled Astra away. "No way, girl. We don't want a repeat of the car ride down when we go home tomorrow."

"We could make her ride with Barclay," Neil said, and I shot him a dirty look as he grinned and we resumed our stroll around the pools.

"Do you wish you could find a bottle of rum like Barclay's?" I asked him.

"I'm not sure. Gramps got me pretty excited about treasure-hunting when I was a kid with all of his stories. There's some part of me that still wants to find a gold coin washed up on the beach. And maybe a rare bottle of liquor, something significant."

I thought of all the violence and shook my head. "Curiosity is great until it becomes an obsession, like it did for Fizz and Arnold."

"Obsession can get you into trouble. So can money, if the treasure in question is really valuable. I wonder if a particular treasure is linked to what happened to my grandfather. I keep thinking about what Val said about something priceless on the *Lord Archibald*. I'm going to look into all of the shipwrecks he recovered when we get home, especially that one."

"Since that's the one he never talked about?"

"Exactly. I have a hunch."

"Neil has a hunch," I joked.

He elbowed me. "You don't have any room to talk, Sergeant Pepper."

I rolled my eyes. "I have good hunches and poor judgment."

He transfixed me with those gray eyes and asked softly, "Am I going to have to hover over you like a guardian angel all the time?"

Be still my heart.

I fluttered my eyelashes at him and smiled. "Would that be so bad?"

Acknowledgments

The idea of recovering lost rum from the great dock fire of 1933 is somewhat academic at this point. News reports from the time provide limited insight into the rums that were stored in the No. 2 Rum Warehouse at the West India Docks, but that's where fiction can step in and make things up.

I'm grateful to the experts who talked to me about rum and this event. That said, any fanciful musings and outright inaccuracies in this novel (it's a novel, people) are completely mine.

Thanks much to rum expert and historian Matt Pietrek (CocktailWonk.com) for his emailed insights into the London dock fire and what might have been lost in the No. 2 Rum Warehouse and shed.

I'm especially beholden to rum collector Stephen Remsberg for his deep knowledge and stories about a colorful rum forger who falls into the "you can't make this up" category. I joked with Steve when I buttonholed him at The Hukilau tiki festival in Fort Lauderdale that I was writing about a rum collector from New Orleans who was far more eccentric than he was, and he suggested that such a character was difficult to imagine. I underscore that Conan Cray is not based on Steve, but Steve is indeed a fascinating fellow who knows everything about rum.

In fact, none of my characters are based on real people in the tiki community I adore, though I might've been inspired by your costumes.

I'm also thankful to Jim "Hurricane" Hayward of the Atomic Grog (slammie.com/atomicgrog), who let Steve sneak us into their wonderful session on "The Rums of the Mai-Kai" at The Hukilau in 2019. It provided a peek into some of the historical rums whose bottles can still be found backstage at the historic Polynesian restaurant and show in Fort Lauderdale.

My fictional Pau Hana was inspired by the beloved Mai-Kai, which was built in 1956. I considered using the real setting in my book, but I didn't want to kill anyone in the kitchen. And this way, I could be a little bit creative with the layout if I needed to be. You really can't miss the Mai-Kai's fantastic Molokai Bar (some of whose "under the deck" ship decor comes from the 1962 film *Mutiny on the Bounty*), the food, the dazzling floor show and the gardens if you go to South Florida.

My fictional Hookahakaha convention is inspired in part by The Hukilau, which I've attended for many years. Most recently this gathering of tikiphiles was held at the Pier 66 Hotel and Marina in Fort Lauderdale, which is under destruction—er, construction, undergoing a complete transformation. Supposedly the historic tower will be preserved. I sure hope so, as it's a beautiful mid-century piece of architecture and a landmark that completely captivated my imagination and inspired the fictional setting of Wicker Wharf.

The *Lord Archibald* is also an invention, though it is inspired by history. I've always had a thing for sailing ships.

The title of this book has multiple meanings, evoking destruction, drunkenness and shipwrecks. Imagine my surprise when I found "wrecked by rum" in the temperance poem Neil recites (thanks, Google) when the book was in final edits. I couldn't resist including a little fragment. It's by L.F. Copeland and appeared in a journal called *School Education* in January 1887.

It was weird to be writing this novel during the pandemic, when The Hukilau was canceled and gatherings of the type described in my book were simply not happening. It's hard to know when they will happen again, but in my universe, the Bohemia Bartenders' events happen before the pandemic or in the much-hoped-for *after.* Or perhaps in a parallel alternate universe where all is well. In the meantime, I can immerse myself in their adventures and dream of happier times.

Thanks to my wonderful writer friends for their inspiration, advice and feedback, especially Maria Geraci, Alethea Kontis, Naomi Bellina and Karen Ann Dell.

A big thank-you goes to editor Holly Martin for her encouragement and sharp eye.

Mahalo to George Jenkins for the bartending know-how, evenings at the Storm Shelter, help in making the cocktail in the back of this book, and great Mai Tais.

And to you, who read and hope: Cheers.

Cocktail Recipe

PIÑA PELE

When the Bohemia Bartenders make Neil's recipe for the Piña Pele, they have at their disposal a commercial kitchen and lots of labor to core pineapples, not to mention a spindle blender.

However, you can make this likeable, frothy, gently sweet cocktail with a regular blender at home. For the coconut rum, I strongly recommend using a good one, such as Siesta Key Toasted Coconut Rum or St. Petersburg Distillery's Oak & Palm Coconut Rum. Please note: Malibu is *not* actually a coconut rum. As for the dark rum, we used Coruba.

If you're not familiar with orgeat, it's an almond syrup that's popular in tiki drinks. You can buy it premade or make it yourself.

Fresh pineapple is essential, but serving this drink in a pineapple is completely optional. I happen to think it's pretty in a rocks glass.

For the toasted coconut: Spread a handful or more of unsweetened shredded coconut on a parchment-paper-lined baking sheet and place in a 325-degree oven. Stir after a few minutes, and check frequently to make sure it doesn't burn. Remove when golden brown, after a total of five minutes or so in the oven.

This recipe makes one generous drink and maybe a little extra.

Ingredients

3 ounces fresh pineapple (about three one- to two-inch chunks)
1 ounce fresh lime juice
1 ounce orgeat
2 ounces dark rum
1 ounce coconut rum
Big ice cube made from coconut water
Toasted coconut and pineapple wedge (optional) for garnish

Directions

Blend pineapple, orgeat, lime juice, and rums in a blender until the pineapple is pureed. Pour over a big coconut-water ice cube in a rocks glass. Sprinkle toasted coconut over the top and garnish the glass with a pineapple wedge.

Cheers!

Next in the Bohemia Bartenders Mysteries ...

VEXED BY VODKA

Movies, murder and too much vodka ...

Mixologist Pepper Revelle is thrilled the Bohemia Bartenders' latest gig is in her backyard: a cocktail-themed film festival that draws all the usual suspects to Bohemia Beach. But good suspects are in short supply when a body wearing an antique gold coin necklace washes up on the Florida sand.

Pepper's colleague and elusive crush Neil fears the worst for his grandfather, a treasure hunter who's been missing for months. Meanwhile, Pepper's big-bearded ex-boyfriend, an obnoxious celebrity mixologist with a TV crew in tow, is convinced someone's trying to kill him, too. To Pepper's dismay, he begs her for protection.

Stir in a couple of desperate Hollywood stars, a pushy producer, dashing distillers, a frantic festival chairman, a garnish-eating dog, vats of vodka and a double dose of danger, and Pepper's patience is poised to pop like popcorn. Can the mixologists shake up a solution to multiple mysteries before they're skewered like the olive in a martini?

Vexed by Vodka is the third book in the Bohemia Bartenders Mysteries, funny whodunits with a dash of romance set in a convivial collective of cocktail lovers, eccentrics and mixologists. These cozy culinary comedies contain a hint of heat, a splash of cursing and shots of laughter, served over hand-carved ice.

LEARN MORE AT LucyLakestone.com

Afterword

Thanks for reading! Want a free story set in the Bohemia Bartenders world? In "Baffled by Bitters," Pepper, Neil and Astra the dog set out to learn the secret behind a discovery they've unearthed in the backyard of Pepper's bar. (Timewise, the story is set after *Risky Whiskey* and before *Wrecked by Rum,* but there are no spoilers!) Sign up for my newsletter at Lucy Lakestone.com/signup to get the story, along with fun original content, giveaways, news and cocktail recipes.

I also have a Facebook group where readers can hang out and chat about books and life — please join us in Lucy's Lounge.

And you can always find me at LucyLakestone.com.

BOOKS BY LUCY LAKESTONE

BOHEMIA BARTENDERS MYSTERIES

These funny mysteries star Pepper Revelle and a team of mixologists who travel to colorful events where life is a cocktail of fun — until it's shaken into madcap mayhem ... and murder.

RISKY WHISKEY

BAFFLED BY BITTERS *- story free to subscribers*

WRECKED BY RUM

VEXED BY VODKA

JIGGERED BY GIN

BEGUILED BY BOURBON

SHOCKED BY CHAMPAGNE

BOHEMIA BARTENDERS COCKTAIL COLORING BOOK

The **BOHEMIA BEACH** Series

Award-winning hot contemporary romance

In a beautiful small city on Florida's east coast, artists meet, create, laugh and love. Where restless hearts are fueled by secrets and imagination, romance is impossible to resist. Welcome to the seductive tropical escape that's home to drama, humor and lots of heat – Bohemia Beach.

BOHEMIA BEACH

BOHEMIA LIGHT

BOHEMIA BLUES

BOHEMIA HEAT

BOHEMIA NIGHTS

BACK TO BOHEMIA *- story free to subscribers*

BOHEMIA BELLS

BOHEMIA CHILLS

Bohemia Beach Series Boxed Sets:

Books 1-3 | Books 4-7

The **STORM SEEKERS** Series

Writing as Chris Kridler

FUNNEL VISION

TORNADO PINBALL

ZAP BANG

Storm Seekers Series Boxed Set: Books 1-3

About the Author

Lucy Lakestone is an award-winning author who lives on Florida's east central coast, among the towns that serve as an inspiration for the hot romances of her Bohemia Beach Series and the jumping-off point for the Bohemia Bartenders Mysteries. She's been a journalist, photographer, editor and video producer but prefers living in her imagination, where the moon is full and the cocktails are divine.

She also writes storm-chasing adventures as Chris Kridler, and in her spare time, she chases tornadoes.

Learn more at LucyLakestone.com

facebook.com/lucylakestone

instagram.com/mslucylakestone

amazon.com/Lucy-Lakestone

bookbub.com/authors/lucy-lakestone

goodreads.com/lucylakestone

pinterest.com/lucylakestone

youtube.com/@lucylakestone